PRAISE FOR
DAVID MOGO, GODHU

'Vivid, visceral and with a strength to the voice that
pulls me right in. The god-littered world of
David Mogo's Lagos just won't let go.'
Jeannette Ng, author of *Under the Pendulum Sun*

'A fantastic adventure of gods and mortals—
highly recommended.'
Tasha Suri, author of *Empire of Sand*

'A riveting debut... this story is captivating.'
Publishers Weekly

NO LONGER PROPERTY OF
SEATTLE PUBLIC LIBRARY

'It's a fun fresh ride brimful of adventure, showcasing
great new talent. Wholeheartedly recommend if you love
Zen Cho, Tade Thompson or Nnedi Okorafor.'
Liz de Jager, author of the *Blackhart Legacy* trilogy

'A Nigerian Harry Dresden. Okungbowa's voice is
great, and makes Lagos feel familiar.'
Jacey Bedford, author of *Winterwood*

'I did not know I was a fan of the Nigerian
Godpunk genre, but this book convinced me!'
Horner's Book Corner

'This is a refreshing take on urban fantasy,
and definitely worth a look.'
Mhairi White

An Abaddon Books™ Publication
www.abaddonbooks.com
abaddon@rebellion.co.uk

Published in 2019 by Abaddon Books™,
Rebellion Intellectual Property Limited,
Riverside House, Osney Mead, Oxford,
OX2 0ES, UK.

10 9 8 7 6 5 4 3 2 1

Creative Director and CEO: Jason Kingsley
Chief Technical Officer: Chris Kingsley
Head of Books and Comics Publishing: Ben Smith
Editors: David Thomas Moore,
Michael Rowley and Kate Coe
Marketing and PR: Remy Njambi
Design: Sam Gretton, Oz Osborne and Gemma Sheldrake
Cover Art: Yoshi Yoshitani

Copyright © 2019 Rebellion.
All rights reserved.

ISBN: 978-1-78108-649-0

No part of this publication may be reproduced, stored
in a retrieval system, or transmitted in any form or
by any means, electronic, mechanical, photocopying,
recording or otherwise, without the prior permission
of the publishers.

This is a work of fiction. All the characters and
events portrayed in this book are fictional, and any
resemblance to real people or incidents is purely
coincidental.

Printed in Denmark.

SUYI DAVIES
OKUNGBOWA

DAVID
MOGO
GODHUNTER

GODHUNTER

CHAPTER ONE

THIS IS GOING to be a bad job.

I know it from the angular smile of the wizard-ruler seated before me. I know it because I should sense the icy heat of his godessence on my collarbone, but feel absolutely nothing. I know it because right outside this handcrafted palace, the rest of Lagos mainland is a dank, brooding, perilous hog pen; yet this foyer smells like orange air freshener, and you can only ignore the stink of your own shit for so long.

Let's start with how my new client remains the Baálẹ̀ of the long-abandoned Agbado community, retaining his palace right past the slum's railway crossing. From the outside looking in, you'd never picture such a sophisticated interior. I'm seated in a soft couch under ceiling lights. Ceiling lights oh, not hanging bulbs. D'you know when last anyone was able to get ordinary power in Lagos? Papa Udi and I haven't seen a blink of power in our house since The Falling over a decade ago. We run a 650VA Yamaha generator for three hours every day; just enough to charge our phones and watch the evening news.

But here, Lukmon Ajala has everything. There's a minibar and coffee-maker in the far end of the reception where I'm sitting. The floor-to-ceiling glass windows show halogen lamps piercing the night outside. But it's the silent thrum of a large 30KVA generator that really tells me this guy is mad wadded and true royalty.

The white babariga he wears is layered with exquisite gold embroidery. I almost burst into laughter when I first saw it. Anyone who lives in nowadays Lagos knows he can't step outside this compound in that shit; the streets out there are grimier than a mechanic's workshop. This babariga belongs in Upper Island. Little wonder he has this many aides and guards.

It's not just his clothes. His perfume is exquisite too, the kind that invites you to inhale rather than makes you sneeze. He wears a filà that's half embroidered headpiece, half regular cap, and a tiny smattering of greying hair peeks out from underneath, even though he's young—fiftyish. His eyes are white and piercing. He watches me with them now, smooth hands folded over each other in astute calm.

"So, three million naira on delivery," he says. "If you think about it, that's one-point-five-mil per god."

Yes. Lukmon Ajala One, Baálẹ̀ of Agbado, wants me to go to the epicentre of The Falling and find Ibeji, the twin orishas—high gods. He wants me to capture them both and bring them to him.

"Why not just send your men?" I gesture about at his security detail, a 70/30 split between sergeants hired from the Nigerian Police Force and local hired hands. The policemen mostly run outdoor detail and convoy security, hoisting worn rifles; the meathead boys are mostly palace hands. The three in front of us now, one at each entrance, wear placid faces and carry no visible weapons; but visible beneath the sleeves of their bicep-hugging t-shirts are written wards, like henna tattoos.

He smiles. "This boy, you just want me to massage your ego." He sits forward. "We both know I'm hiring you because you're no ordinary man. You handle these things everyday, and I've been told you have quick turnaround. I also hear you're more skilled in hand-to-hand than all my men."

"And you, sir, are the most powerful practitioner this side of Lagos," I say. "It won't be difficult for you to prepare something and give them to do this job. Or even better, go yourself."

He laughs and fingers his babariga. "You think this atiku was made for tussling with gods at Èkó?"

I shrug.

He snorts. "The way you're behaving, somebody would think you don't need this money."

He obviously does his homework; I can't even start with what three mil will do for my current situation. What's worrisome is how Ajala knows it. It couldn't have been Papa Udi—he won't touch this man with a stick. This is the first thing wrong with this job.

Second thing: I just can't get over that twinkle in his eye when we talk about Ibeji.

A woman, likely one of Ajala's wives, comes and kneels beside him, setting a small bag by his feet. He pats her on the shoulder, and she bows, rises and scuttles off. Not for one second does she take her eyes off the floor.

"Look sir," I say, "my work is simple housekeeping: godlings lose their way and make home in people's garages or pawpaw trees, and I chase them out. I don't capture anything, not to talk of a high god."

"High *gods*. And that one is not a problem." He opens the bag, pulls out a squat, iridescent vial with a stopper and a small, carved ceremonial mask and lays them on the coffee table between us. He points to the flask. "This is a Spirit Bottle, made from Yasal crystals. A Santeria priest gifted it to me when I visited Brazil. All you need to do is ensure Ibeji don't stray too far from their centre and materialise. Then you trap them."

"How will I see them if they're dematerialised?"

"That's why you need this," he says, pointing to the mask. "This is emi boju."

A spirit mask. I don't speak Yoruba, but I understand it well enough.

"I need those gods, Mr Mogo," Ajala says.

I don't like his smile. I don't like it at all.

"What're you going to do with them?"

Now he frowns. Something flashes across his face, hard and pulsing, then he breaks it with an icewater chuckle. For a moment, I'm reminded this man is a wizard; he not only carries a good enough dose of godessence in him to cause some harm, but is also twice as knowledgeable about the practice as Papa Udi. He's not to be toyed with.

"I thought you had a *don't ask* policy with your customers?"

"Not if they're hiring me to kidnap gods."

"It's not *kidnapping*, Mr Mogo," he says. "Think of it as borrowing."

Borrowing gods. Makes no sense.

"Sir, you know what?" I rise and smooth down my t-shirt and jeans. "How about I think about it and get back to you tomorrow?"

"Ah." He rises with me. "To confer with your pa?"

I chuckle. Confer, indeed. Papa Udi can't even know I came here.

Ajala laughs. "Wizards. We never like each other. Remove our code of practice, and we'd have finished each other since." The way he says it, it sounds like *I would've finished everyone off since*. He has that glint in his eye again.

He picks up the bottle and mask, places them back in the bag, then hands the bag to me.

"I'll get them when I make my decision," I say.

"Of course," he says, not withdrawing the bag. "I'm confident you'll make the right choice."

I take the bag from him. When my hand brushes his, his fingers are cold, like a corpse's. The thought makes me shiver, and when a demigod shivers, you know what that means.

GETTING BACK HOME is war, as always. I drive a motorcycle—a proper Bajaj okada, not those powerbikes you see in Hollywood thrillers—and every bump rattles me on the route from Agbado rail crossing to our house on the fringes of Ìsàlẹ̀ Èkó (the local name for Lagos Island, loosely translating to *the bottom of Lagos*; there isn't a more apt description for Lagos Island—in fact, the whole of Lagos even—in recent years.)

The undulating dirt road out of Agbado is just as difficult to navigate as the potholes pockmarking Iju and Isheri, abandoned by the state government and all the governments before it. You would think that gods raining down on our heads would inspire the political elite to look kindly on the people, to band around them in their time of need. Obviously, they had other plans.

The whole idea to clean up Lagos was simply an exercise in gentrification—shove all the poor people here, move all the rich people there (and of course, only show the investors and media the fun parts). The Falling was the perfect excuse, especially because it happened in Ìsàlẹ̀ Èkó, which divides the mainland and the island proper. Once the deities took over Ìsàlẹ̀ Èkó and the exodus followed, it was easy too for the government. All who could afford Upper Island moved there, and the mainland became a dumping ground for all else.

Lagos used to be a small elite class, a sizeable working class, and a massive poverty class. Since The Falling, all of that working class who couldn't slide into island suburbia or move away—to Abuja, London, Houston, Mumbai, Berlin, Toronto or Sydney—disappeared into the mainland jungle. Now, it's a matter of picking one of the Lagoses: the good, the bad, or the ugly. Papa Udi and I are among the few people crazy enough to still live in the ugly, but our reasons differ from most. Usually, the decider is money: you either have it and leave, or you don't and stay. Every single cog in Nigeria is greased by hard currency.

I join the Lagos-Ibadan Expressway. Riding an okada also means I feel every chill of the early night, the dust in my eye. It's typical early November, so the harmattan is peeking around the corner, and since I never saved long enough to buy a jacket or sweater when they were cheap, I'll have to make do with the thin Peak Milk t-shirt I won at a promo in Upper Island last year. I tie my nose with a handkie, because man, you don't want this harmattan dust in your lungs. I might be a demigod, but this shit can still kill me.

I gun down to the Third Mainland Bridge. My phone says it's almost 8pm, and that explains the empty streets. People have wisened up—anytime after 8pm, and you're fair game for the gods.

Most of these things have chosen to remain at Ìsàlẹ̀ Èkó, the epicentre of their Falling, where the connection to wherever they came from is strongest. It is fabled that there's still a gateway back to their pantheon there. Literally no one knows because who ever goes there?

Well, okay, I have. There's no gateway.

A lot of godlings have strayed from there in the last ten years though, more idle wandering than any sense of purpose. Some are interested in some sort of symbiosis, resigned to their fate with us, seeking acceptance in our world. Some have less noble intentions. It's those ones that make us replace our wooden doors with iron ones, reinforce the bars on our windows, and retire to our fortresses before 8pm. It is also those ones that keep me in a job. People stop fearing these things, and I'm done for.

Straying from their centre also forces the deities to materialise and take on human forms; which makes them even more dangerous because you can no longer tell if that guy pissing by the roadside is the real deal or not.

The bridge is empty too. I burn rubber over the lagoon and turn off at Simpson, into the peripheries of Ìsàlẹ̀ Èkó. The population thins to nothing here. The colours follow suit, melding from the vibrant LED billboards advertising Coke and Samsung, and the flapping Èkó *Oni Baje!* feather banners of the bridge, to Ìsàlẹ̀ Èkó's cold, atomic-fallout-grey. I slow my bike and ease in, keeping the silence as if in a graveyard. The towering ghosts of the abandoned UBA and Union Bank skyscrapers, silhouetted against a rising moon, always remind me of tombstones. There are cricket and frog sounds and no human ones. It's dark as fuck because no power; the last working street light was midway down third mainland.

Happily, our house on Ojo Close is the first turn off Simpson. It's the last and only occupied house down the lane, which means I ride down a short stretch of abandoned buildings taken over by weeds on both sides of the close. We never get any visitors.

I park the bike next to a now-useless power pole.

The house is pitch dark, but I know Papa Udi is in there, waiting for me to come turn on the gen. He used to act like he was the strongest man in the world, but lately, he's all but given up on everything. Except this house, of course.

The real question here is why a one-thousand-year-old man (Payu never tells me his age) chooses to live on the edge of a dead zone; there's a history to Cardoso House that makes Payu stick to it with his life, and he never tells me that, either. You would think maybe there's something special about this house, but you would be wrong: little separates Cardoso House from the other pieces of fallen Afro-Brazilian architecture in Èkó, other than that it's still standing. Which is not going to happen for long if I don't get some money and fix up.

Cardoso House is a one-storey duplex with swinging windows and a balcony decorated in old-style arches, patterned with mortar and highlighted in white. The walls are old, strong, and the bottom floor has been repainted by grime and soot, so only patches near the top tell us the walls were once a tepid blue-green. Its pillars follow the arty style of the window arches, giving the house clean edges, like a matchbox. We like to tell ourselves we have a roof, but the wind reminds us every night that we'd better do something about it.

Inside is pitch black. I feel my way under the stairs, stuff Ajala's bag and hide it there, then find the gen. I take it outside, plug it, and pull it once, twice, careful not to rip the cord or the whole engine out (this happens sometimes, when I forget what I am and do things like normal people). The thing comes to life. I switch over, and the house is bathed in yellow warmth, a far cry from the cold, silent onset of a harmattan night outside.

When I get in, Papa Udi is seated on the one ratty settee in our sparse living room, staring at nothing. A bottle of ogogoro, the local South Nigeria gin with like 70% ethanol, rests on the sofa's arm.

"Wetin happen?" I ask him.

Papa Udi rises in creaks. He's a gangly old man with pockets of thinning grey hair, no beard. He's wearing his usual raffia-resist àdìrẹ̀ shirt and matching shorts. His tired old eyes are set deep in their sockets, retreating, as if they've seen too much.

"Why you dey siddon for inside darkness?" I ask.

"Ungh." He chews slowly, showing me his yellow teeth. As a child, I used to be scared of his bursts of irritation; that air of calm that glides over an impatience about him, like a dog kept in check by its tamer, capable of anything once the patting hand is removed. You never knew what he was going to do next, especially when he was wasted on this shit. I still never know.

He waves a hand, starts to move, then stops, forgetting why he got up in the first place. They don't call the drink *push-me-I-push-you* for nothing.

"Eh." I kick off my boots. I consider telling him about Ajala and his proposal, but that's obviously out the window now. "As you be like this, you go fit run ebo for me this night? I gats work tomorrow."

Before every hunt, Papa Udi douses my hunting weapons of

choice—two handcrafted ceremonial daggers the Yorubas call ọbẹ iṣèṣé, capable of penetrating spaces less than, er, human—in his famous ebo, an alchemical spiritual penetration potion that's so good he sells it to the Lagos State Paranormal Commission. Ebo puts anything short of a heavily-warded wizard or a mega-mega-deity at risk. Kind of like the green kryptonite to all godessence.

Papa Udi munches a bit and says, "Mmn." He gives up trying to remember what he was going to say and sits back down. I fling my t-shirt on the back of the couch, take the remote, turn on the TV and start flipping through channels.

"Wetin you chop?" I always ask about Payu's food; it is too easy for me to forget he must eat thrice a day because, as a demigod, I only eat thrice a week.

"Indomie and suya," he says. "Plenty pepper."

"And you dey drink on top?" I shake my head. "Na die you wan die be that."

"Mmn." He's definitely thinking about something.

"Payu, for real, any problem?"

He sighs heavily, suddenly remembering what he was going to tell me.

"Go up go see."

I toss the remote, go out to the now-lit stairs and take them in leaps. There's nothing of note at the landing, neither is there any at the corridor at the top. But then I open the door to my room.

"Ah ah!"

I hear Papa Udi snicker downstairs.

My little room looks like the site of a hurricane. The whole roof has caved in on my bed in the middle. Zinc, splintered wood and termite dust dig into the mattress. A few nails have found my clothes lying around and left deep, long tears in them. One whole half of the room is wet with mildew or something. Early moonlight filters in through the new aperture, casts a bluish hue and a look of ruin over the room.

I lean over the railing and scream into the living room: "Wetin happen na?"

"Small wind oh," Papa Udi croaks back. "Small wind."

"Eish." I run my hand over my head. "When e take happen?"

"Afternoon."

"You call Suleiman?"

"Yesso. Over 200k to fix am. I juss say make him no bother."

I sigh. Now I see why he was drinking in the darkness.

"No worry, I go fix am," I say, to no one in particular. If Papa Udi hears it, he doesn't acknowledge.

Right. So we sleep on the couch tonight, then. Tomorrow, we go jobhunting.

CHAPTER TWO

THE THING ABOUT getting new gigs in the godhunting business is that you don't just go out asking, *Well done oga; please, do you perchance have a godling in your bathroom you'd like me to get rid of?* Not like the police is going to come after me or anything, but a black market is black for the very reason that you don't go about announcing yourself.

First, the client will usually seek me out. There are no telephone books in Lagos, but some online business directories had me hooked up back when they were still fully functional, and my phone number did spread over the internet for a bit. Some find me through Google searches, or my several-years-behind Facebook account. Most, however, find me the same way they find weed and codeine dealers: through recommendations. They call me, gimme details, I send them a quote via SMS, and we have a deal. I collect payment up front. Truth be told, it's the only way to deal with Nigerians: money for hand, back for ground.

So the next morning sees me on my Bajaj a little after dawn, turning out of Simpson and circling the fringes of Èkó Ìsàlẹ̀. Specifically, to Muiz's place at the divineries in the old Sura Shopping Complex.

The rise of divineries was a natural result of The Falling. Not like they've never been there—men calling out a string of ailments and hailing their cure-all elixirs as sent-from-heaven have been as much a staple of Lagos as yellow danfos. A decade later though, and everyone suddenly accepts the existence of something beyond their comprehension. Yes, the religious institutions tried to capitalise on it all to spew prophecies and talks of Armaggeddon, but it was the divineries who offered practical solutions. *Rub this on your skin, and they won't see you. Use this chalk to draw around your house, and nothing go disturb you for night. Drink this, and the gods can't touch you.*

Of course 99% of them are scams, but people need a solution they can touch.

Typical Lagos morning in the days before The Falling, and I might've not been able to make it down this route, which would've been packed with cars stuffed with workers, their windows rolled up, crawling in early-morning traffic on their commute from the mainland to the island. These days, however, no one goes this route anymore. In fact, no one who works on the island lives on the mainland anymore, or if they do, they find some alternative route that's not already laden with highway robbers. Or police, who're pretty much the same thing.

My phone vibrates in my pocket. I check it: Ajala. No message, but I'm pretty sure he wants to know if I've made a decision. When the next call comes, I let it vibrate to voicemail in my pocket.

At the entrance to the divinery, I encounter a sizeable number of touts lingering about even this early, their sunburnt skins cracked and scarred by gutterside brawls, bottle daggers and squalor. Most folks around here know me, but these boys seem like a fresh squirt from the mainland's slums. Their eyes, red from smoking weed, take me in, wondering if I'm prey. Maybe because I don't drive a car, or they decide my skin is not soft enough, but they bare their teeth at me and let me go by.

The buildings themselves, rows of three-storey shops, closed a long time before The Falling for lack of business, but since the clearout of Ìsàlẹ̀ Èkó (and a sudden availability of illegally rent-free shops), Sura Shopping Complex quickly became the commercial hub for all the things no one wants to buy or rent. Like a godhunter, for instance.

I park the bike in the empty parking lot and stroll in. Most stores here sell recipes: herbal, alchemical or godessence-fuelled. Of all three known ways to make use of godessence to affect things, recipes are the least difficult: you tap into the godessence inherent in all living substances, following very specific procedures to create powerful combinations that can do anything from forcing a god to materialise to breaking spiritual barriers. And no, I'm not talking about reading a grimoire or instruction book for wizards (there *are* those, and it's not wizards who wrote them, trust me). I'm talking of arcane recipes that've been passed down orally for generations. What these people sell here are mostly herbal remedies and scams, one-hit-wonder dusts and elixirs. Papa Udi and his ilk are the ones who know the real deal, and they never rent shopfronts and put up signs.

As for the other two ways of wielding godessence, let's just say performing a ritual is something only people exquisitely skilled in it should do (or else could easily end up harming the wrong person, if not themselves); and charmcasting—well, currently no human is known to have cast a charm out of their own godessence without running mad or self-combusting on the spot. They simply don't have enough of it in them, and you can't cast a charm out of someone *else's* godessence.

Muiz's Place is on the second floor of the third building, right past the stairs at the far end. The store itself is locked, but I know Muiz has never left it. Unlike all the illegal occupants here (whom the police raid every now-and-then), Muiz has lived here since the old days, along with the bales of àdìrẹ and ankara fabric he used to sell and got poor on when everyone stopped coming. His real job now, as with many others here, is as an agent: he gets a freelancer like me work, he gets a cut.

I rattle the gate a couple of times. "Muiz!"

An oblong head pokes out behind the bales of clothing.

"Who be that?" Muiz's voice betrays a tickle in the back of his throat.

"David."

Muiz comes to the gate, the frown of sleep unsettling his smooth forehead. He's a slight boy who only managed to finish secondary school before taking on the textile business to support his family. Sometimes, I suspect this is the reason he won't return to the mainland—too much shame to contend with.

He unlocks the gate and swings it open. "Oga David. Kaarọ sah."

"Yes, yes, kaarọ to you too," I say. "Look, any work don show? I need something bad."

"Ah yes, yes." He retrieves the hardback notebook he uses as a register, licks a finger, flips. "Ah yes, Boss, one of my guys na gateman for Ibeju Lekki. Him oyibo oga say something dey make noise inside their tank."

An immigrant. I can't believe my luck. "How much?"

"Fifty grand."

The oyibo is Frieda Lange, a young German lady who turns out to be the spokesperson for all the immigrants in a row of five terraced duplexes in uptown Upper Island, close to the Lagos-Ogun boundary. She hugs her slight frame, presses her thin lips together, and says she will go nowhere near the gate. The sounds have been intermittent, she tells me, so she doesn't know for sure if whatever-that-thing-is is in there right now, but they think it comes to sleep at night after emptying the water through a hole in the tank.

Immigrants are the best customers. In a foreign land, dealing with foreign gods; you can literally charge these oyibos anything. Problem is, they're so few and they mostly live in Upper Island, so I only get gigs once in a blue moon.

"Two hundred grand and I take it out now," I tell her.

Frieda studies me through narrow eyes, wrinkling her nose as if I smell. Every single family has moved out of the house, she says, and is currently wearing down the company with hotel bills. An additional fifty can be argued relative to the hotel bills, but a 300% increase? Don't be stupid. She hands me the first fifty in cash. Go in there, get that thing out, and I give you another fifty and that's that.

The affected plastic water tank is behind the house, occupying the second level of a triple-platform steel scaffolding as high as the roof. I've seen lots of these kinds—godlings wandering so far out of Èkó Ìsàlẹ̀ that they end up disoriented and need somewhere to perch. They're crude and simple-minded, operating mostly on instinct and emotion. An upset godling is as dangerous as a rabid dog; worse, when it's still immaterial.

I climb the metal ladder welded onto the platform and tap the tank. Frieda says there's no water, but it doesn't sound hollow, so my guy is definitely inside. I can feel him, sense the godling signature. The top is still screwed on, and the tank has scratches, telltale signs of an earlier scuffle—someone tried to flush this roach earlier, and obviously didn't succeed. I tap it again, hoping for a response, some movement. Nothing.

I climb down, lay down my bag and pull out a length of slim chains, the kinds used to leash mongrels, except these have been soaked in Papa Udi's *ebo*.

Then I push the tank down.

It's too easy. The cover pops off as the tank hits the ground, and the godling comes wriggling out, scrambling to its feet. This one has strayed much too far from its epicentre, and been forced to take on material form. It has chosen a naked, malnourished boy—for the convenience of fitting into the tank, I suppose. It lets out a high-pitched howl and a string of syllables that sound like all the languages of the world put together. The thing plants down on all fours and stares back at me with the soft eyes of a teenage boy.

No, no, don't do that, no.

It makes a loping move, ready to hightail it. I already have the chain wound around one hand. I whip it out and catch the godling's calf. It screeches, a sound that has no business in a human throat. The chain goes around, slides down to its ankle, hooks. The godling pulls and whines aloud, a dog on a leash. I pull back.

Of course I win, I'm a demigod.

Damn, I should've asked for more money.

After I've gagged the godling's mouth to prevent that hair-raising embarrassment to the ears, I lash it across the back seat of my okada with the chains, cover it with some tarpaulin, and leave it to get tired of struggling. Frieda, who'd gone to withdraw my balance from the ATM earlier, hands me the remaining fifty.

Inside my pocket, my phone is vibrating.

THE SUN IS well in form when I brave the afternoon traffic back from Upper Island. Bearing a demigod and a godling for twenty-five kilometres of the Lekki-Epe Expressway turns out to be too much on my okada, which overheats. I turn off to Ahmadu Bello and park by the bridge interchange to let the bike cool off, and sit by the silent roadside to eat some fried yam and sauce I'd bought off a streetside seller. I call Papa Udi to find out if he's eaten, but he doesn't pick up. Typical. I leave some food for him.

My phone vibrates. It's not Payu calling back, but Ajala. I put it away.

Once the bike's cooled off a bit and I've fed the radiator some water, I'm ready to gun it back to Sura, but voilà: as I turn the interchange, I run into a police roadblock.

The Nigerian police are a fucking menace. There's five of them here, dressed in the customary black combats and ratty boots, each hoisting a rifle. They've blocked half the road with their van and a couple of tyres. They flag me down instantly.

Now, what I do isn't entirely illegal. Yes, technically, the government—specifically, LASPAC—are there to deal with stray deities, so *technically* black market godhunters like me shouldn't exist. It's never a fun run-in with the police for me.

So when the first thing a policeman does is rip open the tarpaulin across the back seat to find a teenage boy bound and gagged there, imagine what it looks like.

The five of them cock their guns and train the barrels at my head.

"Good afternoon, officers," I say, smiling brightly. "Great day, yes?"

"Shut up," says the one close to me—his badge reads Ibrahim Momodu. "Identify yourself and what you're carrying."

"David Mogo," I say. "Godhunter." I tap the godling just enough for it to make its clearly inhuman sounds. "And this, right here, is something you don't want on your hands."

The men look at each other, and an understanding passes between them.

"Get down from this bike," Ibrahim says. "We need to search you."

This is all pointless shit. They know who I am and what I do; they've heard stories. They're not looking to keep the peace. See, this is one of those times I wish I could speak Yoruba, convince the man in his native tongue. Too bad I never got around to it.

"Look, officers," I say, planting myself firmly on the bike, "I don't need any trouble. I'm just doing my work."

"My friend, get down," Ibrahim says. "Don't you know your work is illegal? Everything about you is illegal—no ID, no visible source of income, loitering Èkó axis without aim. You are illegal just standing here." He hoists the gun higher. "I said, get down."

I've been shot once before. By the police, actually. It hurt, but not much. It healed quickly too, even before Payu's recipes hastened the process. I've never been shot by five people at once, though, and I don't know what that will do to me. Even so, I'm still thinking I can take them. I mean, it's the Nigerian police—they're as useless as shit. All five will be kissing the dust before anyone can fire two shots. And the first one will definitely miss.

But then I'm looking at Papa Udi's food in front of me and thinking he won't get to eat if I don't get home tonight. So I get down from the bike.

Ibrahim just pokes around, really. More a performance than a real search. When he opens my bag and finds my tools, I see him shiver a bit. Then his eyes light up when he spots the hundred grand in cash. He turns about to me.

"We're confiscating your bike until we can ascertain that you're not a danger to the public," he pronounces finally. "Let's go to the station."

I laugh. This is just ridiculous.

"Are you laughing? I'm not afraid of your useless juju oh."

I laugh even more. That's what people say when they're afraid.

"Oya drag him," Ibrahim says, waving to his boys. None of them move an inch. In fact, they've all lowered their rifles.

"I said drag him!" When no one obeys, Ibrahim turns to me and grabs my upper arm. It takes all the restraint in my bones to let him. Assaulting weaklings has never really been my forte. But does that mean I have to move? No.

This guy tries to shove me, first with one arm, then with two. He would have better luck pushing a brick wall.

After a minute of futility, he steps back and stares at me for a bit. "You can go," he says finally, panting. "But your bike is not leaving here until—until you give your—your boys something for pure water."

Forty grand. That's how much they take from me, after threatening multiple times to shoot me in the ankle so I can't make it home. I let them have it, if for no other reason than so I don't end up killing anybody. I'm so pissed when I leave the checkpoint that I wish maybe I should've just beaten them all.

Muiz's agency fees eat another fifteen grand into my paycheck, so at the end of the day my pot of gold is only forty-five grand strong. Take out the cost of supplies and petrol for the next couple of weeks, and I'm left with maybe ten grand. Just 190 grand left for our roof: nineteen more jobs or two new immigrant jobs, neither of which is going to happen anytime soon.

Great stuff.

Before I turn into Simpson, I park and release the godling as I always do, taking off the gag. It's quiet now, watching me with those soft eyes, as if asking permission to go.

"Shoo." I wave at it.

I watch the thing lope away, into the graveyard of buildings silhouetted against the evening sun.

The phone in my pocket vibrates. I look at the screen and sigh at the name, then press the green button.

"Hello, sir. David Mogo at your service. Yes, yes, I've decided. I'll do it."

CHAPTER THREE

IF ANYONE WANTS to hunt a deity in Lagos, the most sensible place to begin is the stretch of city between Broad Street and Marina Road. This is because the very first place where a god fell was right on the roundabout at the end of Marina, in front of the former United Bank for Africa Tower, the most distinctive building to catch the eye upon stepping on the Third Mainland Bridge.

This is where I start.

It's nearing evening when I arrive at Broad Street on my Bajaj. I don't know if it's preparing to rain: November should be all dry season, but the clouds above look moody. If you've ever witnessed a storm this side of Lagos, you'd know to trust the clouds, harmattan season or not.

The streets are a rapture. Since the pandemonium of The Falling and ensuing evacuation, Èkó Ìsàlẹ̀ has quickly settled into godland; meaning black, cold and dying for human warmth. A lonely crossing guard's post stands at the intersection of First Baptist Church. A Pep shop is half-secured by a mucky chain, as if the owners decided last-minute their goods weren't worth it. A chubby sewage rat perches on the chain and doesn't move, even when I pass by, too busy munching on its business. Dry season dust blows about the unlit streets, coating sidewalks that haven't known human feet for a long time.

In the darkness beyond, shadows move.

While no one can attest to ever seeing two high gods in any one place (those who see even one high god are damn lucky), Lukmon Ajala was very specific about my search zone: he thinks Ibeji—the twins, Taiwo and Kehinde—are right in that band, on a link road between Broad Street and Marina. Google Maps lists about ten of these: Brook to the east, through Joseph Harden and Kakawa, and ending at Balogun on the west, right under the looming UBA tower. My plan is to ride down Broad, circle about the tower, then ride down Marina back here, all the while scanning for divine signatures.

Unlike human mothers who harbour the regular amount of human godessence—which is only slightly more than the average plant or animal (except cats, of course)—my mother is a high god—well, *was;* I've never been sure which to use. Anyway, this means I stock more than your average guy, if slightly less than a high god. The other catch, however, is that mine doesn't sit in the bottom of my belly like everyone else's. Mine is ingrained in my flesh and bones, my physical. So while others have to reach into themselves to cast a charm and affect the corporeal world, I come factory-fitted, always constantly interfacing between the corporeal and spiritual, even when I'm not conscious of it. Very much like peripheral vision.

No one tells you that when you combine a god and a human, you get wacky results.

My skin carries a sort of extra-sensory perception—an *esper* as Papa Udi calls it. If you need to find anything with a good dose of divine, I'm your walking radar (I should put that on a flyer).

I ease my bike along, slinging the bag with Ajala's spirit mask across my torso and hanging the Yasal bottle from a line on my neck. My daggers are sheathed at either hip on my belt. I tap to check they're secure, and the smell of garlic mixed with local scentleaf—the principal ingredients of ebo—hits me. Papa Udi happily made me some after eating that fried yam.

Unfiltered evening breeze from the sea on the far side of the marina caresses my face. I ride without looking left or right, scanning for divine signatures. I'm picking up a good number of them as I near the fifth intersection. They register as hotspots across my collarbone, low lightbulbs, if lightbulbs were icy; like intuition, if intuition gave you clear, exact numbers. Sometimes, these things come with smell or taste, sometimes with sound.

The signatures are weak—godlings. I can't normally sense humans at all (they don't have enough to pick up), and the signature of a high god is much, much stronger.

I met a high god once, at the parking lot of the Onikan Museum, while on a job to retrieve an abandoned artefact for a client. His signature was a white hot core, burning bright, but with a fire like ice. I couldn't see him, he never told me his name, we never spoke; but I could sense so much of his godessence that I could almost say I knew him, that there was a kinship between us; the way you know when you stumble upon a kinsman in a foreign place. One more minute, and I might've even known his name.

But he never said anything. He just looked at me, confused, most likely by my weird demigod signature. Then he turned and went away, towards Tafawa Balewa Square. I didn't follow him. I told Papa Udi, and he thought it was the wisest decision I've ever made.

How Ajala knows that Ibeji is situated here is both interesting and not my concern (he *is* a wizard, after all). I don't know much about the orishas (no one does), but there's one thing I do know: no one ever just stumbles upon a high god. If you come across one, they definitely wanted you to.

The godlings sense me now, sense something confusing—a whiff of that pure godessence of high gods they're used to, but abominably mixed with filthy human?—and are converging, coming to see what manner of creature this is. The first one peeks out of a small First Bank with a lease banner still hanging over it. More follow, peeking out of streets, of ATMs, of old parking lots, of trees, of abandoned yellow danfos. I can't see any of them—this close to their centre, they're basically invisible; humanoid forms covered in a shimmer sheet, like when you look above a fire. I imagine them watching me ride down, blinking, chattering in their gobbledegook godspeak.

I'm almost at the end of Broad Street when my collarbone starts to throb and my neck warms up. The image is clear in my mind. There is only one thing that can emit so much spiritual energy.

I brake right into Martin Street, and the maze of broken buildings that used to be Balogun Market.

This is the farthest I've ever come in my five years of godhunting. I'm flying blind for the first time. Balogun Market wasn't even a good place when humans inhabited it, and if there's a place the worst of the worst deities would reside, especially those interested in manhandling humans, Balogun Market seems like a perfect fit.

I park the bike, unsheath my daggers, and put on the mask.

You know those Virtual Reality stuff them folks abroad are wearing these days? I swear this is what they must be like. At first, Martin Street is a long stretch of darkness, skeletons of the former shops jutting out of its sides. Then everything is bright, too bright; then everything is back as it was, except those tiny warm-cold signatures have become corporeal bodies.

This mask was def produced via a ritual. Rituals differ from recipes and charmcasting, in that their power lies not in living biology, but in language and the stories told with them. The ancient tongues of gods themselves are powerful carriers of godessence, and if the right stories are woven from them in the right way—through invocations, incantations, song, or writing—they can be used to make massive, massive change in the corporeal world. Of course there's the part where you have to know these languages to the very last, which is no small feat in itself. Papa Udi uses Nsibidi, an ancient divine system of thousands of artistic symbols depicting words, ideas and concepts. It's more common with wizards from Eastern Nigeria, but Payu says his dearest friend, a wizard called David Mogo (yes, this is who he named me after; ridiculous, I know) taught it to him. With it, he weaves stories and crafts charms, amulets, wards. All he needs to do is draw the right symbols.

This mask, however, was not built with Nsibidi, as far as I can tell. Same with the Yasal bottle. I have no idea what tongues were used, and maybe the less about Ajala I know, the better.

I go down the street, ignoring the unblinking, unsettling stares. Godlings, in their true form, are the oddest things. Bipeds like humans, but only a close approximation. Their lower limbs look like arms, their toes like thumbs. Their arms themselves are spindly, willowy things with tiny appendages. Complete with lashless round eyes, plastered flat noses and conspicuously rounded torsos, they'd only need to be green to finish up the classic alien look.

If I were them, I'd want to remain invisible too.

I'm picking the massive signature a fair ways down the road, close to the now decrepit Oluwole Urban Mall, where textiles used to be shopped. It's like, what, 800 metres? I roll my daggers, breathe into my mask and continue the trek.

A line of abandoned mannequins suddenly moves, and rodents and godlings alike scamper out of the ground floor shops, shrieking. Tattered cloth from ruined umbrellas follows the wind and blows across in their wake. Above, the skies have turned sour as darkness fully descends.

I now have a clear point on the signature. It burns bright, not from the mall, but from a small building next to it: triangle-topped, five pillars, topped with moon-and-star symbols—a mosque. Typical. Fallen or not, gods love to be worshipped, don't they?

I crouch in a corner and reach out with my esper, projecting it slightly, hands feeling for spiritual energies in the dark. I immediately start to feel dizzy and nauseous, the usual side-effect, but I hold steady, struggling not to puke. The esper shows me there are more godlings in there, but there's definitely a high god among them. Just my luck. I pull my senses back, rise and tiptoe into the mosque.

My eyes adjust to the darkness. The room is small, dark and quiet. No seats, but rolled-up mats are piled against a corner. There's a dais at the opposite end, raised like a throne room. One creaky chair stands in the centre, its back to me.

Someone—something—is seated in it, humming softly and mumbling words in a weird language, tapping a drumbeat into the chair handle with its fingers. There are three to four godlings on each side of it, statue still, listening with rapt attention and unblinking eyes.

Then its fingers stop mid-air. I swear I feel it sniff before it jumps up and swirls.

Taiwo is almost seven feet tall, lithe, dressed in a red-and-white robe that dances slowly, always a fraction of a second slower than normal. I smell bark, humus and fresh green off him, and I'm not sure whether the smell is real. His skin glows translucent, and he shimmers, so I see two things at once, juxtaposed—the willowy man in front of me with the long, young face; and also a wooden carving, a dwarf with a long head, unblinking eyes and a crown.

I swear he sniffs again and frowns.

"Yeah," I say. "I get that a lot."

I move faster than he expects, the Yasal bottle bobbing at my chest. He's slow to respond, slower even than the godlings, who shriek in godspeak and scamper, stretching their limbs and legging it. Taiwo is stuck to the spot, so stunned that I have time to thrust the Yasal bottle at him.

Nothing happens. It takes me a few seconds to realise I forgot to pull the stopper.

With a *pop,* the form in front of me dissipates. I catch a brief taste of salt on my tongue. Someone laughs: not the full, chesty laughter of an adult, but a childlike giggle, mischievous.

Then the voice says in Yoruba: "Who're you?"

I project my esper and pick a signature above me. As I look up, Taiwo comes falling down, landing on my shoulder.

Dematerialised, he's light for seven feet, and does only enough to knock me over. I roll and flash my ọbẹ iṣẹ̀ṣẹ́.

Man, the way this guy's eyes light up when the smell of ebo hits the air. His faces change, suddenly overrun by childlike, primal fear—of mortality, it seems, something he has probably never had to deal with before.

And like that, he starts to run.

I jump up and follow him out of the mosque, down the street. He's running like an old man or a child, swinging his legs too high. He's screaming in Yoruba, asking what he's done. I press my arms to myself, duck my head and sprint.

He makes a turn and I follow him, panting, LSPDC House looming in front of us. It's a narrow street, empty caricature shops scattered about and silent, monolithic shopping complexes frowning down on us. More godlings shriek and shriek, as if alerting others, and the noise intensifies, distracting me, making it difficult for me to see Taiwo properly. I have to keep my esper extended in front of me, which slows me.

Taiwo gets further away from me, makes another turn right.

I suddenly no longer have any bearings. I'm definitely lost now. I'm not even on a street; I'm in a narrow space between two buildings, within some tattered clothes spread on lines, long abandoned by their owners. Then I see Taiwo gliding between the clothes, barely disturbing them. I sweep them aside and push on.

He's giggling, muttering things, but also worried, screaming, hysterical. If he were human, he'd have passed for schizophrenic. I don't care, though. Cardoso House needs this money.

He turns again, and again, and I follow him, keeping his signature within sight, so that even when, twice, I lose sight of him, I relocate him easily, and he shrieks each time. Now he's suddenly run into a wide open road, and as soon as I jump out, I recognise it: we're back at Broad, only a few yards from where I parked my bike.

I turn back and sprint the remaining yards of dimming light, jump on the Bajaj, kick, swing the bike in a quick circle, and I'm on my way back up Broad.

People say gods are wise, and I've always believed it. Today, I don't think I've ever seen a more stupid god. This guy looks back, sees me coming at full speed, and what does he do? He yips and continues to run *in the same direction*.

It's too casy.

One hand off the throttle, I yank at the Yasal bottle on my neck as I approach. The line snaps and, other hand on the brake, I swing a wide arc about Taiwo, cut him off. *Now* he realises he could turn into a side street, but it's too late.

I pull off the stopper and thrust the bottle at him.

First thing I think the bottle does is immobilise him. He struggles to move, but is failing. Then the juxtaposed dwarf image vanishes, and I'm staring only at the lean, young face. Slowly, he starts to fade in bits. First, the parts closest to the bottle: his right ear, his right arm, his right foot. Then the rest of his body, including the mouth he's opening to say something, but the bottle is sucking it away, snatching his words, snatching him.

It takes less than a minute. Soon, every scrap of the essence of the once gleaming high god is gone.

I put back the stopper, rest on the bike handlebars for a minute. After catching my breath, I rise, tie the bottle back to my neck, then rev the bike again.

One down.

CHAPTER FOUR

It's a little past midnight when I find myself back at Agbado rail crossing, fagged out and aching in my joints. A silent policeman at the palace gate lets me in.

There's some activity to the far end of the compound. A handful of policemen and palace guards are roughing up a line of kids, boys and girls no less than fourteen and no more than nineteen. They're being filed into a room through the side of the house at gunpoint; I can see the shiny reflections of tears on many of their faces, hear the stifled whimpers.

Now, I'm no soothsayer, but that doesn't look good to me.

"What's happening with those children?" I ask the policeman.

He looks at me incredulously, as if I've just asked for his wife's hand in marriage, then shakes his head, mutters something, and directs me to a large shed behind the palace, his eyes never leaving me for a second.

The room is long, and piled with herbs in every corner, low-lit by a lone yellow bulb, like a stable. Ajala is there, his back to me, elbow-deep in selecting herbs. He's a far cry from the man I sat with yesterday night and this morning. All the royalty and elegance is gone, and he now wears a flowing black robe without embroidery, his feet in simple slippers. When he turns to face me, without all the distractions of knuckle rings and cashmere shawls, I see him for what he truly is: an aging wizard, with his best days behind him.

"Ah, David Mogo," he says, then waves the guard away. He's frowning, as if he didn't expect to see me. "You're early."

I shrug. "When I say I'll deliver, sir, I deliver."

He nods, studying me. "I knew I underestimated you."

I sigh and pull the Yasal bottle from my neck. "I got just one, though."

His brows dip. "I asked for the twins."

"I know," I say, tired, extending my arm with the Yasal bottle swaying from the string. "I searched the extent of Ìsàlẹ̀ Èkó that you said: Broad, Marina, Breadfruit, Williams, down to Nnamdi Azikiwe and Ereko. Nothing." I shake my head. "A waste of an evening. I didn't meet a single orisha except Taiwo. Are you sure your information is correct?"

A flicker of irritation passes across his face, then is replaced with a cold smile.

"It's fine, it's fine." He sniffles, returning to his herbs and waving his hand at a nearby table. "Drop it there."

I lay it down. The heat in the room is stifling, and I start to sweat.

"I'll manage with the one for now." Ajala is saying. "Come and get the bottle tomorrow and find Kehinde."

"Hm," I say, then shuffle my feet. He pauses his work to look at me.

"Your money?"

I shrug. "I've brought half of the delivery."

He takes a long time to look at me again, then sighs and says: "Fati!"

A teenage girl, dark-skinned with deep, fat tribal marks etched into her oily cheeks, shuffles into the room. She's closer to fifteen than thirteen, and wraps herself in a black chest-length hijab and black robe that make her look like a floating ghost. She kneels before Ajala, and he places a hand on her head, caressing. The way he moves his hand, the way he looks at her—it's not like a parent or carer, but something more like a lover.

Cringe.

He speaks to her softly in Yoruba. Something about something under his bed. She leaves the room without so much as a glance in my direction. Ajala wants to return to his herbs, but sees the distaste in my rigid posture.

"You don't approve."

I shrug again. "That's not why I came here."

He chuckles and dives back into the herbs. "You must've seen the kids outside, yes? The police pick them up every now and then. Illegal hawkers, petty criminals, loiterers. The stations are filled with them, so I've decided to take some off their hands. When they brought Fati in, I knew she was special. She can't talk, but she's smart, you know? She doesn't belong with the others." He sniffles again. "Who knows, I might just go to her parents after this, eh? She can be my fifth." He chuckles when I don't respond. "Don't worry; I'm not marrying her for fucking."

I wish he could see my face, because it's clearly saying *stop now, man, stop*. But his back is to me, so he keeps going.

"When you've reached a certain place in life like me, you

can't trust anybody, you understand? Especially women. They become your weakness, see? You stay far from them. But then again, after all the wives I've had, I'm used to companionship. So I need something, somebody to love. Fati will do that for me."

I've been trying to settle upon the reason Papa Udi detests this man, and I think I've found it. It's not because he's powerful, but because he can charm his way through anything, and is willing to walk over everyone.

Fatoumata comes back in the room, lugging a small Ghana-Must-Go bag. With the sound it makes when she thumps it on the ground, I know there's only one thing that can be in there.

"That's one-point-five," Ajala says without looking. "Come back for the bottle tomorrow and find me Kehinde, then we talk about the rest." Then, to Fati: "Mu fun."

The girl hands me the bag, lifting it with both small hands. She's bowing her head, refusing to look at my face. I see her fingers and arms painted in black, swirling henna, snaking under the cloth.

Our fingers brush when I take the bag from her, and hers are cold, like something sickly, something with a fever. Simultaneously, something ignites within me. A memory, a thought, a premonition; a flash of fire, gone as soon as it had come. In its wake, I taste fine sand, the kind that's whipped up by a storm.

I won't be forgetting those fingers in a long, long time.

THE BAG RESTS on my fuel tank between my arms as I ride back to Cardoso House. That musty, bittersweet smell of hard cash filters through to my nose. But excited as I am that I'll soon get a roof back over my head, maybe a bigger gen, a refrigerator (cold beers, man!), the coldness in Fatoumata's fingers, the lingering image of her henna-painted hands, of the memory or vision that is not to be remembered: it unsettles me and sours my victory.

So all through the journey out of the mainland, I'm telling myself that the reason I'm this way is that I'm a softie. I've left myself grow weak in this world of men, adopted the feelings of these humans, adopted some of their bad traits too (like maybe being greedy, capturing my own kind for roof money, right?)

Yet as I ride over the Third Mainland Bridge, the lagoon breeze of wee morning slapping at my shirt and filling my ears, I think maybe that's not true at all. Maybe my tongue has suddenly become sour with this Ajala man because I understand what it means to be Fatoumata: what it means to be lost, abandoned by the people who're meant to love you most, left alone to fend for yourself in a strange place. Maybe I understand what it means to settle into a world that doesn't suit you, but to also be too scared to leave because you don't even know what's out there, if it's better or worse. I know what it is to be caught in the interstices, to be liminal, to be half-and-half.

It's not like I could've just pulled her, or those kids, out of the house, right? I mean, I don't want to think of what an angered wizard is capable of. But at the same time, I do this job because I want to save things from their helplessness—godlings and people alike. Shouldn't I be running in the opposite direction, then?

I brush off the thoughts as I approach Carsodo House. It's dark, because Payu has not put on the gen, as usual. After parking the bike and tossing the Ghana-Must-Go bag under the stairs, I'm about to retrieve the gen when I feel it on my collarbone. A white hot icy signature.

Upstairs.

I take the stairs in threes, flashing my daggers as I bound down the corridor, screaming Payu's name.

The door to his room is closed. It's never closed.

I would break it down, but too much of the house is already in ruins. Slowly, I turn the knob and ease it inwards.

Payu is seated on the bed, chill as anything. Behind him, a woman, a god, stands with her hands on his shoulders. There's the stench of humus, of rich earth, in the room, alongside a smell I don't recognise, yet somehow know is the smell of birthing, of childbearing.

She's taken on the form of a young woman, twenties or thirties, light-skinned, with massive coffee braids that sweep down to her waist. Her neck and arms are layered in blue markings that give the impression of beaded jewellery, and her dress is a rainbow of blue and white over denim trousers. Behind her, within her, before her, like superimposed imagery, is the exact wooden carving juxtaposition of a dwarf with a long head and a crown that I saw with Taiwo.

Her eyes are white cold fire, and they're glaring at me.

"Orisha 'daji," she hisses. "Where is my brother?"

Her voice sends thoughts of salt and stone and fields and graves through me; thoughts of markets and mines and nurseries and chasms. I blink it all away, trying to concentrate.

"Kehinde," I say, slowly, my palms out to signify I mean no harm. "He's not here. But calm down. Maybe remove your hands from Payu, right? Let's talk."

She breathes, says: "Okay."

Then she kicks Papa Udi across the room.

The old man flies and crashes into me. Payu is not heavy enough to knock me over, but him falling into me means I toss my daggers out of the way, which is exactly what Kehinde is counting on.

The woman sails across the room, too fast for my human eyes. I shove Papa Udi out the doorway and roll out of the way myself. I catch a glimpse of Kehinde's shoes as she lands— carton brown, suede, monk buckle, not at all godly, not at all made for fighting—and then her foot is coming for me and I have to duck and roll again.

I get up to face her, my arms in front of me.

"Wait, wait, wait," I'm saying. "Lemme explain."

Kehinde yells and claps her hands once, thrice, once, thrice. A drumbeat rhythm. She chants in a language akin to the one Taiwo had sung in. She bends, links her arms as if cradling a baby, then opens up, as if for an embrace.

The air crackles. A soft whoosh.

Something slams into my chest.

I'm picked up a few feet and my back slams into the wall; I drop to my hands and knees, the wind knocked out of me. My head pounds, mega migraines, like someone installed a nightclub in my head. My skin tingles, like my blood isn't sure where to accumulate.

Charmcasting. She's charmcasting.

She chants and beats another charm into form, blasts it against me. I roll away just in time. The spiritual energy smacks the wall, leaving a huge dent.

Then she screams.

I push my hands to my ears, opening my mouth to contain the

pain, but her screaming just gets louder, louder. She stamps her feet, claps her hands, chants something between a playground song and a war cry. The pounding in my head grows so that I can no longer hear her, lost in a world of agony. I don't know when I drop to my knees, to the floor, clasping my ears, squirming as a wetness trickles through them into my fingers, in too much pain to even remember to appeal.

Then, the sound of dull impact, of something slamming into something.

A thud. The pain quenches.

Papa Udi stands over me with a piece of broken rafter in one hand, dripping something that smells of garlic and scentleaf. His other hand is on his waist. He grimaces, shakes his head and tsk-tsks.

"Gettup," he says. "See how you don' go put us for wahala?"

WE ROUSE KEHINDE in Payu's tiny workroom, an old garage annexed to the side of the house. We do this after Papa Udi writes a ward ritual about her.

He does it in the usual way: first we cast a circle to keep the spiritual energy contained, but using salt as our material instead of an ọbẹ iṣẹ̀ṣẹ́ or candles or chalk or a censer. We do this because Payu believes the things my esper picked up reveal that Ibeji are earth gods.

Next, he invokes Kehinde into the circle, writing her into the salt with Nsibidi script. He uses what the Yorubas loosely term an oriki: a sort of True Name and/or title, sung in poetic verses that carry the embodiment of one's past, present and future. Anyone knowledgeable enough in a godtongue to weave a story using one's oriki can weave a charm to affect their very character. Hence, why Nigerian mothers frown at kids who're too forthcoming: tell the wrong people enough about yourself, and they can harm you with your own name. Technically, one mustn't use an oriki to weave a ritual; if one is versed enough in a godtongue, they can cast a general ritual, and if particularly powerful, can do this by simply speaking the words. But Kehinde is too strong for that.

Papa Udi narrates in song as he writes; and I listen, catching the little Yoruba I can. The story tells of twin gods who came down from Orun and made home on earth. One is hunted and captured by a demigod (he uses the expression orisha 'daji, *half orisha*, something I really hate to be called). The other twin is angry and vows to get him back, but ends up also captured.

Then he binds Kehinde into the tale, drawing an earth pentacle across the ward to seal her in. That about does it. With the subject ensconced within the circle, the ritual is complete. Payu tips a few drops of peppermint oil into a handkerchief and holds it to her nose for a few seconds. She comes to, coughing, her braids wild and feral.

Instantly, she lunges for Papa Udi, smacks the edge of the circle with a *pop*. She's taken aback for a second, confused, then she's back up again, smacking herself against the air about its circumference, hysterical. She chants, beats a rhythm with her hands and feet. The ward does its work well—containing not just her, but also whatever spiritual energy she's exuding.

After one final try that throws her to the ground, she sits up, takes one good look at herself, at the ward, then starts to sob.

I look at Papa Udi, who shrugs, as if to say, *this is your problem.*

"Kehinde," I say, squatting.

She covers her face in her hands, her body racking with real, human sobs.

"Kehinde."

"You took him," she says between sobs. "You took him."

"Listen, *I* didn't take your brother. Someone hired me."

"But you took him?"

"Yes."

She drops her hands and looks at me. "Why?"

I'm not sure what the answer is. I could say I did it for roof money, but is that really true?

"Who is this person?"

"He's the Baálẹ̀ of a former community in Agbado. His name is Lukmon—"

"—Ajala," she completes, then starts to wail again. "You've killed us, you've killed us."

Papa Udi stares pointedly at me, crosses his arms and *hmphs*. I breathe, then:

"Okay, so you know this man."

Kehinde shakes her head, long, slow. "You do not understand for how long we have fought, how long we have fled, how long we have evaded this man and his kind."

"Wizards?"

She shakes her head again. "He is much more." Then her face emerges from the mass of braids. "But you are worse, orisha 'daji, for bringing Taiwo to him."

I flinch at the name. How many times must I tell people I'm not half of anything?

"Look," I say, "calm down. This is how I make money, okay?"

"Do you care at all?" she says. "I know you're half them"—she motions to Papa Udi—"but do you care for your people at all?"

Papa Udi senses my rising anger and pulls me back, eases me aside, then faces her himself.

"Ajala. How you know am?"

There's a command in his statement that even Kehinde recognises. She calms a little.

"He has been hunting us," she says. "Taiwo and I migrated to Tafawa Balewa Square after we came down. First, he sent men. But our charms, it bled their ears, drove them back. Back in Orun, we could've swiftly destroyed them, you know? Bound them into earth or called on their bodies to rotten. But Orun left us only this one way to defend ourselves. Somehow, this man knows, and it makes him relentless; he keeps sending and sending. Once, he came by himself. He was very strong; too strong. He uses charmcasting."

Papa Udi and I look at each other.

"That one no possible," Papa Udi says.

"Are you stupid?" Kehinde says. "I know what I saw."

"Humans can't charmcast," I tell her. "They even die if they try too hard. It burns you up."

"Yes, I know," she says. "This is how I know he's not ordinary—he has something... *more*. He chased us deep into the island, then gave up. We believed he feared us rallying other orishas and defeating him. We didn't know he was rallying one of us against us instead."

She looks at me then, in a way so unsettling that I go perch in a corner.

"So una two separate," Papa Udi says.

She nods. "For safety. I didn't want to leave him, but Taiwo is stubborn. He thinks himself my elder." She sniffs again. "He stayed on the island, to be more connected, so he could defend himself better."

"And you?" I ask. "I searched the whole island and you weren't there."

"I'm strong enough without a centre." She twists her lips. "Plus I was busy hiding, from the likes of you. If any one of us got captured, I felt I'd be in a better position to retrieve Taiwo than the other way around."

Papa Udi shrugs and looks at me. Did I have more questions to ask?

"Ajala wants you," I say. "So unless there's something I'm not understanding, give me a good reason not to deliver you to him."

Kehinde's eyes narrow.

"You think you know what you're playing with," she says. "You think you know what this man is. You think you know anything."

"You're right. Maybe I don't. So tell me."

"Do you know what I am?" She's rising now, the weeping woman gone, the authority of a god returned to her voice. "Do you know what we are?" She stands tall, towering over me at almost seven feet, staring me down. Her tattooed beads ripple, shimmer. "We are Ibeji, orisha of the Divine Abundance." She steps forward to the edge of the ward. "We are the keepers of the essence of all things. We are wisdom, growth, prosperity, fertility. We are life. We are existence."

Papa Udi is nodding to me, telling me she's right.

"So," I say again, "why does Ajala want you?"

She shakes her head. "If we are the keepers of existence, why else will anyone want us? Why else have people hunted us for ages long before you were born?"

Papa Udi blinks. Disbelief is written all over his face. "Ajala wan—"

"—make orisha, yes," Kehinde says, sitting back into the circle, hugging her legs to herself. "He wants to make gods, and you, orisha 'daji, have just given him the ingredients."

CHAPTER FIVE

WE LEAVE KEHINDE in the ward and try to catch an hour or two of sleep before dawn. It's a pointless venture, because my mind ticks like clockwork, my belly roiling from hunger. Half of my bed is still wet with dew, and though I lie in the dark corner of the moonlit room—thanks to my new skylight—aiming for sleep ends up a pointless venture.

I go downstairs and mix cocoa and milk into a bowl with garri and sugar. As I eat it with lukewarm water, I'm reminded again that if we had a bigger gen and a refrigerator, this snack-meal would've turned out much better with chilled water. This causes my thoughts to run the gamut from Ajala to Fatoumata to Taiwo to Kehinde, and back to Papa Udi and—you'll never guess—my mother, whom I barely think of.

Pacing and restless, I find myself back at the workroom, garri bowl in hand. Kehinde is seated in the circle in a lotus position, her eyes shut and her breathing even. I don't know if she's asleep (do gods sleep?), so I just sit in a corner and munch my snack quietly, watching her.

"How did you become so?" Kehinde speaks suddenly. Not even her eyes twitch or a braid moves, just her lips.

"I don't understand."

"How did you become so corrupted? So much like them? So much that you turn on your own people?"

I slam my bowl on the floor. "First of all, you dunno shit about me, so end this *your people* talk right now. I don't *turn* on anybody. I do my job—I relocate the infestation you people brought down here. I help! Is it my fault they go where they don't belong?"

She opens her eyes and frowns. "What're you talking about? That's not what I asked."

I breathe out. "Know what? Forget it."

She studies me for a second. "You're conflicted. You think yourself misjudged."

"Whatever."

"Of your parents, who is divine?"

"My mother."

"I see. And the other?"

My shoulders stiffen. See, of all the questions that should truly require asking, this is one I've never asked myself. I've broached it with Papa Udi a few times. He's as clueless as I am. My father might as well have fallen off the face of the earth.

"I don't know."

"Hmm," she says. I suddenly feel like I'm at an interview, like I need to defend myself.

"I don't know *anything* about where I came from, about who I am. My mother is—or was—a god, that's the much I know. I don't know what pantheon she's from, or where she is. Papa Udi doesn't know either—everything about me was revealed to him by Aziza, a whirlwind god he used to proxy with back when he was in Urhoboland. They've long parted ways, he and this god, and all he knows is what was revealed to him, and how he came to find and raise me. Our best guess is Aziza was a friend to my mother's, and simply helped deliver a message." I look to her face. "So, there. Story of my life."

"Hmm." She nods again.

"What?"

"Nothing, I'm just thinking," she says. "You're definitely not of Orun. Where I come from, things like you are curses. We seek your halfbreed kind and slay you instantly. That you're still alive says your mother is definitely not from my place."

I stop eating and just look at her. I've been called many names, but never *thing* or *curse*.

"Your pantheon is probably looking for you, if they know you exist. Especially if they've twisted the truth out of your mother."

The thought of this makes my ears hot, but I swallow down my anger and ask a more reasonable question instead:

"What d'you know of other pantheons?"

She shrugs. "Not much. I'm the warrior half of Ibeji. Taiwo is the knowledge half." She says this wistfully. "My brother knows the songs of a thousand pantheons. He would entertain with their stories and histories. He was a scholar back in Orun, pooling knowledge for the growth of your earthkind and the peoples of other worlds." Then she stares at me, filled with purpose. "Help me get him back, and maybe we can find what song holds your oriki."

I scrape the last garri out of my bowl, gulp it down and smack the plate on the floor.

"So." I dust my palms together. "I believe you need me to help you confront Ajala. This means you believe Ajala is too strong for you alone. I'm curious: is this why you came for me instead? Because you think I'm weak?" I chuckle. "That hasn't worked out well for you, has it?"

"I came for you because your very unique essence is all over Ìsàlẹ̀ Èkó," she says. "From the chatter of the godlings—I understand them, if I listen just right—I gathered what happened. I tracked you to your wizard's house."

"Or you're just afraid of Ajala."

"I fear no one. I am Kehinde."

"Says the god who can't handle one-and-a-half humans."

I'm riling her up, I see. Her fists clench, then release.

"Taiwo and I, we are connected," she says. "I sensed my brother's distress throughout the time you hunted him. He was afraid, confused, just like during the war. I knew he was gone the minute I could no longer feel him. May you never get to experience that; but then again, may you."

"You held Papa Udi when I came," I say. "I've felt it plenty."

"I see," she says. "So you're on their side now? Do you think the same thing they do? You think us alien, an infestation of parasites come to take over your world? But you see, there's no difference between how you, David Mogo, find yourself in this world, and how we find ourselves here."

"How so?"

"We didn't ask for it. We're both here by accident."

"I'm not an accident."

She stares at me, unblinking.

I breathe. "How did you come here?"

"You don't know?"

"We know you guys fell from the sky, and that's it."

She frowns. "So you don't know about the orisha war."

"A war? A war brought you here?"

Kehinde looks up at the ceiling. "It is a long story, and my brother tells it better. But I'll try." She clears her throat. "One of us, Aganju, was a thinker, a philosopher. He did not share the raging fire that was his brother, Sango. For this, we considered him barely a menace, and thus we did not see his search for the meaning of life, not until it had consumed him. First, he brought his case before Obatala—what if we recreate the divine, form life of life? Imagine all we could do, all the ways we could make Orun better. Of course that would require drawing from a fount of the essence of all things—there are other sources besides us Ibeji, you see, but not a single one is easy to procure.

"Now Obatala—Obatala is our supreme guardian, yes?—he was having none of it. But Aganju has a thirst that cannot be sated—the fire that burns in his brother burns in him, after all. He was determined to make Obatala see how much better things could be if he could bring beings to fruition. And like that, Aganju, aided by his brother Sango, conspired to take a healthy dose of godessence and cross it with the weakest of us whom they could suppress by their strength." She shakes her head. "He made these... these senseless things you have running around, failing woefully. And, unlike you humans believe, one's creator does not hold supreme power over the created: such is the freedom of being. Aganju and Shango wielded their essence over them, but they were too much. Some got away, many wreaked havoc in Orun. It was a mess."

She sighs. "Obatala's judgement was swift and firm. Exile. But Aganju and Shango are revered, powerful, influential. There were too many who loved and stood by them. What was supposed to be simple punishment gave rise to defiance, revolt and, finally, mutiny against Obatala's supremacy.

"Like that, the whole of our home was thrown into chaos. The war was long and hard, and became the end of Orun as we knew it. In the wake of our pantheon's destruction, some of us fell here, many others in other parts of this world, and in parts of other worlds. What you people call *godlings* are Aganju's creations, falling alongside us. No one knows where Aganju or Obatala fell. Good riddance to rubbish, if you ask me."

"So how does this connect?" I'm really not here for a history lesson. "To us, right here, right now?"

She chuckles. "Humans. You too have inherited their stupidity. Can't you see this is the exact same thing your Ajala is planning to do? He must have gained knowledge of Aganju's feat and found a way to achieve it. Whatever his plan, it begins with us. And if he is going the way of Aganju, I can promise you it will not end well, for you or whatever little slice of this world you wish to protect." She stares pointedly at me. "We did not ask for this war, but we became victims anyway. We are refugees in a place we cannot call home; we cannot go back to the place we *should* call home." She pauses. "This will be you if you don't do what is right. That is, if this isn't already you, orisha 'daji."

"My *name* is *David Mogo*," I say, rising. "And you don't know shit about me. I didn't cause your war, and I didn't bring you here. Don't try to guilt me into anything."

"I'm only telling you a story."

"Whatever. I'm going to bed."

When I'm at the door, Kehinde says to me: "Whatever you seek, David Mogo, you know some of the answers lie here. You know what you must do to get them."

Then she shuts her eyes and goes back to 'sleeping.' I stand there for a while and watch her, then return to bed.

I do not sleep.

CHAPTER SIX

THE NEXT MORNING, we have to beg Kehinde to come out of the ward. She folds her arms and crosses her legs. *You people think you're wise, trapping me? Ooooh. Just let me sit here and watch you all die by your own hand.* I spend an hour convincing her that we only want to talk, to put together our best intentions and see if we can come to a consensus. Eventually, when she has promised not to harm us in any way, Papa Udi wipes the ward and she steps out safely, tossing her braids in triumph. Her material form is much prettier when she isn't scowling.

Now in the living room, we stand around the one large table occupying the empty side of the room—a table we like to think is a dining table, but really isn't. Kehinde is perched on the edge of a tall stool. Papa Udi offers to make her tea; she scoffs and tells him higher beings do not drink filthy human shit. Papa Udi goes into a sullen silence from then on.

"You and I," Kehinde says to me, "we're going to that Ajala's place. And then you're going to help me get Taiwo back."

Papa Udi makes a click at the back of his throat. "Is like this one never understand."

"I understand fully," she retorts, perched on the edge of a tall stool. "He might be a more powerful wizard than you are"—she juts her chin at Papa Udi—"but we must get my Taiwo. Because if he starts to use Taiwo's essence…" She shakes her head.

"So," I say, drumming my fingers on the table, "explain this thing again. What does he want to make deities for?"

"I don't know. What I know is that he will take of my brother's essence, cross them with mortal lifeforms and create gods he will force to bow to his command. They might or might not be akin to Aganju's, but considering how savage your kind can be towards one another, will definitely pose a major threat. You could suffer the same terrible fate we suffered at Orun. Or worse."

Papa Udi frowns in confusion, but I brush it aside.

"What's in it for us?" I ask. "Why don't I just take this money and enjoy my life?"

"It depends," she says, "on if you really want answers to the questions you seek"—she looks directly in my eyes when she says this— "and if you're ready to live with the guilt when your people crumble under Ajala's hand."

Papa Udi chews, sucks the bitterness from whatever's in his mouth and says: "But una know say wizard no fit attack wizard, abi?"

"What is the basis of this?" Kehinde asks.

"Practitioner ethics," I say. "If any of them fights another using their skills, everyone turns on that person."

"So that means Ajala won't attack us if we go with him?"

I turn to Papa Udi in mock dramatics. "What a wise thought I didn't have!"

Payu shakes his head. "No, no, no. Na die two of una dey and I cannot follow you for such a thing. Good luck if you wan go die, but you cannot drag me along. David, no. I say no. No!"

IT TAKES ME the remainder of the day to persuade Papa Udi to come with us. Kehinde spends the time going about the house, *mmhn*-ing and *aah*-ing at articles of interest. Papa Udi pretends to cook beans, and spends a lot of time in a kitchen he barely spends time in, slicing lots and lots of onions that he actually hates but pretends to like in his old age. I throw in incentives: we get to find Taiwo and see if he knows anything about my mother; we'll be doing Lagos a favour; we'll add it to our portfolio and use it to wring more jobs out of Femi Onipede and her Lagos State Paranormal Commission. I would tell him about Fatoumata too, but something holds my tongue.

"Fine," he says at exactly 7pm. "But I must carry things follow body."

By *things*, Papa Udi means his War Kit, a leather briefcase belonging to the '90s that he says he'll carry for consultations, but never does. It contains compartments stuffed with recipes—powders and potions alike—and a number of artefacts made through rigorous rituals. Some are wearables, some throwables, some consumables. I don't know how half of them work, because Papa Udi sent me to school instead, back when he still went on consultations. He said that life wasn't for me.

Well, wasn't *he* wrong?

I, on the other hand, carry only my daggers. My plan is for us to solve this as amicably as possible, so I'll go with nothing else but my wits. What with me wearing my godessence on my sleeve (literally), I'd better look like the least possible menace;

anyone working on the back of a good recipe or ritual will earmark me as first target.

We leave close to sunset, when the sky is split into a dichotomous rainbow: half a sharp orange, half a numbing deep blue. Papa Udi's bony knees dig into my waist from the backseat of the Bajaj, as I ride through the Lagos-Ibadan Expressway to Agbado rail crossing for a fourth time in three days.

Of course one god, one human, and one in-betweener cannot fit on my Bajaj, so we asked Kehinde to find her way there by herself, giving her instructions to meet us first at the railway crossing.

The plan is, only Papa Udi and I will go inside. She might be a god, but I can't trust her not to turn hysterical in there, and I can't trust Ajala to not have some trick up his sleeve and capture her on the spot. The kind of diplomatic discussion we're going to be having, we need the coolest heads ever.

Papa Udi chews behind me, the breeze in his face, nonchalant in that way one becomes at his age. His mouth is turned down so that I know he thinks he's doing something distasteful going to Ajala's house—someone he detests. Still, I think he relishes it, in that way you do when you're so old you don't care anymore.

We arrive at the railways and park to wait for Kehinde. Papa Udi, in the meantime, checks up on his charms. He has three Nsibidi ward amulets on: a bracelet and two rings, one on the middle finger of each hand, all baptised in ebo. He downs two other herbal potions as well—one that prevents him from being manipulated, and one that enables him to disapparate, to get out real fast, if he absolutely needs to. He used to sell the latter to interstate bus and truck drivers, so they could disappear right in the moment before an accident. He insists he only does honest work now, so I wonder why he's still making these.

We stay another hour with no sign of Kehinde. Papa Udi is starting to tire, and no one wants a tired old man on their hands, so we move ahead without her.

Another two minutes, and we're at Ajala's gates. I honk and park my bike outside the compound, in case I need to make a quick escape. The policeman at the gate, same guy from last night, is not happy to see us, especially Papa Udi and his case. He lets us in anyway.

We're back in the foyer. Ajala keeps us waiting for about thirty minutes, then rushes in, his steps light, as if he's happy to see me.

All that vanishes the minute he sets sights on Papa Udi.

He stops short, tucks his hands into the pockets of his jalabiya, studies Papa Udi's ward charms and nods.

"Odivwiri."

Papa Udi doesn't nod back. He just chews and chews, watching Ajala, who sits opposite us, slowly, carefully.

"So, you're here for the bottle," he says to me.

I blink. "Not really."

He nods. "I see." He's waiting for me to explain, but he's looking at Papa Udi.

"I'm reconsidering," I say. "I think maybe I won't take this job. So, I'll give you your money back, no problem."

"No problem," Ajala repeats. His fingers are stained black at the tips, his fingernails bitten, stubbed. Has he been digging through herbs again? His eyes look darker, shaded, like he hasn't been getting much sleep. He looks tense, on the edge. That look is not helping me right now.

"Yes," I say.

"And you'll like what in return?" He looks to Papa Udi. "This one that you brought, Payu here, it can't be for nothing."

I stiffen at that name.

"No ever call me that thing," Papa Udi says, speaking up for the first time. "Ever."

I'm looking at Papa Udi, confused. That name is intimate, in-house. The ease with which Ajala says it tells me there's some history here, something Papa Udi hasn't really been forthcoming with. What else has this man been hiding from me?

"Oh, he never told you?" Ajala says, reading my face. "Ah, na wah oh." He leans back now; he has the upper hand. "Payu was my Baba na. He trained me for a while when I was just coming up."

I watch Papa Udi, who's refusing to look at me, slightly narrow his eyes.

"Call me that name again," he says.

"Okay, okay," I'm saying, my hands out. "We just want Taiwo back. That's all. We give you your money, I get him from the Yasal bottle, we go on our way. Everybody's fine. What about that?"

Ajala is dumbfounded for a second, then starts to laugh. As he does, the palace guards about him snicker too, and that's when I notice them for the first time—one at each corner of the foyer, like on the first day. Six in total, I count.

"You think I care about the money?" he asks finally. "Measly one-and-a-half million is nothing compared to what I plan to build when I'm through with my work. Ibeji is very critical to what I'm doing here, okay? So, no; no returning."

I breathe. "I understand that, sir, but maybe we can reason something."

"Oh, there's nothing to reason," he says, then rises. "If you won't provide your services anymore, no problem. I have what I need to begin my work." He beats his chest. "Me, Ajala One; when I'm done, you won't recognise Lagos again."

He's saying this when a chorus of shouts rise at once, from somewhere within or behind the house. One or two voices first, then a good number, commanding someone, something to stop.

Then a gunshot, loud and rattling. We shoot to our feet. Ajala flashes us a sharp look.

"Sit," he hisses. His men move in sync with his command, and he looks to them: "If any one of them moves, finish them." Then he's gone off.

The ruckus increases. Now there's a rush of feet. The men stand stoic, flexing their muscles.

Papa Udi nudges me and whispers in my ear: "See their rituals."

Again, I notice the tattoos peeking out from beneath the sleeves of their t-shirts. This must be how he forces them to work for him, probably tying them down with charms. I'm uneasy in my seat, being cut off from something important happening about me, and guarded by warded men. I feel the tensing of Papa Udi's shoulder next to me.

"We gats to commot here," he whispers.

A collection of screams reaches us—children's voices. Sounds: a stampede, a tumult, a chase. The clatter of something climbing the zinc roof above us. More screams, objects shattering.

A second gun report. More shouts.

Then, amidst these, a voice starts to beat a rhythm, chant something from somewhere deep in the rooms of the palace; something manic, something between a war chant and a playground song.

Papa Udi and I look at each other, eyes popping.

"Which kain stupid—" Papa Udi says.

"Shet. Trap." I yank his wrist. "Time to go."

The closest guard moves just when I do. He's real close, though, so I grab a fistful of his bushy hair. He's thick and buff like me, but is he a demigod? No.

I crash his head against my knee, and he falls.

The remaining five come for us.

"Cover your nose!" Papa Udi screams, then opens his palm and flings a powder into the air.

A strong, unpleasant odour like weed mixed with bitterleaf hits the air. I know this thing. Salvia, a powerful hallucinogenic, mixed with ginkgo. Worse yet, he's ground black pepper into it. It's like tear gas that makes you go gaga in under a second. All you need do is breathe.

These men might be spiritually warded, but this isn't a spiritual attack. They reel back once the dust hits the air, then start to cough and scratch at their eyes. We don't wait to see what else happens.

Out in the yard, the sight that greets us grabs hold of my chest and doesn't let go.

Children of all shapes and sizes run about, making escape wherever they see. Half of them are midway over the fence. Some look around, barefoot, confused. Some are without shirt or shorts or blouse or skirt, running in no direction at all.

The same kids I saw the other day.

"Who be these—"

"Move, Payu," I say. "Get the bike, I get Kehinde."

I'm off before he can protest, trying to make my way through the sea of children and in the direction they're emerging from.

The sounds of Kehinde casting her charms increase. Some screaming, thuds, whooshes and bursts, followed by a voice I recognise: Ajala.

The rumours must be true. He and Kehinde must be fighting by charmcasting.

But how could he possibly—?

Out in the corner of my eye, someone covered in a black dress is helping a child over the barbed-wire fence. Despite her slim frame, she is heaving the burly child up. She turns to bring her shoulders into play, to give him one final hoist, and that's when I recognise the oily tribal marks on Fatoumata's cheeks.

Then a loud report, and something strikes the fence above her head where the burly child has just gone over. Fatoumata screams and covers her head in her hands. I look in the direction the shot came from and see the policeman who let us in cocking a rifle, readying himself for another shot. He raises the gun to his shoulder again.

Fucking bastard.

I pull one dagger from the sheath about my belt, take aim, and fling before his finger moves. The blade strikes him deep in his shoulder and knocks him over stat.

The gun goes off.

Fatoumata screams.

More children are criss-crossing the yard, but I can see her clearly, crumpled on the ground, gripping her upper arm which I know is bleeding before I can even see it.

I rush over to Fatoumata, pick her up, and throw her over my shoulder. Her skin is hot under the robe, and she is whimpering, weeping, hurting. If I must keep her alive, I'll need to take her to Cardoso fast. Will she even make the long trip? I have to go now, now.

I still hear Kehinde singing, beating. The thumps, the crashes, Ajala's grunts.

She's a god; she can handle him, right?

I hoist Fatoumata properly—she whimpers a little in response—and then head for the bike. If I'm going to save anything, might as well be things that can't save themselves.

The gate is padlocked, but I give it one well-placed kick and the padlock gives way. I fling the gate open, and like that, the children pour out of the gate into the wet night of Agbado.

Papa Udi has already guided the bike over. I lay Fati in front of myself as I get on, kick it and rev. Payu gets on behind me and we zoom out, leaving the fracas in our wake, and the fading voice of Kehinde frantically beating and singing for an escape that might never come.

CHAPTER SEVEN

It's been two weeks since we tried to give Ajala his money back, and everything's changed.

For the first time ever, Cardoso House has three occupants. Papa Udi has been treating Fatoumata's gunshot wound, which has begun to heal nicely enough so that she now gets out of bed and stares out the window in my room upstairs, looking at the old Union Bank and UBA buildings in the distance. She never says anything—it takes me a while to realise she's actually speech- and hearing-impaired. She signs with her hands to us sometimes, but neither Papa Udi nor I have any idea what it means. However, Papa Udi, a man of few words himself, somehow manages to always meet her needs. I've asked her questions a couple of times—*Where are your parents? Will they be looking for you?*—but all she does is blink back at me, and sometimes sobs, so heavy and racking I become uncomfortable and leave her to herself.

Papa Udi has also, for the first time, drawn a ward about Cardoso House. There's never been a reason to do this: everyone's too scared to go back to Lagos Island as it is, and the few who try are roughed up so bad by rogue godlings that it's enough to deter others. Armed robbers have tried to visit us once or twice. It did not end well for them.

Now, though, we're harbouring the intended wife of one of the most powerful wizards in Lagos. To say nothing of having delivered a divine weapon into the hand of said crazy wizard. Now Papa Udi has to do something he hasn't done in a long time. He pulls out his four staves etched with the Nsibidi stories for a large ward, then plants one staff in each corner of the compound, completing a makeshift enclosure. He writes invocations in native chalk dipped in saltwater and dried by burnt scentleaf, and dares anyone or anything he hasn't cleared to cross those boundaries.

I wonder what happens if it's Kehinde, though. We haven't seen or heard anything from her since the incident, and I'm starting to think she's been captured just like her brother, and that doesn't spell well for anyone, not even us.

My suspicions are confirmed on the midweek evening news of the third week. Fatoumata's not healed enough yet to take the stairs, so Payu and I watch the evening news alone in the parlour, the gen chugging outside. The presenter is a slim, bright lady with a large forehead that makes her grim frown even more pronounced.

"Residents of Agbado Oke Odo Local Government Area of Lagos State today visited our studios with complaints about missing children in their community," she reads. "A spokesperson, identifying himself as Mr Frank Okunola, says that the community believes the current Baálẹ̀, His Royal Highness Lukmon Ajala I, is responsible for these disappearances, in collusion with the police."

Papa Udi and I sit up. The camera cuts, and a small man

wringing his fingers appears onscreen.

"Police arrest our children, and we don't know what happen to them after that," the man says, his voice quivering as if he's just been asked to stop crying. "My son Majid, he is only twelve years. They take him—they say he is loitering, he is wandering. They say I must pay bail money, but after I pay, they say they have already release him. I go home, he's not there. I wait, two days, three days, no Majid. Then one day, Majid come home, running. He say police take him somewhere, but he cannot say where. He say they keep him and many other children in a big, dark room. They feed them bread and water only one time everyday. They give him one medicine to drink in the place where they keep him. They say the medicine is so that if he talk about that place, he will die."

"And what does this have to do with your Baálẹ̀?" the interviewing reporter asks.

"Because people say they see many children in Baálẹ̀ palace," the man replies. "What Baálẹ̀ is doing with them, we don't know. But our children are there, we know this. We want the police and the government to help us to bring our children home."

The TV cuts to a small crowd protesting outside the TV studios, demanding their voices be heard. A couple more people get their stories in, all the same—the police is selling their children to the Baálẹ̀. Some kids have returned, but for most of them at the TV studio, theirs have not, and they're here to seek justice.

Payu and I look at each other. This is *not* good.

"We spoke to the Police Public Relations Officer, Ademola Daramola," the reporter's voice-over continues, "concerning unanswered complaints made at the Agbado Police Division."

The scene cuts again to a light-skinned slim man with a big smile that has no place on a Nigerian police officer's face.

"Ah, you know how children are with fantasies, eh?" he says. "Yes, we do pick up some young ones who're wandering around—to keep them safe and keep them from crime, really. But we *always* send them home, once they have been identified by family members. Some of them we pick up for illegal activities—hawking and selling in traffic, for instance. Most of these parents complaining now, they send their children out for these illegal activities, expose them to criminals and unscrupulous elements. Then when they go missing, they blame the police and the great Baálẹ̀."

"So you're saying these allegations are false?" the reporter asks.

"Yes," he replies confidently, that smile still planted on his face. "Some of our men are stationed at that same palace. If anything is happening there, we would know. I know Ajala personally; he would never hurt a fly. He has the best interests of this community at heart. You can see it from the good things he's done already."

The screen cuts again, to a group of youths gathered outside the palace, chanting in Yoruba and carrying placards reading *LEAVE OUR BAÁLẸ̀ ALONE* and *THANK YOU FOR WATER, YOUR HIGHNESS* and *WHEN THE GOV'T LEFT, YOU STAYED*. Ajala, looking very out-of-place in a suit, like an aged, respected professor, comes out and pats them on the back as they bow to him.

"We made attempts to reach His Royal Highness for comments, but he was still unavailable as at the time of this report."

The screen cuts back to the sombre news presenter before Papa Udi takes the remote and mutes the TV, shaking his head with disapproving click from the back of his throat.

"This is my fault," I'm saying. "This is all my fault."

"No," he says. "You don do your own. Make them handle their wahala. You no come fit die on top craze people matter." He gets up and shuffles his way upstairs. "Make LASPAC handle am. Everything go dey alright last last."

Maybe he's right. Maybe we should let the LASPAC handle this one. Everything go dey alright last last, eh?

Wrong.

Next day, Femi Onipede comes to visit, That's when I know it's really, really bad.

I WAKE UP the next morning to hear Femi downstairs in the parlour with Papa Udi. Out the window, I see she's come in her sleek 2016 Highlander, bulletproof (maybe even godproof, considering her relationship with Papa Udi). Parked next to it is a navy-blue Hilux, where two men sit—one in the driver's seat, and one in the open back with the tailgate closed. They wear navy-blue combat police uniforms, with the LASPAC logo on their breast pockets, as well as on the side of the vehicle. The one in the back carries an AK-47 assault rifle, which I'm pretty sure houses not just ordinary bullets, again, considering Femi's relationship with Papa Udi.

Over the years, LASPAC has become the only arm of federal or state government that has even acknowledged that we have a problem beyond the realms of physical solutions. It was a parastatal squeezed out by the last governor to combat the deity infestation, right before he was ousted from his own party. Recruits brazen enough to sign up had to undergo two sets of trials: first, pass the eighteen-month police college curriculum in three months; and second, undergo a six-month attachment with a recognised wizard, one of whom Papa Udi used to be until he retired to become a consultant. The third trial, that of being disowned by family for devoting one's life to a profession sneered at by society, was an unwritten one.

Mostly, these men are taught a few key recipes for combating anything with a good command of godessence. But let's be honest: one either wants to be a wizard, or one doesn't. Even I who live with one don't want to, so I'm not surprised only one of every thirty of these men ends up knowing anything about making recipes. The few who do quit the LASPAC right quick and set up shop at Sura. Some become apprentices to the wizards they interned under. All the LASPAC is left with is a bunch of regular boys with their bullets dipped in ebo.

Since the last governor, the commission has been on a downward spiral, receiving a total sum of zero naira in financial backing from the government, which has instead placed all focus on rebuilding a newer, better Lagos closer to Ogun state. I'm not surprised that, now that Ajala has declared war on the state, all government eyes have instantly turned to Onipede, the current director, as if she herself is a wizard. I'm pretty sure, if I were her, I'd turn my eye to the real wizards as well.

I go downstairs.

Femi Onipede looks exactly how the director of a state parastatal should look: smart of build, coarse of voice and sharp of eyes, mostly through years of pushing government papers to places they shouldn't be pushed. She has deepset tribal marks like Fatoumata, terribly out of place under her scholarly spectacles. However, I've never let that plump frame deceive me. Papa Udi says she's ex-military, that she used to be a long-range shooter. I've seen her fire a rifle once before, and everything she did—her stance, her grip, her assurance—spoke to this truth. I don't doubt her ability with a firearm for one minute.

She rises when she sees me, bows slightly. No matter how many times I explain to this woman that, apart from the fact that she's old enough to be my mother, I am not a god and do not deserve worship, she does this every time.

"You saw the news?" she's saying to me, or Papa Udi, or us both. She never looks us in the eye when she talks. Sometimes, I feel she brings those guys outside over for protection—from us.

"Yes," I say. The room falls silent. For a beat, I think Papa Udi is going to go all Nigerian Father on me and rat me out to her, but he just chews and says nothing. Femi Onipede breathes and counts the tiles on the floor. It's as if we're all processing the weight of the storm that's coming, before deciding who's going to go out and pack in all the clothes from the washline.

"He's gone very far," Onipede is saying, still standing. "We believe he's trying to take over Lagos—whether he's going to run for office or launch an outright attack, we don't even know. He's started a movement he calls 'Operation Save Lagos.' The Agbado youths are solidly behind it. There's a hashtag on the internet and everything."

"Hmm," Papa Udi says.

"The children," I say. "The stories. Are they true?"

Papa Udi described them as *taboos*, what Ajala wants to do with those kids. Apparently, the man bumps up the godessence of these kids using the distilled essences of Ibeji, but not before invoking a ritual into the process, binding them to himself via his oriki, so they remain under his control. Payu says he's seen over the years that nothing good ever comes from these sorts of experiments, that the results are always bastardised versions of whatever was planned. If Kehinde's story about the godlings is true, then it means he's simply going to make more of them.

Onipede sighs. "Some of those policemen at Agbado, they live in shanty barracks. They have four, five, six children. They will do anything for money. Pinching children off the street and selling them to the Baálè for fifty, hundred grand is nothing. They do worse. But I cannot confirm or deny anything, because I don't know for sure. The Inspector General says he'll look into it, but that doesn't seem like it'll happen in time for what is coming."

"What's going to happen now?" I ask.

"We're going to have to deal with him," Onipede says, as if repeating someone else's words. "Somehow."

"You go need ebo," Papa Udi is saying. This, of course, is all Onipede ever comes here for.

"Lots and lots of it," I add.

Onipede nods meekly. Then the room falls silent again, all of us knowing that even with all the ebo we can get, we might not be able to defeat Ajala. If what I heard that night was right, then the rumors are true: the man *is* using charmcasting somehow. Fighting that with just ebo will be like spitting on a fire.

"How many men do you have?" I ask.

She shrugs. "Same."

So, little to nothing, then. "Have you spoken to any of the other divineries or wizards? Will they get people to join you?"

Onipede sighs and, though she doesn't shake her head, I feel her do it mentally.

I understand her distress. Trying to get the owners of divineries to band together for a common cause is like asking Hausa northerners and Igbo easterners to come together and eat from the same bowl. The divineries are too busy fighting over themselves for the little belief left in the populace (now that almost all religious conglomerates, churches and mosques alike, have been relegated to the background). Same deal with the wizards, with the added wrinkle of a code that prevents them from attacking Ajala. Trying to bring him down is too much trouble for no reward. It's simply easier to pack up their load and go to Epe or neighbouring states like everyone else.

"Tell us," Papa Udi says, finally returning to his conversational voice. "Wetin you want make we do?"

"Help us," Femi Onipede says, her eyes shiny with almost-tears. "Help us, please."

PAPA UDI AND I spend the next few days preparing a large drum of ebo, the largest he's ever made in one go. Back in the day, I used to enjoy helping him make recipes. He didn't have many tools at the time—like a hand-grinder, for instance—so he used to make me chew ingredients like garlic. Killed my interest fast. The final ebo also tended to be slightly harmful to me, a bit like cigarette smoke to humans. Making a whole drum of ebo is too much on an old man, though, so I agree to help him this time.

We prepare the in the usual two major stages: first, there's measuring the purest forms of the ingredients in the right amounts—weights, volumes, number of leaves, whatever.

Then, there's the mixing, and whatever boiling or burning or any other process involved. The biggest problem here, of course, is remembering all the details; getting every step and measurement right. Get them wrong, and you might make something that could kill you just by smelling it.

Our base ingredient, the one carrying the most godessence, is the local scentleaf, *Ocimum gratissimum*: a massive carrier if harvested the right way. Sometimes, Payu *speaks* to the plant to give of its leaves freely, harvesting them with the utmost tenderness and care so its power is retained. Scent leaf is not so hard to find either, with wild weeds taking over half of Ojo Close, so Payu gathers enough of that.

Next, we need a boosting agent—something with its own dose of godessence but carrying a sharp scent or rough texture. Sometimes, Payu adds sound too—a gunshot, a cat's meow, a song—but only for more complex recipes. The boosting agent latches on to the base ingredient and channels the effect. We use ground eggshells for touch (eggshells, being boundaries themselves, work as boundary eliminators, which help negate whatever spiritual boundary has been set up) and garlic for smell (to perforate said spiritual barrier and reach the entity on the other side). My job now is to help Payu grind a whole BagCo sack of garlic using a large hand-grinder.

After this, we'll need something to connect to the godessence of the user. Recipes work like a chain: the user's godessence connects to that of the recipe, then on to the target. Papa Udi usually uses anything I can give him, from body hair to nail clippings. Sometimes, it's a personal artefact, like an old shirt or even a favourite animal. (I kept a stray pigeon once— couldn't find it after one particular dose of ebo that turned out very potent. Payu and I never talk about what happened to that bird.) For this batch, I give him a battered pair of old shoes and my backpack from secondary school.

The last agent, the binding agent, makes everything meld together evenly. Usually, Payu employs palm oil or ogogoro when mixing small amounts. Given this quantity however, we opt for saltwater, and plan to boil it all to help the mixing along. We just have to watch it carefully to ensure we don't lose the boosting agents' properties.

We grind the garlic in the afternoon, outside in the narrow space between the house and the low fence. The sun beats down on my bare back as I wind the handle of the grinder continuously while Papa Udi adds more garlic when the current batch goes down and comes out the other end in paste.

"So," he says, clearing his throat. "You go follow them go?"

I wind and wind, processing both the garlic and the question. I'm not sure what he's asking me: if I'm going to go because I'm the one who caused it, or if I'm going to go because LASPAC stands a better chance with me leading them.

"Maybe," I say finally. "I dunno."

"Mmhn," Papa Udi says. "E go make sense if you go. That Ajala no be small man."

Again, not sure how I fit into this. I did learn streetfighting back after secondary school—roadside gym, crude weights, makeshift boxing gloves made with mattress foam, wire and tape. Punch, kick, duck, grip, throw. Nothing special that can be used against Ajala. Not like I can charmcast either, or use my always-on godessence somehow. I mean, the thing isn't just going to start firing on all cylinders after all the years I've spent taming it so I could appear normal in school and civil society.

"Yes," I say. "So what're you saying?"

"Join them," he says. "Do something whey make sense. For once."

Our relationship has always been this way. You know what they say about old people, how they tend to pour their frustrations and regrets into the youth around them? Payu always tries to force me to *become something better* than him. He worked his ass off to ship me into King's College, and if not that he couldn't afford it, he would've sent me off to become an accountant or something too. His dream has always been for me to live in Upper Island. He never asked me if that was what I wanted, and this is why we always argue.

I finish grinding the batch and watch him heap new measurements of garlic into the feeder. He supports his waist with one hand as he bends, then sits on a stool and pants after a while. He truly is an old man, it dawns on me now, on the last embers of his life. It dawns on me too, that maybe all he wants is to exit honourably, while helping people. I mean, that's what he'd always done: training apprentices, taking on LASPAC interns. He talks about setting up a divinery here at Cardoso—a real one, not like those charlatans at Sura, to help people. Maybe this is also why he lets me hunt? Help people vicariously through me? Maybe this is the reason he wants me to go with them.

"Wetin happen with you and Ajala?" I say, my bicep shiny with sweat as I work the grinder handle. "Na your student before, ba?"

Papa Udi shrugs. He's trained a lot of people in his prime, and he's filed away and archived that part of his life, never to be spoken about, like with lots of other things. Ajala is the first time I'm encountering one of his students, alive and kicking.

"Did he run away?" I ask.

"No."

"Steal?"

He shakes his head.

"Then what?"

Payu shrugs again. "Just... he no like to face work."

I pause for a moment, stretch my back. "So na dull boy then."

"At all oh," Papa Udi says, and looks up, unfurling the memory by the edge. "Smartest boy whey I don ever train, in fact. But the training no even last two months."

"You send am commot."

"Yes." He adds more garlic, shutting the memory again.

"He do something?"

"Mmhn," Papa Udi says. "Grind."

I grind some more.

"So, what did he do?"

Papa Udi chews for a minute, then says: "The only thing whey concern am throughout na charmcasting."

"I see."

"And that kain talk, I no wan dey hear am for my ear," Papa Udi says. "But the boy—na small boy then, short like this, can raise shoulder, ehn? Anyway, he go dey pepper me with question. I go say, *I no know, shey your Papa na practitioner, na Baálę? Go ask am.* But the boy go pepper me, then him go steal my things go dey mix for house." He clicks the back of his tongue in disgust. "No be with my name pessin go dey do that nonsense. I send am commot fast fast."

He throws in another heap of garlic, continues: "Me, I don see this kain thing before. I no wan hear say any repeat dey happen."

"Where you for see am?" I ask. "Isiokolo?"

And then Papa Udi goes silent and doesn't speak for the next two, three hours.

We cover the bowl of garlic paste with a tray, sit on small plastic chairs, pull out our large stash of scent leaves and start to pluck the leaves from the stalk so we can chop them into our ebo. Papa Udi is statue quiet, not even chewing anymore. I don't even bother. Since I was a kid, I've found a thousand different ways to ask Papa Udi about where he came from and why he moved to Lagos in his thirties. The answer that has always greeted me is silence. I know he's been exiled in some way from where he once called home, and prefers not to speak or think of it, lest it remind him of what he's lost. I respect that. But I'm his foster child (grandchild? Whatever). There are some things he should be able to trust me with.

One night, in those days when he would do a whole green square bottle of Seaman's Aromatic Schnapps in a go, he was drunk enough to tell me he hailed from Isiokolo of Delta State in the Niger-Delta. Now, years after that Night of Shame, as he calls it, whenever this town's name comes up in conversation, he goes cold and quiet like an opossum playing dead.

When he finally speaks, it's something unexpected that comes out of his mouth.

"Your mama," he says. "She too for like make you go."

"Whadda fuck, Payu?" I slap the scent leaf down. "Which kain blackmail be this na? Because of ordinary small mistake?"

"No no," Papa Udi is saying, placating. "Listen. Na just because of wetin she tell me. You know, that night."

That night is the night he received the dream vision from my divine mother that led him to me.

There's a squat guava tree in the backyard of Cardoso house, its slim branches stretching out like an extended yawn. Balanced in the middle of a connection of three branches of that tree was where he found me, swaddled in fine, silky hair the colour of fire and the lengths of which he'd never seen.

Over the years, his aging brain has produced various iterations of the story, and they have all muddled up into an unrecognisable story that is definitely much farther from than closer to the truth. The only thing that remains a constant is the last part of the story, the part where he brings me out of a tree.

After waking from a dream whose details he never tells the same way twice, the story goes that he stumbles down the stairs of Cardoso House in the dead of night, feeling under the stairs for his axe. The cry of a baby pierces his ears, much too loud inside his head, so he follows where it leads, out of the house, around to the tiny backyard. The image of an old wizard with an axe at midnight is something that always amuses me. Apparently, after squinting hard enough into the darkness, he finds me cupped between branches, covered in falling leaves, bawling my eyes out in a swaddling of hair.

The tree is still there, by the way. Whittled down to a bare skeleton after all these years. Payu says he thinks the life of the thing was sustained only for the purpose of delivering me, and now that's done, it's been discarded. He says that's why he won't cut it down, that it deserves to go on even if it's now useless to all. Sometimes, I think he really is talking about himself, that if he lets me go, he too will be done and discarded.

"That night," he's saying now. "For that dream. She tell me say I gats commot you from that tree. Say you big pass to dey hide inside there."

"I see," I say. "As opposed to every other human being who will fit right inside those branches, ba?"

"Shut up," he says. "Listen to me. Your work no be to dey go pursue godlings from people house, okay? You big pass those things. Na wetin you come here for be this. Go do your work."

"Whatever," I say. I slap the last of the leaves down. "Lemme know if you need any more help."

I go around the building then, to the same backyard, and stare at the withered tree with leaves and no fruit, surrounded by concrete flooring. I'm not angry; maybe a bit irritated. If he wants me to go fix a mistake, that's a different thing. But telling me this bullshit story that I'm made for "greater things" is just one fabu too far. When I'm not Harry Potter and some such nonsense.

I'm supposed to go back and help him for the next item: a binding amulet, a necklace made of wooden beads, which we're meant to prepare to help negate Ajala's power. Writing a ritual into an amulet is hard work, worse yet for someone whose oriki you don't know. Papa Udi will need to write the whole ritual into each wooden bead, one at a time, but what do I care? I don't know Nsibidi. Let him handle it.

I feel a presence about me, and I look up, at the back window to my room upstairs. Fatoumata is framed, waist up, by the window, dressed in an oversized t-shirt of mine. Now out of her hijab, I see her hair is cropped very short, her scalp weirdly shiny underneath, just like her cheeks. She's staring at the horizon as she usually does.

That lost look in her eyes, I recognise it. I used to look that way, during our one-hour break period back in King's College, when Payu still did good work as a natural herbal solutions salesman and could pay for my schooling. Not everyone knew who I was, but they *sensed* it, sensed I was *mixed*, just didn't know what with. I did click with a few people, as youngsters are wont to, but I was realistic: it couldn't really last. How many people could I truly explain to that I was half human, half divine? Who would I talk to about my esper? Who would find it okay that that my foster grandpa was a part-time wizard?

I realised too early what a kid never should: that I truly was alone, and that it was okay. I made my peace and spent the rest of my school breaks alone under a tree, like an abandoned baby. And then these things came down and polluted the whole place and ruined Payu's business because everyone thought it was the wizards who did it. I couldn't go to school again, so I went and learned to fight and became a godhunter, and that is okay too.

I look up at her again. Possibly feeling my gaze, she looks down and her eyes find mine.

I smile and wave.

She blinks at me once, twice.

Then she smiles back, a tiny, tentative smile.

And I say, *yeah*. Now *that* is a reason to go blow that bastard's head off.

CHAPTER EIGHT

I'M A BIG man, but I can get around lightly if I want to. So, where stepping on zinc will be a problem for anyone else trying to infiltrate the palace of the Baálè of Agbado at a quarter past midnight, I'm least concerned by that; more bothered that I can be smelled or discovered by people within that building without them even hearing or seeing me. If Ajala can charmcast, let's not put a lid on what he can do.

My thoughts are more focused on the kids who didn't get away, or the new ones captured since then. If they truly end up as taboos, I'm not yet sure how I'll handle that. I won't harm them for the world, because they're something they did not ask to be, and don't deserve to answer for someone else's questions. Half sane, half not; part human, part not. Aside the fact that I'm crawling up this gateman's shed now with a very human body, what really separates me from them? What really stops Femi Onipede's men, stationed underneath the railway tracks opposite the palace, from standing up and shooting me down like everything else half-human in this place?

I ease down from the gateman's post, my daggers out and ready. I expected them to have replaced the last man since I basically ruined his legs, but they seem to have not: the door to the gatehouse is open. Not at all weird; if you were a very powerful ruler of a town with an army of gods and humans under your finger, you'd get complacent from time to time and leave your gate unmanned.

I put the chunky little mobile phone in my hand to my lips.

"The compound is empty."

I stretch my neck to look over the fence. Outside the big gate, in the distance beyond the old railway line that runs in front of the palace, shadows bob up and down. About twenty-five of Onipede's strongest men, armed to the teeth with one rifle each and bullets and vests doused in ebo. I was offered a gun, but I refused. I've never shot one and I'd rather not.

Their heads come into full view, crouched beneath the railway line for cover, a few yards from the gate. They have no reason to fear: no train has come this way in years.

"Ready," a voice says through the phone.

I creep across the compound, listening for sounds other than those of frogs and crickets, peeling my eyes for anything more than the one or two lone fireflies I see. The front door is locked as expected, and all the windows in the house are dark. There's no sign of life. The side of the house, however, leading to the evil back shed, has another door I didn't spot the last time. I creep over and examine it. A padlock is hooked over the bolt, but not locked. I slip it out, slide the bolt and push the door open without a creak.

Bingo.

"I'm inside," I whisper into the phone.

The plan is simple. First, I go in. I make sure I get directly to Ajala as quickly as possible, quickly enough, before he can pull any stunts. Once I can get this warded necklace about him, it'll glue to his skin so tight that getting it off will be like slicking off an ear. It should sever his connection to his godessence. Then, in that window of complete humanity, with zero dose of the divine, I can hold him down. The rest of the men will pour in and take over the house. We can easily rescue the kids who haven't been turned yet, and find a way to revert the taboos and free Ibeji while at it.

Not the best plan, truly. We did consider other ways to try and get him, but the man barely ever leaves the house. When Mohammed doesn't go to the mountain...

I step into the house.

It's pitch black and I have no idea where I am. My intel says I enter into the lobby from the front door—same lobby he entertained me in, the last two times. It used to be a throne room, back when people took the Baálè seriously as a local ruler, but now it's simply a place for receiving guests. From here, three doors go into other areas of the house: courtyard, kitchen, store, wash room, etc. The stairs up to the residential floor are meant to be at an edge of the courtyard.

It seems I'm in one of the working rooms. I sidle close to the wall, feeling for a door, wary of knocking anything over. I find one towards the first corner of the room, unlocked. It leads into the courtyard, a square opening in the middle of the house. There's a clump of blooming yellowbushes in the middle of the courtyard and a couple of graves: Ajala's father and grandfather, if I were to guess by the statues next to them.

The stairs are not hard to find; moonlight leads me to them. Still I haven't set eyes on anyone, and I find it very difficult to believe the house of a man of such importance would be filled with such silence. I look around carefully, taking time to check for signatures again. Nothing.

I go up the stairs. Finding Ajala's room shouldn't be a problem; in standard Yoruba family house planning and architecture, the corridor is lined with doors opposite each other in the *face-me-I-face-you* style. I seem to have entered at the beginning of the corridor: the doors are thin and cheap. The servants' quarters. Next should be the children, then wives, then the head of the agbo'lé at the very end.

I don't care for their arrangements.

By now, I sense something on my collarbone—a nagging absence, like a signature should be there, but isn't. I figure this is some after-effect, or I'm picking up traces of old godessence accumulated here over time; it happens sometimes.

Better get to it, then.

I move quicker, trading stealth for speed now. In a beat, I'm at Ajala's quarters, the large double-swing doors at the end of the upstairs hallway. I put the phone to my lips and whisper:

"Going inside."

Then I kick the door open and jump in, daggers and necklace at the ready.

An icy-white-hot blast of signatures blinds me. My collarbone sings and rings. The heat of too many bodies packed in a room whooshes out of the door.

Then, *raar*.

The taboos lash out as one, blinding hot, icy-white rage. Their eyes are light, fire, blood, essence. Their limbs are whips, teeth slashing, biting, chattering.

I pull the door against me just as the first one nears, back out of the room and fall onto my buttocks. The phone topples out of my hands and into the darkness.

"Trap!" I'm screaming, hoping they still hear me. "Trap!

Then I bound down the corridor. Snarls arise from all over the house, whispers, hisses. A gunshot echoes outside. Another. Another.

Then the rattle of gunfire fills the compound.

As if on command, the taboos burst out of the door behind me and give chase, hissing unspeakables, like the godlings in the streets. Then the doors to the other face-me-I-face-you rooms crash open, and out pour more taboos, some dressed in rags of school uniforms, some bare and naked, wild.

The doors in front of me slam open and a couple of taboos jump into my way. I don't slow down, throwing a knee that catches the first one, a little scrawny child, on the jaw. I wince, not from pain. The second one lunges at me, flashing teeth, catches my arm. It's hanging on to me as I go down the stairs, into the courtyard.

They're dropping from the balcony above; onto the landing, onto the stairs.

I snatch the one off my arm and fling it away as I hustle my way out of there. Then I'm back in the washer room, out the door and into the yard, their hissing in my wake.

There is blood about the ground in amounts I've never set eyes upon in my life. Half of the LASPAC men are lying in the front yard sand, lifeless, guns discarded about. A lone officer is trying to climb onto the gateman's house, but there are four, five taboos on him, pulling him down.

I raise my hand, one dagger in it. The things are pulling him down, and he's losing his hold, struggling to cling on, but for the life of me, I cannot throw it.

Then the night is punctured by the roar of a nearby vehicle. With a loud report, the left side of the LASPAC man's head explodes. He falls, slowly, into the hands of the taboos, who drag him to the ground.

I'm still trying to understand what has happened when the gate bursts open and a large van charges in, lights blaring in my eyes.

I move, not as quickly as I thought. Three shots follow me: two strike the wall and raise mortar dust, then one strikes me in the leg and I go down.

It doesn't hurt, the bullet; not while I'm still trying to get away. But as if on cue, the taboos pour out from the washer room. One dives on me and the next follows, and soon I'm carrying three, four on my back, still trying to make a getaway.

A taboo sinks its teeth into the back of my neck.

"Stop!" a voice commands, and another shot follows. Something punctures the wall next to me. Someone shouts not to hit the taboos.

A taboo drags its fingers across my back and I feel something wet drip down. I swing one, two off me, but that just makes space for the horde pouring out from the washroom and raining down from the roof above.

I go down on one knee, unable to bear the load. A searing pain runs up my leg into my groin, and I can hold it no longer.

I crash to the ground. Taboos pile over me.

"Hold him down," a familiar voice says, then Ajala's face appears over me. He's wearing his professor glasses, as if he hasn't been doing any work tonight.

"One day, bush meat go catch hunter, eh?" he says, then holds a piece of cloth over my nose. My last thought before I go to sleep is wondering why the cloth smells of ogogoro and household bleach.

CHAPTER NINE

I WAKE UP dizzy, my tongue heavy and sandpapery. I try to swallow, but can't; try to see, but can't. My ears are ringing, and I can't smell a thing. I feel like puking.

I'm sitting up, my back to a cold wall. I can't blink my surroundings into focus, can't get a grip of where I am, can't get a fix on any of my five human senses, much less my esper, which I feel is present, but so far away from me, and for the first time ever in my life, out of reach.

My hands and legs, too, I can't move them. My wrists are bound behind me—steel chains, from the feel of it—and no matter how hard I pull apart, I can't snap the binding. Either these must be superior chains or I've lost all of my strength too. My legs are the same, bound together at the ankles and knees. My joints ache from long misuse—minutes, hours?

I remain this way for a time again—hours, minutes?—drifting in and out of consciousness, weak, a persistent ache in my joints. My back stings where the taboos scratched it, but should heal soon, within a day or three. Maybe a bit longer with the gunshot wound on my right leg, which throbs like a chorus of dull, tiny hammers.

From nowhere, a bright yellow light washes over me and the room, blinds me for a moment. I blink back into focus—or not really focus, because now my vision is like two photography negatives overlaid—there is a man I don't recognise in front of me, offering me a bowl of what looks like noodles. Ignoring him, I survey the room: I am in the washroom from before—I recognise the entrance door and the door to the courtyard, from which this man has just come—and there's nothing but a large washing machine in the corner, leaving wide open space in the middle. My back is to the east wall, opposite the door.

The man thrusts the food in my face without saying anything. He's small, a tad old, wearing nothing but a singlet and shorts, but he has a smattering of protective Nsibidi hennas tattooed into both his arms, from shoulder down to wrist. His face is lined and fucking ugly.

I try to tell him I don't want food, that what I really need is water. Yet no matter how far I open my mouth, I can't make any words. I try and try, but something has yanked away my voice. This must be how Fatoumata feels everyday.

He lays the food and water down on the floor within the circle and walks away.

Oh. A circle.

Now I see why I've lost all my senses, and my strength with them. First, on my neck is the binding necklace from Papa Udi. I can't take it off because I'm bound, but also because it clings to my skin like tissue. He has then drawn a general ward, meant to affect the physical—which I currently am, it seems. The ward prevents me from leaving its confines, and the necklace prevents me from accessing my powers. Since my powers are grounded in my senses, there goes my esper and everything else.

"Yes," a voice says, coming into the room. It's vague, distant, though I already know it's Ajala.

For the first time, I see him dressed in the full regalia of the Yoruba medicine man that he is. An Oníṣègùn; the ancient name Papa Udi uses for him, a name that identified his kind long before The Falling. He's in a small round cap, the kind worn by Imams, but more intricately embroidered—he's a Baálẹ̀, after all. His nose is painted black and his eyes yellow. He wears a flowing white robe, on which rituals are written in red stitchwork. Piled high on his neck are beads that clack against each other when he moves. The Yasal bottle hangs from his neck as well, glowing blue with the godessence within. He walks with a staff, and he is barefoot.

I'm glaring at him, my mouth working, unable to find the words to voice my anger, to explain my plans to snap his neck in two if I ever get out of this circle.

"Oh, you're angry," he says, then snorts. "Is it not me that should be angry? I mean"—he tucks the staff in his armpit and counts on his fingers—"I offered you serious money to work for me, but instead you come into my house, steal my intended wife, then come back to steal even more?" He snickers. "What exactly were you planning to do? Take my essence with that Ẹ̀gbà?" He points to my necklace and tut-tuts.

"If you're going to do something behind my back, David Mogo, you must be smarter than this. Your plans, I mean, they made me laugh. Even my wives can plan better than that."

I frown, watching him. He doesn't look okay. He's rocking, unable to stand still. His fingers tremble, like he's high on drugs. The staff is more than ornamental; he really needs it for support. His eyes are bloodshot. He's talking as if reading from a script. He's not... himself. As if he's—dare I say it—possessed.

He leans on the washing machine and watches me coming to this conclusion.

"You think you're smart, oga, and that's where your problem is. You think because you're big and strong and the bastard son of a god, that you're better than me, than all of us?" He frowns, becoming serious now. "But you see, orisha 'daji, you're not."

And at this point, he makes a shrill noise with his mouth, something like a whistle from the back of the throat. His robe flaps at the edges, as if a wind suddenly rose into the room. There is that same taste of fine sand on my tongue as the day I met Fatoumata, only sharper now, the grains grinding against my hard palate. The pungent smell of sulphur follows in its wake.

Then he casts a charm, and the divine energy balloons into the atmosphere about us.

It's like a near-death experience where your life flashes before your eyes. Except, what flashes before my eyes is not *my* life.

It's a god's. An orisha's. It's...

Aganju's.

It's like being backstage with a famous celeb, going through a fast-forwarded interview of their life. I'm in a formless place; a place built upon a divinity imperceptible by my human senses, devoid of life but full of spiritual energy, like TV static. I'm speaking to someone whose face I cannot see, who berates me for going too far, whose voice sounds like speaking into the wrong end of a woofer. Someone else is defending me, someone whose voice is gravel, is rage and flames. Then we are at war, fighting, swatting away charm after charm aimed against us. Everything is burning, flames too high, too hot. Boom.

Then I am falling, falling. I am in a strange land, one I cannot place, cannot find my centre. All my powers are gone, except a few. I am alone, lost, and cannot make sense of this new place. But I am a thinker, a philosopher, yes? I seek a way to proxy to other spiritual energies, latch on to something. I try and try, but there seems to be nothing else in this place I have fallen. So I extend as far as I can, seeking openings in other worlds. Then, I've suddenly latched on to something, onto the much smaller essence of another, who is feeling in the dark, seeking something bigger to latch on to. Then, I'm taking control slowly, eating into this space, prodding, nudging.

Then suddenly, I am meeting with—David Mogo? Then I am fighting Kehinde, defeating her, trapping her essence into the Yasal bottle. Then I am feeding the children the recipes I've made from the knowledge I have amassed, spiked it with a good dose of godessence. I watch them contort, connect to me like a web, like we are a hive and I am the queen—

I shrug myself out of the charm, quickly. It slips off me like a silk nightie, though something remains, like the weight of a slight headache, telling me that the charm is still there, working. It is there that I feel it, Ajala himself struggling to settle Aganju's essence back into place, to hide it behind the curtain, like having two minds inside one body.

Activity from somewhere in the compound jerks me back to the present, the sound at first distant, then growing louder as it approaches.

Taboos pour into the room.

They're a legion now, so many that I can't even count. They flock to Ajala like ants to a lollipop, like *he* is their centre. Now that I see them up close, they're unnervingly familiar: they're indeed exactly like godlings, if godlings had permanent material forms. Theirs are no longer the soft, round faces of innocent children, but hard-edged things that belong to something much more ancient. Their limbs are longer than their bodies, spindly; their lips are thin lines and their broken teeth are the colour of rot. Most of their hair has fallen off to reveal smooth, inhuman scalps. Only one childlike feature remains, and as my eyes roam through the taboos in the room, I realise what it is. That sparkle I saw in the eyes of the twins—it's there, behind every eyeball on each taboo's face.

Ajala rests his weight on his staff again. He looks weak, frail. He's muttering to himself, or to me, I can't tell anymore. The charmcasting is starting to take its toll on his mind.

"You see it, don't you?" he's saying. "His power is greater than you all put together. Only for a small duty, he will help me get the Lagos I've always wanted." He rubs his hand over the head of one taboo, which purrs with a guttural groan, like a cat with a broken throat. "See how they answer when I call them with my Reveal charm? They will never let any harm come to me. They know their master. Aganju will not let his servant come to harm."

I'm staring at the man, my mind racing. How the fuck does a god control a wizard by proxy? How?

"Ibeji are still fine, for now," Ajala is still rambling. "They are the fount of all abundance, yes? They're of the purest of Orun, and I will have to make a million armies for their essence to run out. So you have nothing to fear for them." He pulls the nearest taboo close in a paternal gesture which makes me think of Fatoumata.

"Besides, since when did you even start caring about these things? I mean, you were so ready to put Taiwo in a Yasal bottle."

My chest is pumping now.

"No need to be vexing," he says. "If you hadn't done it, I would never had brought Kehinde out of hiding. If anything, I should thank you for that."

My head spins. I'm unsure if it's the wards or what he's just told me.

"Oh, so you think your roof spoilt on its own?" he asks. "Or that Kehinde was able to get into this compound and release that first batch of children because she's so smart?"

He played me, played all of us. The bastard.

"I know Orun to the core," he says, and I no longer know if it is Ajala or Aganju speaking. "I knew Ibeji since they were children. Kehinde will always come for her brother. Ibeji have separated many times, long before your existence, and each time, they've known no life until the other is found. Do you know twins are one soul in two parts, not two separate souls?

"Anyway, I ensured those children were here, made sure she found them easily. It was the perfect distraction."

He adjusts on his seat. "Actually, you—David Mogo—have been my biggest problem. I expected you to die trying to capture these two, which unfortunately you didn't. Then after bringing me a half a delivery, you wanted to take it back? Not only that, you also stole Fatoumata! What kind of man does that to someone who has only shown him kindness, eh? You became a liability that very instant, and all I wanted was to slice off your head." He wags a finger at me. "I knew then that you were ready to oppose me, and that you must be *something* to do so." He laughs dryly, then coughs. "I can't let you combine with those nonsense supernatural police people. I will take them out first, then you, then I can settle down and do my work."

It looks like Ajala talking, the way he shakes his head and clicks his tongue. "Your weakness has become your undoing. I saw the way you looked at Fati that night. I put that sponge ritual on her because of you. You opened my eyes, David Mogo. Thank you."

Wait, what?

"Oh, so you didn't—" He laughs now, maniacal. He coughs, sputters, but doesn't stop.

"Ah," he says, wiping his eyes. "Of course you didn't know! Pure boy, afraid to look at a small girl's chest. That's is exactly why I wrote the charm there! I thought your Papa would see it, but obviously, he too is too afraid to look. I'm happy I did it, now. You know small girl like that, a lot of people can use her to reach me, you know? I have to keep track."

Of course this was how he found out about all our plans— about the attack! The sponge ritual, actually called a Listening charm, Papa Udi says is one of the most difficult charms to execute, mostly because it's a combination of a recipe, a ritual and charmcasting. First, he would've had Fati ingest the right recipe, or smear it on her like an ointment, to establish the link between them. That was the fine sand I tasted on my tongue the first day I met her—that was Aganju's godessence. I couldn't sense it because it was an extension, not the source. Then he must've invoked some sort of ritual: whatever she sees, hears, feels, so does he. Hence, 'sponge'—it used to be thought that it soaked up all the spiritual energy around the affected person, although in truth it duplicates it. To retain this connection over a long distance, however, he'd have to augment it with a charmcast, which he could, what with having the godessence of three gods.

Fucking. Genius. This man had a bug in our house, and we and the bug both had no idea.

A wave of despair washes over me, heavy and desolate. My shoulders are all of a sudden slumped, resigned. Ajala sees it and beams.

"Ah." He smirks, rises. The taboos gather about him like nightflies about a light. "Aganju and I are the same, you know? Our goals align. We both believe a few cannot dictate the undertakings of the many. And you, David Mogo, are the few. You and Obatala and Papa Udi and the supernatural police and the government of Lagos.

"You're not as hard as you think. You're soft in places a gunshot cannot touch: a weakness for helpless and abandoned things, since you were once a broken, helpless child yourself. Isn't that why you chase godlings for a living? Hoping to chase them into finding their homes?"

Don't talk like you know me, I say inside. *Fuck what you know. Fuck you.*

Ajala chuckles, walking away. "I hear you have a very powerful mother, that you have her passion for fire and rage. No wahala. I'm taking no chances. You'll be here until I'm done, then I will decide your fate."

And with that he takes all my hope out the door with him, trailed by a multitude of child-monsters.

CHAPTER TEN

THE WORST THING about being in captivity too long is that you make up stories and start to believe them. You know they're rubbish, you know you shouldn't be listening to yourself; but you do it because if you don't, it becomes too difficult to convince yourself that you're alive.

Many hours after Ajala has left me to my helplessness, this is where I find myself.

I've tried to get out of the ward circle. I can't clean it or touch it. If the ebo in it doesn't burn through my skin like melted plastic (and no, this won't heal quickly like other injuries—this one burns gods wellah) then the ward barrier will leave me in a daze for hours.

But of course, this was the first thing I tried to do once the taboos evacuated the room.

I didn't touch the chalk, but I did try to step out of the circle. I've seen what happens to warded people before—besides Kehinde, Papa Udi has had one or two over in my lifetime—and I'm always confused about why they get so stupefied when they try to cross the threshold. There was this one guy who did it, smacked right into the air above the threshold, knocked himself out for almost a day. Papa Udi even got scared, withdrew the ward and had to revive him.

Well, let's just say when I closed my eyes and tried to jump over the ward circumference, hoping to the high heavens that maybe the rules were different for demigods, the clapback I received was, uhm, significant.

My hip smacked into something solid, like a wall, and if I was a lesser man, my bones might've shifted. There was pain, impact-dull like someone took a sledgehammer to my waist, but also sharp, like electricity was fired into my buttocks. I recoiled from the circle and crumpled to the floor. For the next hour or so that I lay there, I was grateful Ajala drew the circle large enough to contain me prone.

And now as I lie here, I begin to fall into that place of crazy. All has finally become grave silent in my ears. It is in this silence that I begin to curse myself, to ask questions like: what the actual fuck drove me to take that shitty money and get involved in this nonsense? To give Lagos over to a sadist maniac, all for the price of one roof repair?

And then, for absolutely no reason at all, I start to remember my mother. In the way of dreams, it seems normal: I remember her so clearly, as a woman with big arms, soft, but also firm and solid. She is light-skinned, with flowing hair. Her lips are made for smiling, a natural lipstick red. Her hair is wild and fire and coral and sea. The image is sharp and imprinted in my brain.

But of course it cannot be my mother, it occurs to me almost an hour later. How can you remember something you've never seen or heard?

But then I *have* heard her before. I do get flashes like these from time to time. It's like spiritual adrenaline: when I get scared, or angry, or sad enough, my body reacts, and then my godessence reacts, and I get these visions. Papa Udi says it's a memory not fully formed, that I must've been too young when it happened for me to remember it normally. But it doesn't feel that way—it feels like a reaction to the stress, like she's reaching out of my past and soothing me.

Sometimes the images are sharp and vivid, sometimes blurry. Sometimes there are smells, sounds. Sometimes, I cannot remember anything at all. But one thing that always sticks is that I know it's my mother talking to me.

And isn't she always, really? Through Papa Udi, through the stories he tells? They change every time, but isn't she always telling me the same things? She might've left me in the middle of a tree, but didn't she instruct a crazy old wizard to go take me in? Didn't she scrape out all traces of my identity in order to cloak me from who-knows-what?

So I find myself thinking about her, about what she would say if she saw me here, about what she would want me to do. *E get why you gats commot from that tree. You big pass to dey hide inside there.*

And then I'm thinking: am I not inside the tree right now? Should I be cowering from the edge like so? If I somehow get out of here, what do I do? Do I still want to go back, still want to fix the city that I've given over to be broken?

Am I bigger than the tree?

I'm still trying to answer when I drift into a fitful doze.

THE HOUSE IS not empty after all.

A piercing scream wakes me from my nap. I say piercing but

it's not that loud at all; what really startles me is that, for a second, I regain my hearing. The yowl doesn't last long.

Then, as if from a distance, all the sounds in the house start to come alive. Shouts. Commands. Feet moving.

There's a gunshot from very, very far away.

Then the air presses against my skin with a force, like a very large hand is stretching my skin taut on a cold, dry harmattan morning. There is another piercing yowl, and another, and for a second I hear, smell, feel everything—the generator, the smell of petrol, the damp of the washer room—then I'm back to oblivion, with a pressure in my ears that I have to pop by swallowing.

More shouting. More gunshots, three or four, closer still. Then the feeling comes again, tugging at my skin, as if trying to remove something from beneath it. It's stronger, like whatever's causing it is right in front of me.

Until it is.

The door before me, the one that leads outside, slams open, and a man flies through. A long rifle falls with him, but he's up quickly, recovering enough to settle his gun into a good firing grip. He points it to the silhouette in the door.

He never gets to shoot. A hand reaches out of the darkened doorway and touches his skin.

The feeling hits me, stronger than ever, like my skin is stretched to pain now. My ears block completely. But the guard is having it harder. The gun clatters from his hands, falls to the ground, and he's jerking, emitting that long yowl I heard before, the cry of a wounded animal.

Then the feeling goes *pop*, and he is still.

The little shadow steps from the doorway into the light of

the room, dressed in a black hijab and robe, and walks up to my circle.

Fatoumata smiles.

Then she puts her hand forward, into the ward.

The air vibrates, as if someone is taking a wooden bat to a rubber wall, and the space in front of me shimmers, like when you look above fire. Fatoumata winces, but keeps her hand there, eating up the essence of the ward into her body. She bends by the waist, braces to accept more pain, but she keeps her hand up.

Then, all at once, the circle breaks. She reaches into the circle and grasps the necklace.

It feels like someone is pulling my skin out of my body. My bones ache like a wisdom tooth. My brain pounds in a migraine, and I feel my mind, my consciousness leaving me, slipping away. I scream in pain, for the first time in my entire life.

Fati goes down on one knee, but by all that is of sky and sea, she keeps her hand up.

Slowly, the chalk on the ground fades, wears away as if washed by age. The necklace breaks, the warded beads rolling across the floor.

The ward is almost greyed into the floor before Fatoumata can't keep it up any longer. In slow motion, she crumples into a faint and lays still.

It takes me two, three minutes before I gather enough strength to flex my arms again. Finally, I pull at the chains; they resist for a moment, before opening up at the links. I slip them off my hands easily, then snap off the chains at my ankles.

Tentatively, I stick my hand over the ward circle, teeth

clenched and braced for the pain. When it doesn't come, I put my arm, leg, and finally my whole body over the boundary. Nothing.

I stand outside the circle, my mouth open, staring at the girl on the ground. I want to look at her chest and confirm, but I don't need to. Papa Udi is a genius, isn't he? This is where the beauty of the ritual lies—a smart practitioner can turn it against the user, and this is just what he's done. Not only did he take Ajala's Listening charm on Fatoumata and re-write it to become an actual sponge—I didn't even know he could do that!—he made it a sponge for *everything*.

I was wrong afterall. Ajala might have Aganju behind him, but he still isn't the best wizard in Lagos, because someone else has just done what he's spent his whole life trying to do.

Papa Udi just made Fatoumata a god.

I kneel and gather the girl into my arms. Outside in the yard, palace guards are scattered about on the ground, motionless. I try to concentrate on the moment. Right now I should be grateful to be alive and free, but I'm angry that Papa Udi put a teenager at risk of being shot.

But—he made her a full sponge.

By the front gate are two bodies still standing—one leaning calmly on the bonnet of a parked Hilux, one with a gun in hand, pointing at us.

"Na them," Papa Udi says.

"Oh, thank God," Femi Onipede says, lowering her gun.

I set the girl on the ground and embrace Papa Udi. "Oh, you fucking brilliant man."

"Haysss." He shoves me aside, embarrassed. "Put the girl inside motor."

We lay Fati down in the backseat. She stirs a little, finally coming to.

"How you do am?" I ask. "Where you learn that kain thing? How did you—" I clear my throat. "You know. Write it *there*."

Onipede frowns and says, "*Hmm?*" Papa Udi blinks and refuses to acknowledge, but motions to Fatoutmata in the vehicle.

"Na she say make I do am. I just close eye do the thing."

"I told him he could've killed her, sending her in there like that," Onipede says. "I mean, I took care of these ones out here, but what if there was someone hiding in there with you?"

Papa Udi smells the air, then frowns at me. "Blood."

"Mine," I say. "Only a scratch. They shot my leg earlier, but it's healing."

"Good," Onipede says. "Because we need your help. Right now."

"Yes, yes," Papa Udi is saying. "We gats go there sharply."

"Where?"

"LASPAC command," Onipede says. "Ajala is there right now."

"Doing what?"

"Taking out the one organisation that can stand in his way," Onipede says. "And you know if he succeeds, we're all well and truly dead."

CHAPTER ELEVEN

81 DIVISION OF the Nigerian Army was formed in Lagos during the colonial era, and replaced the Lagos Garrison Command in 2000. The Nigerian Army's long-abandoned website says its responsibility is securing Lagos and Ogun States, and that the division is a "mechanized infantry with affiliated combat support and combat service support units." But the real truth, over fifteen years since the website was last updated, is that 81 Division is now a cold, dark nook on Ahmadu Bello, right off Onikan, a little ways off the Lagos Island marina. The command, an abandoned cluster of barracks, has long since been handed over to the under-equipped infantry of the Lagos State Paranormal Commission.

In time, the LASPAC Command has become the last hope for Lagos. Everyone lives in the little hope that LASPAC will one day hustle up arms and take on cleansing Isale Èkó once and for all. As with most things Nigerian, it's a pipe dream. LASPAC officers can barely tackle the actual menace of deities fallen from the sky, never mind a mad wizard with three gods and an army of monsters behind him.

So when we arrive at Onikan Under Bridge in Onipede's

Hilux, me in front, Papa Udi in the back with Fatoumata—now awake—the sight that greets us is something I'm not shocked to see, yet causes us to gape.

The men must've received word of Ajala's threat, but being Nigerians, did not take him seriously enough. Or maybe they took him very seriously, and bailed. Seeing as their director was busy rescuing a stupid demigod at the time, it makes sense to take the chance. Those who remained must've sat behind their walls without much protection. So, when Ajala stormed the yard with a horde of monster-children, they couldn't have been prepared enough.

The smoke outside the command stings my nose. There's a big fire burning somewhere within its walls—maybe a whole building. There are one or two LASPAC-blue Hiluxes parked mid-flight, some of them crashed into square concrete planters. There are blood smears and hand prints on the walls, like something dipped its hands in blood and proceeded to climb over them.

Fatoumata shudders as we get down from the truck. Papa Udi's mouth is twisted like he's chewing something bitter. I'm not entirely sure what I feel, considering I took this power and handed it over to something that I'm no longer sure I can conquer.

I turn to my army of two. "Okay, so remember the plan?"

Fatoumata nods, then signs something to me. I assume it has something to do with being ready or careful.

"Right," I say. "We move."

The 'plan' is simple. The Yasal bottle must still be hanging from Ajala's neck—it's the source of his power over these monsters. Papa Udi says since the bottle was used to make them, Ajala will lose much of his control the minute he loses the spirit bottle. Get the bottle, free Ibeji, and that power is gone. Then it'll be just Ajala/Aganju versus us all.

Two tiny problems, though. First, how do we get past a hundred taboos? Secondly, once we isolate him, then what?

So Papa Udi suggested we break the plan into two. If he finds a way to lure the taboos, then Fati and I can go for Ajala. If she can sponge off his power for a bit, I'll use that window to get to him—and the bottle.

There are problems with the plan. The only way Papa Udi can lure them involves putting himself in danger. After I told him the story of Ajala's Reveal charm and how he used it to call to the taboos, he's decided he will do the same. I ask him how he's going to carry out the charmcast part without harming himself, and he smiles and says nothing.

"You're not doing it," I say.

"I go dey alright," he says.

"No, Payu. No."

"Look," he says, placing both hands on my shoulders. "I don do am before, you know."

"Charmcasting?"

He nods. "Once, before. The problem no be say people no fit cast am; na say them no sabi release am little by little." He taps his chest. "I don do am, long time ago. I never craze, abi?" He sniggers now. "Trust me, I go dey alright."

"And when those things come to realise you're just mimicking him, what then? They will attack you, those monsters. They're not kids anymore."

He smiles wryly. "No worry. I go ward myself after I cast the charm."

My eyes pop. "Draw a ward around *yourself?*"

He nods.

"No, Payu. There won't be enough time between casting the charm and completing the ward. They will get you. No, no, no."

"David!" He shakes my shoulders. "Listen to me—go get that bastard. No worry about me."

I'm shaking my head. He pats my back, then retrieves his bag from the Hilux. Onipede is still in the driver's seat, making a call: asking for reinforcements from the police, from the sound of it. Then she screams into the phone and slams it down in disgust,

"Fucking commissioner!" She runs her hand through her weave, and I see her eyes are bloodshot. "They say they can't mobilise anyone here tonight. We're on our own."

Behind the command's huge gate, I'm already catching a mad number of signatures, pulsing strong and firm. I look at Papa Udi, whose mouth is twisted as he starts to work out the intricacies of both charmcast and ward, muttering things to himself as he draws on the ground.

I signal to Onipede in the car. "Stay in the ward with him. If he goes too far with that charm, knock him out." I take Fati by the hand. "Okay. Let's do it."

We take the left side of the fence, the one that opens up directly into the expressway. Cars barely flash by these days, but the sound of waves slapping the concrete marina covers our tracks. I seek a spot by the fence furthest from any signatures and stop there, hoisting Fati onto the fence by her haunches. She perches up top, crouching low and making herself small, while I climb over myself. The smoke is more intense now that we're closer, and when I look down into the building, I see why this part of the compound is empty: it is long-abandoned, with a stinky pond of gathered water and algae growing over it. There are buildings close by here, possibly some old command buildings discarded for the new one, visible in the distance.

We crawl a few steps on the fence and I drop down as silently as I can onto solid ground. I hold my arms up for Fati, and she jumps, trusting in me absolutely. Something moves in my chest.

We get around a dilapidated building and study the barracks. I was wrong—the fire is not a building, but a car, a Hilux that didn't make it out in time.

I suddenly realise that horrible smell in my nose is of charring meat. My blood boils, and I suddenly want to abandon the whole plan and storm the barracks. Who does this man think he is, killing and destroying? Who does he think he is, trying to take over Lagos?

And just then, the blast from the Reveal charm hits us.

I'm suddenly somewhere that is not Lagos, somewhere that looks like the south of Nigeria, in a divinery as big as Cardoso house; I'm aloof, pacing, trying to figure something out; I'm running through novel recipe mixes, scribbling down a new ritual designed by me and practicing tiny doses of charmcasting; I'm performing the rituals and charms, sweat running down my head and inside my armpits; fire, blood, whining, screaming, fire, blood; I'm running barefoot, my heart pounding, my feet bloody, but I'm running because my pursuers desire nothing less than my blood; I'm hidden, somewhere they can't find me, and my heart is heavy with loss, desolate and lonely—

I shrug out of Papa Udi's past like out of a thick, stifling robe, and suddenly I'm back behind the dilapidated barracks of the LASPAC command. A tumult greets me, something like a stampede of cattle. Before me, a large number of taboos—fifties, maybe hundreds—are loping towards the gate at the other end, running with their arms and legs like animals. Their mouths are open, their tongues dangling like feral cats, spittle dripping like they've smelled a fresh meal.

Out of the headquarters comes a figure, running in confusion. I recognise Ajala at once, his jalabiya flowing in the night marina breeze. He falls under the illumination of a yellow bulb, and I see his baffled, scrunched up face.

"Stop!" he screams, his hands out. I feel an echo of a charm. He speaks something in a language I don't catch.

The ears of the taboos are pulled back by the wind, too loud for his voice, too loud for his charm. He is angry now, the air stirring up about him as his essence churns, his energies roused. The Yasal bottle is there, hanging from his neck as he struts towards the main gates, the last of the taboos flashing past him at superhuman speed.

He stops short suddenly, and at once I know he's picked up the Reveal charm. The way that air gathers about him, I recognise it: he is preparing to cast something. And I know where and who exactly that charm is going to hit.

I look to Fatoumata, next to me in a squat. Her eyes are glazed over and she's static, unmovable. It occurs to me now that I didn't think of her in the grand scheme of things—the Reveal couldn't deflect and slip off her like it would for me. She is not a demigod. She will experience the Reveal until the charm is yanked back, and is in no state to follow through with the plan.

It's up to me now. I know what I must do.

I bound out of my hideout, slipping out a dagger as I go, readying it before me. The smell of garlic tickles my nose as the wind shifts against me, the ebo on my dagger splashing dots on my chest. It burns like melted plastic on my skin, but I don't care. My eyes are locked on Ajala.

I'm three paces away when he senses me and turns swiftly, taken by surprise. His eyes are cold fire, surging, burning. The godessence within him is brighter, whiter, sevenfold.

I step forward with my dagger and, without a second thought, sink the knife right into his chest, his heart. I push so hard the whole blade goes in, up to the hilt. His mouth opens in a large "O" of surprise, of confusion, of betrayal.

Then he grins.

I first notice there is no blood, that the ọbẹ iṣẹ́ṣẹ́ just stays in there, dripping ebo. Then much more slowly, I feel the halo about him, the shroud of energy pulsing about him, protecting him from everything and anything. I see that the dagger has not at all pierced his flesh, but pierced the shroud only, hanging in the air a hair's distance from his heart. The hilt does not go forward, not being touched by ebo.

His grin widens into a smile. Then he pulls his hand back and slams a backhand into the side of my head.

We make this Nigerian joke about the difference between being slapped by an ordinary person and being slapped by a military person. Military personnel slaps cause ears to ring for days. It comes to me now that I've been slapped within an army command post, as Ajala's backhand takes all the wind out of me.

I find myself on the ground, confused, my senses muted like I'm back in the ward circle. I no longer hear anything out of my left ear other than an incessant ringing, like an explosion just happened on that side of me. Then a hand gathers my shirt at my chest and pulls me up. I lean back, and the whole shirt gives way into tatters. The hand swiftly catches my arm, hauls me back, and then I'm standing in front of Ajala.

He reels his fist back and smashes it into my nose.

A slight *crack*, and fire pours through my cheekbones and into the rest of my face. I find myself falling again. Why the fuck is he so strong?

My left ear is fully deaf now, but beneath the ringing, I still hear the clamour of the taboos. They scream, like there's a fight going on. I hear the *pop!* of a body slamming a ward boundary, and ensuing howls from more taboos.

Ajala stands over me, his black jalabiya tussling in the wind. Suddenly, I'm seeing another image superimposed over him, like I saw with Taiwo at Èkó Ìsàlẹ̀. This one is a face formed of swirling desert sand, given form by molten magma and volcanic ash. The fiery beast is looking right at me through Ajala's eyes, its mouth and ears black holes that spout fire-red magma.

Aganju.

Ajala places his foot on my chest, the sand under his sandal coarse on my skin. I take his ankle and try to pull it away, but I cannot. I breathe in, hunch my shoulders, and with both hands push against his leg with all the strength I can muster. Nothing. The foot is firm on my chest, without any effort. I don't even move it slightly.

Aganju is smiling at me, his lips of magma flowing and forming, sand-eyes blazing with little fires. He says something I can barely hear.

"...think you're smart?"

The wind howls in my ear, and the ringing continues. I strain.

"...you're special? ...show you that I'm bigger..."

He lifts his foot and crashes it into my face.

Or at least plans to. I roll away and miss it by an inch. His foot hits the ground and raises dust.

At this point, I've lost all the decorum I learnt at Cardoso House, at King's College. If this man wants to play hand-to-hand, fuck it. Streetfighting mode on.

I turn on my back, swivel onto my elbow, and with all the strength I can muster, I kick at Ajala's ankles.

A sharp pain runs into my shin, like kicking the edge of a concrete pillar, and I feel like this leg will be useless for a while.

Ajala turns and slams his foot into my ribs. Then he kicks again, and again. And again.

I have never felt more human in my entire life. At this point, I no longer feel pain: the first kick sends waves of pain down my whole side, so great that I'm numb to everything after it. All the while he's shouting, but what I hear is something—or somethings—greater, larger, more ancient than him.

As I lay on the ground, I see that the gate is open, and beyond that, Papa Udi and Onipede huddle next to one another, the ward about them shimmering with taboos throwing themselves against the perimeter. The little fire of hope in my chest blazes, and I suddenly find myself feeling... joy? *They're alive,* is all I can think. The charm is obviously done, but the taboos have smelled the Reveal already, tasted of it, and will not be sated until they get a piece of him for calling. They hurl themselves against the circle, howl when it burns them, but they pick themselves up again and hurl themselves back. They're like zombies.

A kick slams into the back of my head, and my brain stops functioning for a minute.

I'm seeing a woman I don't recognise before me, her hair wild and her eyes fire and her arms strong and firm. She is a warrior, she is home, she is a bosom. Her mouth isn't moving, but I'm hearing what she's telling me nevertheless.

She says it's okay. To be human, to be weak. To not be the only one who can solve all the problems. She's saying it's okay to not be the hero; for now, at least. That time will come. She says this is not the time to despair but to remain strong. This is an example, something to show me that there are greater evils in this world, and dealing with evil requires a special kind of crazy that I'll have to become. That I have to be willing to step outside of the conventional, of the normal. It's a risk I will have to take.

Or, maybe it's just me telling myself these things.

Ajala's eyes are full of fire now.

"I see you won't give up," a chorus of voices say, and then I recognise the undiluted, hot-ice essence of an orisha. Aganju has fully commandeered Ajala's body now.

Oh, that's not good at all—not for Ajala, who's definitely going to die now, if this god ever leaves his body; and not for me, because I'm going to be fighting a full-blown high god.

Aganju does that shrill noise with his mouth, the one that tells me he's preparing to cast a charm. Then he puts out his arm, and the fires from the burning vehicle lean towards him. Then he *pulls*, and a large blob detaches from the inferno and flies towards me.

I have just enough time to brace for impact.

The fire vanishes into smoke an inch from my nose.

The shock on my face is mirrored by Aganju's, his mouth slightly open in astonishment, his eyes focused on me—

No, behind me.

I turn about.

Fatoumata is standing there, a tiny figure in her low-cut hair and one of my undershirts. She has shrugged off her robe, her face a billboard of fury, her chest heaving with the power just sponged off Aganju. Her eyes lock on him, hatred and bile spilling up within them. I sense all the collected energies in her insides, her godessence forming, roiling, burning.

Aganju works his mouth into a grimace, deciding what path to take. I've seen power corrupt often enough; I don't need two guesses to know what he will do.

I dive at Fatoumata before he casts the second fire blast towards her.

It's a pointless dive. Though I catch her in time to shove her out of the way, tumbling us both to the ground, her sponge is still doing its job. She seizes the charm before the fire even reaches Aganju's hands, and contains it. It dissipates into a bulb of smoke. Her body shudders as power settles into her, like an electric current grounded by earth.

"You ungrateful—" Aganju grits his teeth and fires three blasts in succession. Fati rises and collects them all in one great puff of smoke. She shivers again, staggers, and plants herself back, ready. Her brow furrows in concentration.

Then, Fati puts her hands forward and screams.

A hurricane slams into the barracks. All the energies present about the barracks rise in response and rush towards her, *into* her. Every living thing, everything with an ounce of godessence within them, shudders, their godessence yanked from them.

Everything, except me.

The taboos are the first. Their screams are shrill and eerie and fill the compound, like a school of crying fish. One by one, their godessences leave them. I feel them whooshing across the barracks and into Fati's little body. Others follow—the energy in every living thing rises, liberated by Fati's sponge, flying across the yard.

My skin, my bones—I feel the little energies in them agitate, but they do not move. Somehow, she is controlling and focusing the sponge—somehow, she is blocking me.

I realise that if she isn't blocking Papa Udi and Onipede as well, she is going to break their ward. Worse yet, she'll accumulate the whole of Aganju. She cannot survive harbouring such power in her little body.

"Stop!" I stare in horror as divine energy pours into her like a flood. She stands her ground, her eyes locked on Aganju, gritting her teeth through it. Aganju himself remains untouched, the same halo about him that stopped my dagger still standing, protecting him from her charm.

The dagger. The second one is still sheathed in my hip.

I see it now, the solution. Fati's plan to sponge everything will only work if I can get through Aganju's halo, if I can pierce a hole through it and break his shield. And I must do so before she collapses.

I reach down and pull out the second dagger. The blade is hot in my hand, the ebo slowly losing its potency to Fati's charm. I scramble up to where Aganju is standing, bracing himself against Fati's efforts, throwing more will into keeping his barrier fortified.

With all the strength I can muster, I lift the dagger in my two hands, drive it into the air an inch from Aganju's sand-fire eyes, and drag down to his feet.

There is a loud whistling, like a large truck's brakes, and Aganju has just enough time to register surprise before all the power within him whooshes through the tear in the shield, blasting out with such force it kicks him back.

There is a sucking sound, as if a vacuum cleaner has been turned on, and the superimposed image of the god disappears. The fire vanishes from the eyes of the body in front of me, and only Ajala's familiar voice is left, screaming in agony. Energies tear out of him with a fury, growing ever brighter. It breaks his skin, cracks of white fire beginning to appear. I lift a hand to shield my eyes, now understanding what Papa Udi used to say about absolute power: that it doesn't just corrupt absolutely, but will in the end consume you.

The fire of the gods is too much for a body so human.

Ajala falls to his knees, burning slowly without smoke, without smell. He does not scream, he does not wince. Instead, he smiles. And in that smile, I see it again; the flash of sand, fire, magma, ash. And something else, a message. Like the snapshots I receive from my mother.

Congratulations, it says. *You have taken this one. But we will meet again.*

Then Ajala crashes to the ground, and the Yasal bottle hanging from his neck shatters. The energies trapped within burst out like a firehose.

"No!" I scream, running for it. Too late.

The essences settle into Fatoumata, and the girl shudders one last time, then crumples to the ground.

Everything stills.

I stand there, watching embers and ashes settle. Watching the charred body of Lukmon Ajala, the Baálè of Agbado, smoke away without smell.

All around me there is movement. One by one, the former taboos pick themselves up, and suddenly I no longer see monsters, but children in tattered clothing, stained with soot and blood, examining themselves, confused. One begins to cry, and another follows, and another, and soon the whole barracks rings with the cries of children.

Onipede rushes into the compound, gathering the wailing children. Papa Udi trudges in past her, towards Fatoumata, his face falling as only a truly broken man's face can, his shoulders sinking with a new weight as he wears the gravity of his mistake, our mistake.

I pull him to myself into an embrace, his bony arms limp beside him. He doesn't hug me back, but he doesn't object either.

Then, a coughing behind us catches our attention. Fatoumata's eyes are shut, her head rolling, as if in a dream. Papa Udi and I rush and kneel beside her. I shake her shoulder gently.

"Fati, wake up," I'm saying. "Please, wake up."

A smile plays over her lips, then her eyes open. There are no pupils. All that is there is white, icy-hot burning. Ashẹ, the fire of the gods.

"Thank you for saving us, orisha 'daji," the voices say, and though I can't separate them, I will recognise Ibeji anywhere.

CHAPTER TWELVE

I STILL HAVE aches from those blows at the barracks two weeks ago. Suleiman and the boys on the roof of Cardoso House are not helping with their hammers on zinc either. Even though I'm seated as far away from them as possible—under the guava tree skeleton in our backyard, on a small plastic chair that can barely take my weight—the clangs of their hammers still send shock waves through my migraine. My body is healing, but I still ache so much that I can forget about anything hunting-related for a month or more.

Papa Udi moves about the yard with purpose, giving Suleiman and his underlings and clackety-clack tools directions. Most of them are escapees from Ajala's clutches, boys and girls looking for a way to pay us back for our help. The way I see it, it's Papa Udi who's helping them, since he's keeping them in gainful employment in the interim. They get to stay off the streets this way—no more police pickups. Also, I think Payu is really trying to fix their frail and broken trust in wizards, by doing the actual thing Ajala lied to the public about doing.

Papa Udi suddenly looks sprite, stronger. His slouched shoulders are gone, and he marches about, giving commands in a voice no longer frail and hesitant, but rich and round and ready. I've never seen him more alive since the moment Ibeji decided they were going to remain within Fatoumata, riding her body like a shell, until he figured out a way to get them out without consigning her to the same fate as Ajala. *You saved us, so we will save this one,* they said. It sounded more like Taiwo than Kehinde, though I can no longer tell the difference. Now Papa Udi suddenly has a purpose, finally found a way to help people as he's always wanted—a divinery of his own, where he'll work on solutions to an actual problem. I wonder if it will take more disaster for me to feel awakened, unravelled, unleashed too.

Fatoumata (or should I say, Fatoumata, Kehinde and Taiwo) is seated next to me. For a week or so since the barracks, I've struggled with not referring to her as *them*, because I just can't help sensing all those divine signatures within the house. She stares calmly at the activity in the yard, bobbing her head every now and then, her low haircut finally growing in patches. She's ditched the hijab and robe for good now, and wears a cotton blouse of her own size, under old shorts of mine slim-fitted to her size.

Her eyes no longer burn white, but there's a sparkle in them now that wasn't there before. She's still small and is still a teenager, but she's become something bigger than herself, bigger than Cardoso, bigger than Lagos.

She sees me watching her and smiles back. It's not the childish smile I saw at my window that other day. This one is laden with meaning, with knowing, with things much older than my forefathers.

"Still wondering?" she says. Her natural voice is a young

girl's, but I don't know why it comes off as if from someone older. It reminds me so much—too much—of Kehinde's.

"Wondering what?"

"About your mother," she says, looking back to the distance.

"And what about her?"

She smiles. "Taiwo knows."

I say nothing, waiting for her to make her point.

"He hears what she used to be, at least," she continues. "He knows she was born of war, of chaos, David, as are you." She turns her face to me now. "Do you know what this means?"

I shrug.

"You saw her that night, didn't you? You've seen her, other times too. Do you know why?"

"Nope."

"She feeds on chaos, David. She always has. Your connection is strongest at the peak of chaos and despair. You, too, when you come to recognise yourself for what you truly are, will feed on chaos. You *are* here for a reason—whether it is to make chaos, as she does, or to prevent it."

"I don't want any trouble," I say.

"But it will follow you nevertheless, because of chaos were you conceived. For all the times you raise turmoil, you offer a sacrifice to your essence. It is something from which you cannot hide."

I look back into the yard. Papa Udi explains to a couple of young boys how he wants the new extension to be expanded, how he wants floating shelves to fit inside it. One teenager is asking what kind of car will fit in there, and Papa Udi is staring at him, asking if he's never heard of a divinery before.

"How soon?" I ask.

Fati smiles, looking at the sky above, heavily clouded in late afternoon violet, blocking out the lowering sun.

"Soon," she says. "Those who first came for the gods of abundance will come again."

"And I'll have to protect them."

"Yes," she says. "You will need help, David. We will stay with you."

Yeah, but how does that help *me*?

"You are not alone," she says, answering my unasked question. "You have an army."

Is this is a prophecy of some sort? (Do gods have powers like that?) I'm sure she isn't talking about Onipede and her LASPAC men. She means a supernatural army, like Ajala's taboos. I will have to become like Aganju, in order to defeat any more to come after. The thought makes me want to laugh.

Papa Udi gesticulates some more, getting worked up by the young men who still can't understand what he means by a divinery.

"So we'll get more people to join us," I'm saying. "Me and Papa Udi. We'll make better, stronger potions. You'll help us?"

She's still looking at the clouds. "We could. But we won't be enough. You'll still need to decide your fate in the end, orisha 'daji. You must dig deep. *Deeper*."

"I don't know what to do."

The edges of Fati's mouth rise in a little smile. "When you meet your mother, ask her."

Another prophecy?

Who knows? Or really, who cares? I join her to watch the violet-streaked clouds.

Maybe I *will* somehow reach my mother, gain this knowledge

that no one but her seems to possess. Maybe I'll have to engage in more chaos to get there. If there's more violence, war and death coming, well, so be it.

I shake my head, sigh and relax into the plastic chair.

I knew this was going to be a bad job.

FIREBRINGER

CHAPTER THIRTEEN

THE WOMAN IN the white Kia Rio is thinking about killing her husband once she gets home. I see how she'll do it: she will mix otapiapia into tonight's ofada and wait for his body to turn stiff in the morning. The waiting is the part she'll hate. That's why she first thought about using a gun—easy, quick, efficient— before deciding it was too messy. For a moment, as her mind lingers, I feel the oily weight of the pistol she tried to cop under an overhead crossing bridge at Agege on Sunday night last week. It's laziness, you know? She really hates cleaning, and blood is so much work.

"Change, ma," I say, rolling up the cash and ticket and passing them through my toll booth window with the tip of my fingers.

She looks at me, her eyes glazed and distant, her cheeks contoured with several shades of bruises in different stages of healing. When she collects it, she touches me again, because she's oblivious, just like when handing me the money.

A jolt, and a new impression ripples across my consciousness, a barrage of ants marching under my follicles, pressing into my skin and my mind. Now she reconsiders, thinking about

Jasmine, her teenage daughter. How will she raise her without her father? It was him who taught her to play piano. Will she ever play piano again after?

This is exactly why I wear three pairs of rubber gloves. Without such protection (if I can call it that, really), people like these will easily rest their heaviness against my heart, a block of lead on my chest through simple skin-to-skin contact. I don't care much for lugging the weight of the world around. It's really not my business, and it never will be.

I press the barrier open. I don't watch her drive away.

Trying to turn off the impressions is pointless as usual, so I focus on the cars instead. I mean, I did tell this to Ibeji, right? I understand that learning better ways to use my powers is a good thing, but the problem is that uncovering them is like digging a hole. You're going down, down, taking the earth and tossing it above you, and suddenly you're in too deep, can't climb out, no protection, no way to take the sand and close it back up again. Stuck.

The next car rolls into my lane: a shining black Highlander. I recite the classes and fees while the window comes down and the driver's hand stretches out, holding a thousand naira.

Class three, SUV, five hundred.

I pluck the money from his strong grip, roll out the change and ticket from the machine and hand it out with the tip of my fingers. Too many people try to touch me even when I make it clear that I do not want to be touched. This driver is one of them, still managing to brush my fingers, just enough for me to get a whiff of his hard, throbbing anger. Something about overtime hours, delayed wages and an insensitive boss perched in the owner's corner behind him.

I press the barrier open. Nope. No, sir.

"You must learn to embrace it, open up to it," they said. Well, Fatoumata's mouth did the talking, but it was Kehinde who said it. These days, it's much easier to uncover the speaker behind the words without stopping to parse sentences: Kehinde tends to be more commanding, prodding, harsh; Taiwo, more soothing and nudging, more telltale. Sometimes both of them speak at once, and it comes out in a susurrus of sibilants, like a snake pit choir. That sound on Fati's lips always puts me on edge. Fati herself barely speaks, save for a few nods and a couple of gestures. The pockets of silence between statements are the times I think the gods within her have gone to sleep, and Fati herself takes over. I'm not sure if Fati is still speech impaired, or if the shock of having two high gods renting her body for accommodation has caused her to make a choice to remain mute.

"Embrace?" I scoffed. "It *hurts*."

The energy for charmcasting exists on another plane, so if I wasn't a demigod drawing my own power, I'd be fine. But tapping into godessence resident in my own skin and bones? Now *that* is painful shit.

The next car rides up and I take money and give change without getting touched. Since I started work as a ticketing officer a few months ago, only once in every five cars do I manage to avoid being zapped.

"It'll be a good test for you," Taiwo said, when Onipede offered me the job. "You must learn to control it, to turn it on and off at will."

I'm reminded that I don't like Taiwo very much. He sounds like a professor and a father mixed together. I don't want either in my life. Thinking of it, maybe I should've just left the guy stuck in the Yasal bottle.

"You say *turn it on and off at will* as if it's that easy," I said.

"Well, if you're going to charmcast, ever, you will have to learn to do that," he said, so matter-of-factly that I would've reached out and punched him if he wasn't using Fati as a vessel. "That's how charmcasting works: you must shape your godessence into form, and send it across space and time to do your bidding."

Yah. Right. And all the practice we've been doing led to what? The only progress I've made in six months is turning my sensitivity dial right up to a hundred percent, and obviously breaking it after that, because since then, I haven't been able to turn it back down.

I see off the next driver without getting my esper/godessence excited. No further cars line up behind the barrier. I glance at the LED clock on the sign at the far side of the road—7:45pm, below the words *Chevron Toll Plaza*. What this place used to be, before it became what it is now: a screen for any undesirables trying into get into Upper Island.

Six months since the biggest menace to Lagos was incinerated and most of Ìsàlẹ̀ Èkó shut off, people have finally awoken to what's up. The LASPAC Force has finally been beefed up enough—Papa Udi spends half his time in the Cardoso House divinery these days, trying to meet their recipe and ritual quotas—and they literally police the city now, including this tollgate, where a good number of navy-blue combats are scattered around, bullets drowned in ebo, protective Nsibidi amulets on their biceps. Some are in plain sight, lugging heavy rifles and patrolling the entrance and exit barriers. Some stay within the shadows, plants watching out for any sign of trouble.

I'm one of those plants. Femi Onipede doesn't think I'd do very well as a LASPAC officer, but she still wants me helping the force out rather than scouting the city for godlings, even though the majority are now sealed off alongside the Ìsàlẹ̀ Èkó zone. She wants me to consider this job a form of payback for helping deal with Ajala, as well as a new source of daily bread, but I think she really just wants me where she can see me. An idle mind, et cetera. That's her favourite quote.

We haven't had trouble this side of Lagos for a while, that's for sure. Femi ensures that by planting navy-blue combats at every nook and cranny around the perimeter of Upper Island. She herself is stationed full-time at the Upper Island State House, protecting Citizen Number One and his ilk. Can't say if the mainland is doing quite as well, but since when did anyone care for the mainland?

The clock clicks for eight, and I pack up my stuff, my shift ended. My replacement for the night is a thin young man who has so many bags under his eyes he's going to do much more sleeping than ticketing. I want to pat his back, reassure him, but then I don't touch people much these days. Plus, I don't know his name, and it'll be awkward. Mostly, I just call everyone *Chairman* or *Boss* or *Sisteh*. I guess I don't want to build more relationships only to get them caught up in my shit. If chaos will follow everywhere I go, I think I want to take less people with me.

I sign out my shift at the admin office at the tail end of the toll and nod officer whatever-her-name-is goodnight. I pick up my Bajaj, strap on the helmet Onipede gave me as a birthday gift—"So you start learning good citizenship now," she said, and Papa Udi grunted in agreement—and I'm on my way back to Cardoso House via the Lekki-Epe Expressway, the night breeze whooshing through the crannies in my helmet.

It's dead quiet and pitch black by the time I hit Ozumba Mbadiwe Avenue. You would think six months since the biggest menace to Lagos was incinerated—the longest period without a godling showing up somewhere since The Falling—people would've become more inclined to revive the nightlife Lagos was once famous for. But old habits die hard, I guess. Eight sharp, and everyone still barricades themselves in, breath held, as if waiting for something to happen.

Heck, who isn't? The LASPAC Force is setting up barricades everywhere too. Even we at Cardoso House, aren't we preparing for something we think is coming?

Nothing is over. Not by a long shot.

I climb the bridge into Osborne and fire down. Massive unlit buildings, empty, brooding, line the road on both sides. I've always wondered what the owners of these multi-billion-naira structures are thinking right now, caught between staying put in Upper Island and returning their businesses here. *Is it safe now?* they'll keep asking themselves. *Is it safe?*

The sky, though already dark at eight, grows blacker as I zoom up the second bridge, into the turn that takes me to Simpson. Lightning flashes veins across the sky, and thunder grumbles in low registers. I speed up, wondering if I can make it before it starts raining. It's peak rainy season, and no one wants to be caught on a bike in the rain on these slippery Lagos roads. If I'm not home in minutes, I'll soon be battling a flash flood chock-full of refuse and sewage.

I turn into Ojo Close just when the sky turns angrier.

Lightning lashes ferociously now, thunder bellowing death threats. Cardoso House looms in the dark at the end of the close, unlit. *Ah, dang,* I sigh. *Papa Udi didn't turn on the gen agai—*

The sharp smell of smoke smacks my nose right then. I sniff, sniff again. Yes—it *is* smoke, but more like *burning*; like electricity, when a power line sparks. But there's no power on Ojo Close, right?

Crack! A clap of thunder, and lightning slams the earth. A light comes on in Cardoso House.

Not a light. Cardoso House is on fire.

CHAPTER FOURTEEN

PAYU. FATI.

My first thought.

I jump off my okada and let it skitter away from me, into the bush, as Cardoso House lights up the end of the close. The stench of kindling wood and plastic jabbs at my nostrils as I run, the sharp sting of new smoke in my eyes. I'm praying, praying, *please, please, please don't spread.* But the night wind is merciless, fanning the flames, so that the little light that was only a warm glow in the dark is suddenly pouring out of a window, licking the blinds and dripping down its sill, and *whoosh,* there is fire everywhere upstairs: the roof, the doors, windows, coming out of every nook, every opening. Cardoso House is a dragon, puffing death and destruction from the depths of its belly.

No no no no no—

I'm at the door. The smoke coming from inside the house is washcloth thick, almost grabbable. I wave through it into the living room, coughing. My skin is hot in an instant, a boiling sweat breaking over my forehead. My throat is dry. I swallow hard.

"Payu! Fati!"

Heat presses down on me from above. The back of my neck is a hot plate, my eyebrows feel like they will peel any moment. Smoke swirls in my ears, my mouth, my nose, my eyes. I'm coughing, tearing my lungs as I clamber up the stairs, careful not to touch anything metallic. Flames billow on the balcony, smoke and tears blinding me so I must blink, blink, and still not see my hand in front of me, feeling my way up the corridor. I struggle to extend my esper, see if I can reach with my consciousness and touch the rooms around me, locate Payu and Fati. But I am still half-human: my senses are dulled, useless, overpowered by the stench of burning wire and foam. Something under the stairs explodes. The gen.

Is this the roof I almost killed myself for? This should be my last thought, but is the one I actually have. All that suffering, for what? For a mistake that reduces all our lives and investments to black rubble.

Shit. The roof. If I don't get them out now, the roof will come crashing down.

Another boom, thunder rolling with menace. The hallway upstairs illuminates for a second as lightning zags about outside.

And in that brief flash of light, I see them: Payu, huddled over Fati at the end of the corridor, the window behind them framing their stricken, frightened poses. The flames keep them in that spot, bursting out of the doors in front of them, filling the stretch between them and I. The floorboards are burnt through, and there is a black, smoking chasm opening up before me. I can see the wall dividing the kitchen and dining below, smouldering pieces of board falling onto our not-dining-table and igniting its edges; Papa Udi's bowl of onions that he never uses melting from a corner, the onions tumbling to the floor and across the linoleum.

"Payu!"

Their eyes register my presence, but there's something else there—Payu's, wide and filled with horror; Fati's bearing the glazed look of Ibeji coming to the fore. They're looking in my direction alright, but not fixed on me; *past* me, behind me...

There is a sparkle, a snap, the *pop* of something materialising behind me. I get a jolt, an impression of brilliant godessence that puts the sum total of all my impressions today to shame: a thrumming white vibrance in this hell of yellow, a blast of ice-heat in this inferno. I turn, and in front of me, standing at closed to seven feet, is the biggest, meanest orisha I've ever seen in my entire life.

His robes: thick, mousled, rippling here and there into fire, silver and blue lightning running crackling fingers around it, never burning. Translucent materialised godskin shimmers, the brown of amala, muscles sculpted by divine hands. A superimposed dwarf statue with a hammerhead and a thick cross-hatched beard flutters about the god in an afterimage. An overpowering nut odour of bitter kola rises off him despite the smoke.

In his hand: a double-headed axe, its surface gleaming in the light of fire; thunderstone, sparkles of lightning caressing it, running fingers around it, pleasing it.

His eyes: swirling pools of àshẹ, fire of the gods, essence of divinity.

He lifts the axe, points it at me, and a voice like many cannons blasting in sync, says:

"You."

The air between the orisha and I first stiffens, gathers. There is the overpowering smell of electricity, like a steel cable heating up and getting ready to spark; as if the air particles are rubbing against themselves and charging up for something. My tongue tastes like a naira coin.

Physics, I think, right before a bolt of electricity leaves his axe and comes for me.

I've ducked from a lot of things in my life: bullets, hurled weapons, punches and all kinds of blows, even a couple of charmcasts, yeah? But mahn, is lightning fucking fast.

The bolt strikes me clean in the left shoulder before I can shift a foot. Something bursts in my shoulder, and pain scatters through me, shooting fire into every blood vessel. The left side of my body goes numb, my eyelid drooping almost so I can't see through that eye. My knee buckles. I go down, breaking my fall with a palm on the floor. My arm responds with a chorus of pain, and my heart's rhythm changes, fibrillates, panicked. I can't seem to remember anything that happened after the axe, except thinking, *Damn, I wish I had my knives.*

The big orisha sails—dude rides lightning like a staircase— and then he is before me, his axe right in front of my eyes, an icy feather touch on the bridge of my nose. I push out a weak esper, reaching out to read his signature, nausea threatening to drown me.

"You know who I am?" that voice like cannons says.

Yes, I say to myself, the signature coming back with a response. *Yes.*

You are Sango.

"Yes," he says, as if reading my thoughts. "Remember me when you cross to the afterlife."

Then the air in front of my face burns, gathers electricity.

A gunshot goes off. Something rattles into Sango's chest, giving off a splash of liquid that burns into my forehead—*ebo*—and seeps into my skin like pinpricks of melted plastic. Steam erupts from Sango's chest. It looks like it should hurt, but Sango doesn't flinch. He just regards the wound the way one would an offending water spill, then lifts his axe and points it in the direction of his offender.

I look back. Papa Udi is holding the double-barrelled shotgun Femi Onipede gave us to defend ourselves. He cocks it, preparing to fire a second round.

Fati steps in front of him, opens her mouth and bellows a war rhythm. Kehinde's charmcast is stark in the night, puncturing the heat, the smoke, the crackle of wood, the sound of burning.

"Run!" I scream at them, the pain of her charm starting to seep into my head and cloud my thoughts. "Go, go!"

Sango keeps his axe aimed, affected by neither bullet nor charm. He narrows an eye, as if aiming for a bullseye.

I don't see the lightning leave his axe. I hear the *crack* of impact, their silhouettes frozen for a second, then Papa Udi and Fati are falling backward, slipping, tumbling out of the window to the ground below.

No no no no no no—

I rise on my good leg to face Sango. I will my godessence, shaping and loading it into the fist of my good right hand, something Ibeji have been trying to get me to do for a while. My fist feels heavy, charged, and I lean back as far as I can and slam it into Sango's face.

My knuckles meet a brick wall. My wrist shifts; my finger joints dislocate, shooting pain down to my elbow, and I'm reminded once again, just like the last time I fought a god: you do not punch an orisha, goddammit.

Sango shakes his head, as if dealing with a child, then puts his axe on my chest and mutters a word in a language I swear is not of Earth.

Everything freezes for a split second, and the air pauses, collecting electricity from every nook and cranny of Cardoso House. Even the fire seems to burn slower for beat, and I swear it's not my eyes when I see every single flame *lean* towards Sango.

Then, *wham*.

Something pierces me, sends heat coursing through my body. I'm flying backward, crashing into the wall of Cardoso House, breaking through, riding the force of the strike out of the house, into the cold wind of night and under a still raging dark sky, flying, flying, *flying*.

My momentum drops, and for a beat I'm caught, gravity pausing right before it starts to drag me the whole thirty feet plus into the lagoon below me.

Then a long finger of lightning reaches down from above and *pounds* my chest, sending excruciating pain into every nerve ending in my body. I am falling, falling, *falling;* and right before my back hits the hard cement of the water surface, the final image I have is of the embers of Cardoso House, the last of everything I have and know and love, disappearing into the night sky.

CHAPTER FIFTEEN

MY MOTHER IS not a beautiful woman. Her eyes are grey like iron, her arms strong and firm. She wears an Indian sari and her hair cascades to her shoulders like velvet window drapery in an Upper Island home.

"Get up," she says to me, her lips barely moving. "Don't be stupid, lying down there, in the bottom of the ocean. That's not your place, is it?"

"Wh...?" I try to speak, but there's water in my nose, in my mouth, in the back of my throat. Bubbles rise and I sound like a fish.

What?

"Get up," she says. "Or everything is going to turn to ash."

What? "I..."

"Shhh." She puts a finger to her lips. "Embrace it. You must learn to embrace it. It's like the phoenix; you know what a phoenix is?"

What!?

"They rise in fire. Chaos, my son. Chaos."

Then she is in the water with me, floating, reaching out to touch my cheek. Her hand is warm, even underwater.

"Rise, my son. Rise and be renewed."

Then Aganju is kicking the back of my head, telling me to *shutup, shutup, shutup, just die, just die, just die, you little bastard*. And in the dust (dust *underwater*, what?), a few ways away from me is Fati with a bloodied nose, her skull bashed in and seeping red fluid. Next to her is Papa Udi, smoke rising from his àdìrẹ buba and sokoto, his face singed and unrecognisable, his arm burnt and twisted, the multicolour of fat cooking under grilled meat.

Then Aganju is laughing, he and his brother Sango, who is speaking with a British accent, saying: *So I killed them all, yeah? I laid waste to that fucking entire lot of them, ha!*

And their laughter is a charmcast because suddenly it's giving me a splitting headache, and my head is pounding, pounding and I can hear them no more, see no more, think no more, and the lagoon is pulling me under, under, into the blackness where I can find no purchase, so I close my eyes and go to sleep.

SINK. COLD. FLOAT. Pain. Fear.
  Cold. Float. Pain. Fear.
  Float. Pain. Fear.
  Fear.
  Fear.

THERE IS A splash of colour before me when I painfully open my eyes. Mustard yellow, dappled with shapes in purple and green. At first I think it's my bad vision, until I recognise it for what it is: ankara. I wonder how long since I last saw someone wearing something so alarmingly cheerful, select fabric so dedicated to celebration, against Lagos's grey pastels. Is this a happy place? Am I in Heaven, then?

I blink. My vision does not get any better.

Heaven isn't dark like this, though. At least, not in the way them preachers describe it. Or is it my eyes? Do they still work proper?

I cannot make out the face of this ankara-dressed person before me. Smallish, a boy or girl approaching teenage years. The person has a long stick—bamboo—in their hands, raising it every now and then, dipping it back into the water—that's how we're moving. Rowing, yes? That's what it's called.

This is a canoe. Not Heaven.

I want to laugh, but I cannot, because there is a pain in my windpipe that makes me think my voice box will shatter if I speak, but I move my lips anyway, whispering as loud as I can.

"Th—thank you."

There is a loud ringing, garbled by the water that has collected in my ears, so that I cannot even hear myself. I realise the ringing is in my own head, and it has been there all along.

I try to move, sit up, but as I turn my head and make to find purchase for my elbows, there's a *scrick*—I hear this one clearly because it happens inside my own body—and then excruciating pain shoots up my spine, up the back of my neck, into my head, then cascades back down, tingling my fingertips, my toes. The cold and pain have conspired to make my joints static points, my bones throbbing entities. My whole body *whines*, the ringing in my head louder and louder. I would scream if I had a voice.

Then I am going under again, darkness closing in from the

edges of my vision, stretching its fingers to press my eyelids shut, but I am not afraid. I am not afraid anymore.

THE NEXT TIME I open my eyes, I do not know how long has passed.

I first notice I'm no longer cold. Pain no longer comes in bursts, but in one long existence of hurt. My body has accepted it, stuck to numb, but my mind hasn't; not yet. All my senses seem to be back in full force too, because for the first time I'm hit with the sharp smell of open sewage.

I want to rise, but memory warns me against it. I turn my head and look around instead.

I lie on a mat, on a hard floor made of wood—with neither patience nor finesse, because I can feel the spaces between the planks on my back. The mat is the rubber kind, with frayed faux thread on the end. My pillow is a lot of rolled-up cloth tied together.

A kerosene lamp hangs in the middle of the ceiling above, giving off light and heat. The ceiling itself is of plain, exposed zinc, as is the wall in front of me. The other three walls are of wood, littered with tattered old posters of English Premier League football clubs, especially Manchester United. Stacked along these walls are all kinds of books, just as old and tattered as the posters: some packed in Ghana-Must-Go bags and old rice sacks, some stacked openly in all their dog-eared glory.

Outside is constant noise; some of it the intermittent *swish* of water that tells me I'm still somewhere close to the lagoon; but lots of noise from children, chattering away in that carefree manner only children can maintain in a cold world. I listen for a bit, hoping to catch something to give me a hint of where exactly I am, but the language sounds quite foreign. It seems to have Yoruba underpinnings—I catch a familiar word here and there—but most expressions in the language are not Yoruba in the slightest. Or English. Or pidgin. Or anything I've heard in Lagos before.

Then there's that *smell*. Now *this*, I recognise: the classic Lagos smell of sewage, refuse, spirogyra and faeces all commingling in stagnant water. Stick around long enough, and this just becomes part of the air. That I'm smelling it now means I'm somewhere that takes the cake. I can taste the filth on the back of my tongue, despite it being swollen.

Mosquitoes buzz about in my ears, a couple settling to bite into my skin. It's too great an effort to lift my arm and swat them so I just let them take their pound of blood. If anything, I'm happy to be alive enough to be bitten.

My rescuer has taken off my shirt but left my jeans on. They are torn in long, burnt strokes, as if by a fiery knife. I look at my chest and almost scream. There is a branching redness under my skin, pressing against it as if struggling to break the surface. The tree of lines starts from my chest, right where Sango's axe or the strike from the sky had touched me, then spreads out about my body: up to my neck, into my groin, like a climbing vine.

My thoughts hover about the attack on Cardoso House. That's that it was: an *attack*. Sango didn't come to shake hands or discuss; he came to *destroy*. How did he breach Papa Udi's defences? The nsibidi staves Payu stuck in the ground since Ajala were never removed. Now I remember that image of lightning striking Cardoso House and starting the fire, and I realise he might've not needed to breach the ward. He came from *above*.

Where are Papa Udi and Fati now?

I have not cried in a long time, so when the first tear drags warmth into my ear, it actually surprises me more than anything. I would wipe it, but my hands are still too heavy, so I just let it flow, let the middle of my chest cave in and wash me of the heaviness.

A portion of the zinc wall opens—an afterthought: *that's a door*—and a not-yet-teenage boy steps in, wearing an ankara buba and sokoto, deep yellow with purple and green scattered over it. *My rescuer,* it occurs to me, which almost gets me laughing. Do I always have to be rescued by teenagers?

The boy stands there, unmoving, afraid to approach. The open door lets in cold air, bringing with it an even stronger stench that causes me to cough. I suddenly feel embarrassed I've been crying, struggle to raise my arm and wipe my tears. The boy is no longer there when I'm done.

A moment later, he returns with a man so tall he has to bend to enter into the room. He is dressed in old jogger trousers and a faded t-shirt showcasing *Pasuma Wonder*. He has a smiling face, the patronizing kind that immediately marks him as a carer: teacher, nurse, volunteer.

My guess is right; he squats before me, that smile on, and tells me his name is Justice Ayorinde. We are in Makoko, a fishing community hanging on to the edge of Yaba and Ìsàlè Èkó, caught between these landforms and the Third Mainland Bridge. He is a schoolteacher here, a former volunteer medic who stayed on to help the community and the children. This humble abode is his living quarters.

"Thank you," I say. "Thank you for saving me."

"Oh, Hafiz here did all the work," he says, rubbing the boy's head, a gesture so affectionate it feels out of place in this dank, decaying slice of Lagos. "He found you floating in the water while on a fishing trip. I wouldn't have been able to do anything if he hadn't brought you in."

Hafiz reminds me every inch of the first time I met Fatoumata, the way he refuses to look at my face. The thought of her pinches another hole in my chest, but I blink them away.

"Thank you," I say to the boy. He looks away, shy. Or scared?

"Well, I'm happy you're alive," Justice says "For a while, I thought you weren't going to rejoin us in the land of the living."

"How long was I unconscious?"

"You've been lying here for four days," he says.

What?

He nods. "Mnn hmm. My biggest worry has been food. You haven't eaten anything in this time. We force-fed you water, and since it's not like we can fish medicine out of the lagoon"—he chuckles at the thought—"we just had to keep your temperature stable with a sponge bath." He looks over at my body, his eyes hesitating for a moment on my chest and the network of red lines. "You heal quite quickly though. Abnormally so." He frowns.

"Well," Justice says, rising, "rest some more, mister..."

"Mogo," I say. "David Mogo."

He pauses for a second, then something shifts on his face, and he's about to voice it, then he looks at Hafiz, who is still very scared. He pats the boy on the head and says something in that language I've been hearing. The boy nods once, glances my way, and slinks out the door.

Then Justice turns to me and says: "Godhunter."

I nod.

He squats again and helps me sit up, expertly guiding me with a hand on my chest and back. I flinch, expecting the quick jolt of an impression, but feel nothing. I'm not sure if the lightning strike has messed with my system, but for once I'm grateful my powers aren't working right, so I settle instead for listening to Justice grunt near my ear, struggling with the unanticipated weight.

"We've heard about you," he says. "That you're something... different. I suspected when I saw these." He points to the lightning scars on my chest. "Lichtenberg figures. Happens when electric current enters your body, passes through your blood vessels, and leaves at an exit point." He sits on the mat himself. "Now, the first thing that comes to mind that causes exit points for electricity is lightning." He pauses for effect, watching my face. "Do you know how many people are struck by lightning every year in Lagos?"

I shake my head.

"Zero. Lightning strikes barely happen in cluttered places. Which makes me think whatever struck you didn't come from up there."

He pauses again, to watch my reaction, like a doctor delivering bad news in bits. I grimace at a tightness below my ribs making it difficult for me to breathe.

"Why was he afraid?" I say with a nod towards the door.

Justice looks down. He's a young man, aged by work. I place him around mid-thirties, a few years ahead of me, but with the air of someone who's already fed up with the world.

"There's a policy against bringing in outsiders of any kind," he says. "It's bad enough in there that we can't get the basics—water, power, food, medicine, education—so taking on refugees is not in our best interest. The Baálẹ forbids it."

He reads my expression, which asks, *so why did Hafiz do it?*

"Because I taught them compassion," he says. "Hafiz is one of my better students. He had dreams of going to the University of Lagos." He says this with a handwave in the general direction of what I presume will be Akoka, home to Lagos's formerly premier higher institution. "But even though Lagos has become less... habitable, he hasn't lost hope. Yes, we're all here clinging on to survival, but people like me, and my students like Hafiz who listen, we think there's more than just locking ourselves in here, trying to survive."

"Mmn." I get the feeling.

He rises again, a finality to this one. "Rest. You'll need it a lot soon."

"For what?"

"You'll need to leave," he says matter-of-factly.

"I see."

He nods, as if he's sorry. "The youth society here does not joke with these things. They can be ruthless. Me, I'm just an outsider, I can't dictate. I also don't want Hafiz to start life thinking people get punished for doing good things."

Right. "Fair enough."

"Sleep," he says again. "I'll have to wake you after midnight. I have a strong feeling you might be required to meet someone."

"Your Baálẹ?"

"Oh, no," he says, a furrow on his brow, not quite fitting into his face. "Someone much more important and powerful. Our Olùṣó."

I know that look; I've seen it many times in my line of work, mostly with people trying to describe something they've seen, but which their brain is still trying to process. I also know what that word means. It's an old Yoruba word for a sentry, a keeper. I don't need to ask to know he's talking about a god.

CHAPTER SIXTEEN

I DON'T SLEEP, of course.

Insomnia and I, we go way back. I was a restless kid; wide-eyed at midnight, tussling at 3am, screaming out of dreams close to dawn. Papa Udi told me he used to have me sleep in his bed when I was younger. Said he used a ritual on me once, to put a stop to the bedwetting so he could sleep without the smell of urea choking him. Then at ten, when I got my own room, he'd run out in the deep of night, flashing his cutlass, chasing screams that ended up being nothing more than dreams and shadows. He wagered it was my childhood brain trying to process abandonment, trying to understand the things my body saw and felt with its eyes and fingers.

Tonight though, it's because my body aches like I was built by angry carpenters. I stand outside, on what passes for the balcony of Justice Ayorinde's quarters. I lean on what passes for a handrail, built from scrapwood—everything in this shanty is built from scrapwood—and the contraption sways back and forth with my weight. There's a kerosene lantern hanging off a nail on the shack wall adjacent to me, turned off because Justice believes just standing here is a risk, but I insisted it'll be difficult for anyone to recognise me in this darkness anyway. He then went to bed and asked *me* to wake him up once the clock strikes midnight.

I stand here, eye on Justice's mobile phone clock in my hand, trying to convince myself that there's a slim chance a sliver of my old life—Payu, Fati, Cardoso House, anything—has to have survived. Just... *has to*. The only way I'll ever know this is, first, by getting out of here. Second will be to find someone to give me the dirt on Sango and how to find him.

Justice had the right idea. If the Makoko community has been protected all this time by an orisha serving as their Olùṣó— well, well, well, am I not in luck?

A late night grocery canoe goes by on its last round, sending ripples across the water, calling out wares. The paddler is a young girl, as young as Hafiz, navigating the vessel with a bamboo stick thrice her height. Mind flits back to Fatoumata, but I brush it aside. The crier is a woman, her face lit by the kerosene lantern perched atop her heap of wares, over which she waves a couple of alcohol bottles and calls out for late night drinkers (I don't know what she's saying, but calling out wares sounds the exact same way in every language). Justice says it's the Egun dialect, specific to Egun fishing families commingled from Badagry, Ìsàlẹ̀ Èkó and other riverine areas of the Niger Delta—these were the people who first came to Makoko and made it home. The way she pronounces the words though, I sense she might not be an original local. Justice did say there are other African immigrants here as well: Gabonese, Togolese, Beninoise, Ghanaians and Cameroonians.

The heavy stench of wet shit smacks my nose, reawakened by the disturbance of water. I shut my eyes and bow my head, trying to avoid throwing up or spitting in disgust. It reminds me that this place, in the end, is little more than an inaccessible slum. Yes, the people are happy, protected; yes, they've been shielded from the upheaval and destruction likely barraging through Lagos right now, but I can't say for sure if they'd needed an Olùṣó for that to happen. No one wants to leave Ìsàlẹ̀ Èkó to walk on makeshift footbridges of scrapwood plank; no one wants to boast of basic architecture suspended on stilts a few feet above water; no one wants to leave their brick walls in Upper Island to come live in tin-can houses of zinc, thatch, tarpaulin and sacking. The Lagos State Commissioner for Waterfronts literally had Makoko earmarked for demolition right before The Falling.

The stone the builders rejected is now the safest stone.

The phone in my hand beeps the alarm I set for midnight. I look up, and the boat has vanished from sight. The crier too has become quiet, her lamp gone out. All noise stops at once, like someone pressed pause on a record player. The distant chugging of a small generator grinds to a halt. Tiny window-squares of light start to go out, almost in sync.

I open the door and point the mobile phone torchlight into the shack. Justice is awake, his kerosene lamp in his hand, the snuffed out wick giving off smoke.

"We have to turn out all lights at midnight," he whispers.

"Why are you whispering?"

"Shh," he says. "Go now. Try not to make any noise."

"Where am I going?"

"Just follow the walkway," he says. "The channel is widest at the tail end of the waterway. You'll know when you get there."

"You're not coming?"

He widens his eyes as if I've just mentioned a taboo. "No one ever sees the Olùṣó," he says. "Not even the Baálẹ̀."

"So how d'you now know there's one?"

He cocks his head and regards me, like, *Seriously?*

"Okay fine. How do I get back?"

He shakes his head. "Once you meet the Olùṣó, if all goes well, you likely won't be coming back."

I hand him the phone, and he promptly turns off the light. He hands me a polythene bag that smells of fish: inside is a change of threadbare clothing, a pair of shorts and a plain polo shirt with holes in it. Can't complain; I'd rather have this than walk around in lagoon-and-lightning-tattered jeans and a bare chest of Lichtenberg figures, screaming *danger* to everyone I meet.

"Thank you for your kindness," I find myself saying, undressing in front of him. He doesn't look away or show discomfort. Life of a medic.

"No worry at all. Just…" He sighs. "Things are mad out there, from what I'm hearing. It's the reason we stay here, under the Olùṣó's protection. But we can't continue to live like this. I just want things to be better. Can you make things better?"

I want to tell him I'm just an ordinary man like him too, so how can I change the world? But even I know that's not quite true.

"I'll do my best."

Something pricks my mind after I'm done dressing, right before I turn to leave. "Wait. You said *if all goes well.*"

"Yes?"

"So, what if all doesn't go well?"

He pauses for a bit. "Then you *definitely* will not be coming back."

*   *   *

THE CHANNEL IS indeed widest at the tail end as I come upon it. The way the people of Makoko have built their houses: they've laid each shanty along in a row, leaving a sort of 'main street' for water vessels to pass through. The tail end of the channel, the part that opens into the Lagoon main, is devoid of dwelling on either side, clearly by design. The houses don't resume after the break, either: the few buildings here have a clear look of abandonment. A couple of stilts show where houses have been knocked down.

In the distance, the snaky length of the Third Mainland bends away into Ìsàlẹ̀ Èkó, lit up on its sides like a festive Chinese dragon. I see where the lights stop functioning and Ìsàlẹ̀ Èkó begins. The lagoon itself is splayed out in the distance, ducking under the bridge to merge into the shallows of the ocean. Barge and boat lights twinkle like stars as they run around doing late night work, which could mean anything from industrial fishing to sand dredging to contraband smuggling.

The water moves suddenly, yet it takes me a while to notice it. Mostly because it moves without noise. It's dark, yet I can still see a shadow below the surface, waiting, almost pondering, the way a shark contemplates before snapping up its prey.

"They say you'll want to see me," I say. "I'm here."

Then the god below the surface rises, slowly, and stands in the water.

Their dreadlocked hair is held up in different places with seaweed, decorated with periwinkle, cowrie shells and water stones, which glow translucent in a myriad of blues, greens, turquoises, opals. Their skin reflects the water stones, smooth and silky, but not at all wet-looking, which messes with my eyes a bit. They are lean, with muscle-toned limbs that tell of a warrior life past; now withered, like a retired soldier. They stand at waist-level in the water, wrapped in green cloth at the torso and chest, swaying as if dancing with the waves. Their eyes are pure white, their àshẹ alive and kicking; yet there is a look of fatigue in them, of someone who has seen many things and fought many battles and loved hard and cared hard and eventually gotten tired of the world. I know that look, because I've seen it in Papa Udi many times.

The god's signature flashes across my consciousness: the beauty of sunset and waterfalls; the smell of raw incense; the sound of water from a fountain; a bell pinging underwater; a chalice—big and beautiful and royal—made for wealth alone; wine, drunk from this chalice, the back of my tongue tasting of grapes, but also of fish; a bleak day of mist and fog, but which is really a dream; the cry of a big fish, calling to its mates underwater. I reach out, heady with nausea, pushing my godessence, asking the signature questions of its origin.

"Olokun," I say, when the answer comes back.

They cock their head in that jerky motion that only birds and fish have. A membrane slides over their eyes and disappears again, a fleeting fish-blink.

"Orisha 'daji," Olokun says. Their voice is clear, but with a wobble underneath, as if speaking underwater.

"Yes," I say. "I guess that's me."

"You are not welcome here," Olokun says, speaking sweetly but firmly, like my primary school teacher saying, *Stretch out your hand, darling. Stretch out your hand.*

"That much has been made known," I say.

Olokun fish-blinks again, cocks their head, as if saying, *Sooo, are you gonna leave or nah?*

"Are you going to attack me?" I ask. "Kick me out?"

They seem to contemplate for a beat. "No."

"I assume you want to see me for a reason, then?"

They rise completely out of the water, and I see that they have no legs at all, but large, suckered octopus tentacles, sculling themselves through the water with the tips, like snakes dangling their tails over the edge of a pool, swishing without sound. They sail forward and stop a few feet in front of me.

"I hear you defeated the first vessel the Fiery Ones brought forth," Olokun says, scrutinising me like a rare specimen, their head twitching here and there.

"Well, yeah, I guess. Why do you care?"

"You were attacked," they say, sniffing the air. "I smelt Sango's bolts all over you once you arrived in my settlement."

"Yes."

"Which means they will come here for you, soon. They will come here, and they will lay these people and everything here to waste, as they did on Orun. If you care about these people, you must leave."

"Uh-huh."

They fish-blink. "Death and destruction follow everywhere you go, orisha 'daji."

"But what the fuck does that mean though?" I say, my voice rising to puncture the night's stillness. "Why do you all keep saying that, as if *I* am the one bringing all the death and destruction?" I wave at them. "Seriously, aren't *you* guys the problem? Left your own home, came down here and messed up our very nice slice of the world, then you want to pin it on *me?* Me who has literally done everything I can to fix your mistakes, to make life better for everyone down here? Me who has lost *everything* I care about in this world *because of you guys!*" I slam my fist on the handrail. "*You* should be the one to get out of here. These people don't need you; it's *you* who need them for sustenance, who feeds on their worship and sacrifice to relive your wasted-away glory days of Orun or whatever. I'm coming for all of you, especially those Fiery Ones."

My breathing is agitated by the time I'm done, but Olokun hasn't flinched, just blinking at me quizzically, with maybe a hint of sorrow in that stare.

"I am sorry for what you have lost—"

"Fuck your sorry," I say. "Can't you all just leave us alone?"

"They will never leave you alone," Olokun says, looking away from me for the first time. "The Fiery Ones do not take to threats kindly, and you have waged war against them. They have proven this in Orun, and they will prove it here. They will come for you, and everyone and everything around you, until all is ash and dust. Only then will they rest."

"Then I'm ready for them," I say, my jaw tightening.

"Good." Olokun nods, looking back at me. "This is what I hoped you would say."

"Sorry, what?"

"I hope for you to fight, to challenge the Fiery Ones. And I hope to offer you assistance."

The night is quiet, sans cricket and frog sounds. Everything of the river has gone to sleep, defaulted to the master of the waters. I remember I am dealing with a powerful high god, of the same echelons of Sango and Aganju. I could have a powerful ally right here, right now, for the first time.

"So, you will fight with me?"

The high god seems amused. "I cannot fight with you, orisha 'daji. Can you not see me?" Olokun attempts to show off their body, twirling in the water without making any sound. "I am no longer the warrior I used to be. Take this—all of Makoko and everything the lagoon has to offer—away, and I have nothing left."

"So you really only care about yourself, then? Not really about removing the threats to their existence."

"I am their Olùṣó," Olokun says. "I protect them. I do not have to fight to do that."

"So you want to throw me to the dogs instead."

"You will not be thrown to the dogs. Not if you become Amúnáwá."

I translate that in my head: *the one who brings fire.*

Olokun sidles up close to me, as if trying to tell me a secret. They're less than a foot away from the footbridge on which I'm standing, so close I can feel their breath (is this really their breath, or their godessence?) which smells like wet clothes and seaweed and raw seafood. Their waterstones reflect calm, bluish tones on my skin.

"You, orisha 'daji," Olokun says, "are smithed of iron and fire. It is written all over you, I smell it in your spirit. All you need to do is unlock who you are, and you will become an equal for all powers in this world and others."

Unlock, unlock, unlock. Where is this door I should be unlocking?

"So what do I do, then? How do I become this... bringer of fire?"

"You will find the place where iron lives," Olokun says.

"There, you will find fire smothered by bone."

"Will it kill you people to speak proper English?" I can't take it anymore; not from Payu, not from Ibeji, not from my mother in my dream-visions, and definitely not from some half-human, half-octopus god. "Can you, like, break it down for me? What do you mean *where iron lives*? What does *fire smothered by bone* even mean? Do you people think I was born with puzzle-cracking abilities or something?"

"This is what I know of how you will become Amunọwa," Olokun says, unperturbed. "Oshodi will guide you, though it won't be easy."

"Oshodi? Like, the *place* Oshodi?"

Olokun nods.

Finally! One sane thing in all this madness. "Great, then. That shouldn't be too difficult." I pause. "Wait, don't tell me: when I get to the place where iron lives, I'll know it, right? And when I find fire smothered by bone, I'll know too, right?"

"You are not man, orisha 'daji," Olokun says. "You will definitely know."

Of course I will, you incomprehensible ancient bastard.

"Thank you," I say. "However, you have not told me how I will defeat the two gods who brought down the whole of Orun and cast all of you down here. Last I checked, killing a god wasn't possible. Not by me, at least."

"Well," Olokun says. "The truth is, only with the weapon of a god can you overpower one."

"So this Amunọwa is the power of a god?"

"Well, yes and no. It's not as much the power itself, as it is *you*. Only a god can scrape another god off this realm."

"So, to kill a god, I must become one?"

"You can put it that way."

I stare off to the distance, at the lights of the barges and anchored vessels in the distance. These gods and their twisted ways will not be the death of me.

"Fine," I say. "I've heard you."

"But you must go now," Olokun says. "Find what you need, for the safety of all. Keep us alive before it is too late."

I remember Justice's *Pasuma Wonder* t-shirt and his precious books, Hafiz's yellow ankara, and think, *Yes, Olokun is right.* But then I remember that night at Cardoso House, the bolt of lightning leaving Sango's axe, Fati and Payu falling out of the first floor window in the hallway, crashing to the ground below, and I think, *Nope, I'm too late any way. I'm always too late.*

I could go back. Try and pick up the pieces of my old life, try to make something out of it. I could find Papa Udi and Fati—they have to have survived somehow, *have to*—and we could start afresh, maybe move to Abuja or further north or something. We could leave all this behind.

Or, I can fix what I started. Once and for all.

CHAPTER SEVENTEEN

IT IS NEARLY dawn by the time Olokun leads me to where the footbridges lead out of Makoko and into the heart of Yaba, Lagos's once-thriving commercial hub. By break of light, I've arrived at the tail end of Commercial Avenue, one of the main streets in Yaba, and home to the few surviving trees in the concrete jungle. Not a single soul in sight as I pass by the palms and evergreens, rising above building height, swaying in the gentle morning breeze.

The buildings of Commercial Avenue haven't fared as well. Most are in the same state as Ìsàlẹ̀ Èkó's: abandoned, the wind rushing through broken windows and open doors, raising dust. Their walls are cracked, their paint faded to pastel shades and the whole avenue eerie with creepy abandoned things: empty danfos and kekes, vacant shops with banners hanging askew. I pass by an unnamed marquee tent that used to be an event centre. I work out that today is a Saturday, and the emptiness of the event centre says everything: on a regular Saturday, pre-Falling, vehicles parked off-street would've clogged up the traffic so I'd have to weave my way between cars, bikes, and humans in colourful aso-ebi uniforms and matching gele headpieces, flowing agbadas, spit-shined shoes, gold watches and Ray-Ban glasses. Lagos used to know how to party; Lagos used to know how to be wild and fun and colourful. Now, it only remains wild, in a way that brings darkness and grim and quiet.

At the top of the avenue, right before I join Murtala Muhammed Way, I come upon the biggest building on the road: the E-Centre. I have to stop for a while just to look at it: at the tall Tecno banner still boasting *Phantom 8: Capture Your Legend;* at the big signs advertising Domino Mall and Ozone Cinemas; at the smaller signs for banks, telecom companies, electronic companies; all speaking to an audience that is no longer here.

Few months ago, and this place, like Ìsàlẹ̀ Èkó, would've been crawling with godlings. Thanks to the work of the LASPAC, it is mostly a silent, windswept complex now, trash littered about by nature and scavenging animals. I wonder, yet again, why people have not come to reclaim what is theirs; but then it occurs to me that though the godlings might be gone, there are far bigger challenges to resettlement on the mainland, whether god-made or man-made. Anyone with a good head will not return to an abandoned building and resume business, serving an audience that is too afraid to come.

I still haven't come upon anyone, and that is expected. The most habitable zones post-Falling have remained Upper Island and Outer Mainland, the extreme ends of Lagos. Everything in-between is fair game, and no one wants to be the prey in open season (and I'm not just talking deities and their affiliates: some of the former policemen and military didn't take too kindly to being replaced by the LASPAC, and anyone who still has guns at this time will use them to get whatever they want).

This general absence of persons is a good thing for me. I'm in neither the shape nor the frame of mind to fight mindless creatures or silly humans. I just need to get to Oshodi and find what I'm looking for.

I keep thinking I should've called Femi Onipede, who must be frowning so deeply about this whole situation by now that ridges have formed permanently on her forehead. I did think about it, while holding Justice's phone by that handrail in Makoko, but then decided it too risky. Apart from the fact that I'm not really interested in bringing more victims into what's no one's fight but mine, I've also been wondering how Sango knew exactly where and when to find me that night (he's a god, though, of course). I maintain a nagging feeling that there are a lot of ears to the ground on the side of the Fiery Ones, so maybe the more discreet I keep things, the easier it is for me to come out of the dark and sucker-punch them. It's best if everyone believes I'm dead.

Murtala Muhammed Way, much wider and more open, feels even more eerie and quiet. In front of me as I enter is the former Tejuosho Ultra-Modern Market, rows of shops and large, tattered umbrellas now quiet and dusty, just like I remember Balogun Market last year. Rows upon rows of yellow danfos are parked, abandoned. These ones are not empty, though: as I walk past the roundabout, there's scrambling on either side; stray dogs, sewage rats, even a monkey; scampering, knocking stuff over—mostly the trash scattered all over. (Thought Lagos was dirty before The Falling? Try again: Tejuosho is a *carpet* of polythene bags, goods wrappers, degraded organic waste and, unsurprisingly, animal shit.) I half-expect to sense a signature somewhere, but there's nothing.

I breach Ikorodu Road, which an even wider road with service lanes. The emptiness of Lagos really hits home here, its windswept landscape bringing me to the full realisation that if I do not do something soon, every single place in Lagos is going to look like this. The first pangs of hunger hit me here, after a long walk down, and the midday sun tickles my throat with thirst. Under the bridge at Jibowu, I finally give in to my humanness: weak, tired, hungry. Aching joints, hurting sides, tight abdomen, tough breathing. But I must soldier on, mustn't I? I'm Lagos' only hope now, aren't I?

I stop and take a seat under a canopy previously used to house passengers waiting for interstate transport shuttles. Behind me, multiple road transport companies are scattered; all now abandoned, of course. A few of their old, rusted buses are left behind with company names still scribbled on the sides, advertising their destinations: Lagos to Benin, Warri, Lokoja, Abuja, Onitsha, Enugu, Owerri, Calabar. A few go up north—Minna, Kaduna—and westward—Ibadan, Abeokuta, Akure.

The sound of an engine starts in the distance and grows steadily, before I recognise it for a motorcycle. The bike comes into view in the distance, on the opposite side of the road, going in the direction I have just come in. The rider is running at max speed, so I guess he won't have time to see me; but I'm wrong. He slows once he approaches the bridge at Jibowu, and stops completely when he spots me, standing astride his bike, the engine idling. He looks terribly young, probably a teenager, and is dressed in aviator goggles and a windbreaker, both filthy with age like his hair, which is thick and woolly and likely hasn't seen any grooming since The Falling. He regards me from head to toe, then waves a tentative hand as if checking,

Are you human? I wave back weakly. *Yes, I am. Also very tired.* Then he does a salute, his hand flat at ninety to his forehead, as if to say *Godspeed*. I return the gesture and he zooms away.

I think it's this singular encounter with humanness that brings back my strength, my zeal, because I find myself standing up sooner than expected. Maybe in it I see hope, that there are those waiting for Lagos to heal, waiting for it to become whole again, so they can resume their business of being very human in one of the most inhuman cities in the world. And it is my job to try and bring this Lagos back to them.

It's what Papa Udi would have wanted—would want (stop speaking about them in past tense, you idiot; how do you know they're dead?). It's what Fati, Taiwo and Kehinde would have wanted—agh, would want (you're doing it again, David). It's what my mother would want.

Besides, let me be honest with myself: I am not going to find any food or water. I am not going to find shelter or rest. Olokun was right: if I'm going to make it, to survive this, I'll have to be more than human. I'll have to become a god.

IT TAKES ME the rest of the day to get to Oshodi. The route from Ikorodu Road takes me past Fadeyi, where I then decide that rather than going on and on along this major route, which is literally desertland now, I cut through Onipanu main. Thing is, I've decided to go as the crow flies. Yes, I risk clashing with one or two small groups, going through the small streets like Ayuba and Olateju, but that's a risk I'm willing to take.

It is in Onipanu I first start to see signs that people might've tried to return here. There's some fresh trash, mostly human faeces in all the wrong places, and clothing scattered about or abandoned on clotheslines. A plastic doll, more creepy than endearing, cast mindlessly aside. A pair of bathroom slippers that do not look aged. This makes me more wary, so that right before I get to the Illupeju bypass—my legs finally getting my attention, reminding me that they can only work for so long—I find the verandah of a small house to lie down for a while. I fall into fitful sleep, dreaming of the charred, smoking faces of Fati and Payu, scattered amongst the rubble of Cardoso House; of Sango wearing the essences of Taiwo and Kehinde in a Yasal bottle on his neck; of Sango and Aganju laughing, clinking champagne glasses, their fingers delicately manicured, toasting to their new Lagos, their new Orun.

I wake up sweating when the sun has almost dipped behind the horizon. It takes me a few minutes to get my groggy self back on the road, crossing the railway tracks to join the Lagos-Abeokuta Expressway that will finally lead me to Oshodi. At this point, I feel not only grateful and even more extremely tired—typical feeling at the last lap of a race—but joyous that at least one good thing seems to be coming out of this after all.

The highway is silent too, as expected. Nightly creatures yawn and stretch and begin their chorus of noises. I walk in the middle of the road, maintaining a good 360-degree view of everything all round me. More yellow danfos and kekes are lined up along the wire fence before the railway, same way they have at all the big bus stops. I ignore the rattling I hear in some of them—I know human and godling rattlings, and those do not sound like either—and instead focus on the Oshodi Interchange before me.

Many years ago, long before The Falling, the Oshodi

Interchange was known to most as the heartbeat of Lagos, where you could get transportation to literally every single nook and cranny of the state, and even beyond. The interchange is characterised by two things: a lengthy flyover, allowing those who didn't want to have anything to do with the interchange be on their merry way, known to most as Oshodi Oke; and beneath the flyover and pedestrian bridges, where all the buses and taxis and touts and hawkers of wares and hoodlums and pickpockets and every possible godforsaken combination of trade and squalor and vice exists. This underside, splayed across the ongoing railway tracks like a milk spill, was known to most as Oshodi Ìsàlẹ̀, one of the most dangerous places in Lagos.

That has not changed.

I arrive at the place square underneath the bridges. The remnants of a once busy precinct are still here; the danfos, the tattered posters and crooked writing scrawled in yellow chalk on the pillars under the bridge advertising domestic workers and penis enlargements, abandoned makeshift wooden sheds, kiosks and mobile toilets, and a massive combined stink of stagnant gutter water, decomposing refuse and spirogyra.

Right. If Olokun is to be believed, this is where I begin my search for the thing that will make me larger than life, that will enable me rise above myself and become something bigger: Amunọwa, the one who brings fire.

Something is different about Oshodi than the last time I saw it, many years ago. Across the road, right where there used to be a massive freeway, is a blockade of vertical concrete slabs and military sandbags, supported by tractor-size tyres. The wire fences once used to separate the train tracks from the bridge have been moved, now installed on each side of the blockade so that it snakes with the length of the flyover, shutting off everything beyond from anyone arriving at Oshodi from my end. It's a blockade through-and-through, that without a sign in sight clearly says *Do Not Cross*.

I'm standing there, thinking, when there is a swift movement to my right. I spin, but there's nothing but shadows between the pillars under the flyover. I scuttle towards the divider in the middle of the road, so I can get a good vantage point on all sides. I hear the same rattle, the sound of feet scurrying after me, stopping when I stop, from the opposite side of the road. Whatever it is, it's all around me; I feel a choking presence converging. It becomes increasingly clear to me that no matter how fast I run, I'll still get caught.

"Okay," I say, to no one in particular, facing the darkness beyond the pillars under the bridge. "Show yourself."

There is hesitation, a tentativeness to the footfalls.

"I have not come here to make trouble," I say. "I'm just looking for something."

Then the shadows slink out from behind the pillars, moving as a pack. They circle me slowly, cautiously. I count over a dozen of them. They're people, dressed in clothes more worn than mine, with pieces of cloth tied around their noses. A closer look tells me that most of them are women, and all of them hold weapons: some guns, some machetes and knives, some clubs.

Of *course* Olokun sent me into a trap.

What else do gods do but get unsuspecting humans caught up in their quests for personal fulfillment? I am the stupid one for trusting him.

"Okay," I say, raising my hands as the militants circle me. "I come in peace, okay? I'm not here to fight. If you'll just let me be on my way..."

I leave the sentence hanging, hoping the ones who're pointing their guns at me will get the message first and lower their weapons, but they hold them steady. I start to back up then, my hands still raised, keeping all of them in my line of sight as they fall into a rough horseshoe shape, keeping my rear as the only direction of escape, or retreat.

As I come out from under the bridge, a figure rides out from the shadows. *Rides*, because she's on a horse. A fucking horse. She's riding it bareback, her hands clutching nothing but its mane. She's dressed in combat-looking gear, complete with boots. She holds no weapons, but she doesn't *need* to, to look menacing. She stops behind me, blocking my escape. I turn to look up at her.

"Look, I said I don't want any troub—"

She throws something at me. Not a weapon, only a sort of belt made of plastic or wooden beads, that wraps itself around my torso and snaps together with a magnetic *click*. I'm almost chiding myself at flinching, when I realise that I can't take off the belt at all. In fact, it tightens the more I try to take it off, and then I realise: the beads are getting stuck to my skin.

It's fucking warded, dammit.

And then slowly, my senses begin to fade like a camera out of focus, my esper retreating to some faraway place, out of my reach. At the same time, the group converges on me swiftly, like they've rehearsed it: someone knocks at the back of my knees, so that I fall to the ground; another puts a hangman's noose of rope around my neck; and others bind my wrist and ankles. In under thirty seconds, I'm completely immobile.

The horse woman dismounts and stands above me. I can't see her face—I can't see *anyone's* face—but I can tell she's smiling, like she's humbled me in my pride, and it brings a memory from last year, where I last saw this look, the last time I was in captivity; the last time I felt hopeless, helpless and useless to the rest of the world.

And I find myself thinking: *Oh, for fuck's sake, not this again.*

CHAPTER EIGHTEEN

THE NIGERIAN ARMY Shopping Arena was one of the most guarded shopping complexes of Oshodi in its heyday. Now, as I am carried between four members of the militant group like a log—I realise the group that bound me by the bridge, outside the blockade, were sentries. The large, arched gate into the Arena, a half mile down from the blockade, sports even more guards and guns than pre-Falling. The three gates are padlocked with heavy chains. A guard, masked like the others, unlocks one when we arrive and lets us in.

The horse woman leads the troop. I hear nothing of the little conversation she makes with people—what with my senses blocked out with the binding ward written into the beads around me—but I can see from the way she moves, the way the bodies of others stiffen just a little when she goes past them, that she is some sort of leader here. And a wizard, of course.

For the first time since Makoko, I see lights in the former shopping stalls ahead of us, and hear life in the familiar sounds of children at play. For a moment, I'm comforted that I am not in the hands of a deadly militant group intent on carving my skin and using it for rituals (I'm sure *someone's* had the idea).

All that hope evaporates soon when, instead of moving in the direction of that warmth, we veer right, into an unlit portion of the massive compound.

"Where are you taking me?" I ask, barely hearing myself, not quite sure if I make any sense to them at all. "Where are we going?"

I'm taken around back without response, as if they want to keep the dirty work they're about to do with me out of the eyes of the happy children. We walk at least half a kilometre before I hear the sound of a large door being opened. I'm carried into a large building, a warehouse of sorts. It's pitch dark.

They dump me on the ground. Someone turns on a torchlight and points it directly into my face. If I couldn't see for shit before, it's even worse now.

"I'm going to ask you just once," a voice says: clearly the commander's. She sounds older, but firm, like she is used to commanding people. "Who sent you?"

"Sent... What?"

Something hard—the butt of a gun, maybe—smacks me in the temple.

"Every time you respond to my question without the answer I'm looking for, I break your head. Now, who sent you?"

I shake my head to orient myself. "Nobody. Nobody sent me."

Another smack.

"Did the Fiery Ones send you?"

"Did the—What? The Fiery Ones didn't send me, what the hell?"

Smack.

"*Can you hold on?*" I find myself shouting. "Can you just, like, wait for a second?"

There is a pause.

"Sango and Aganju didn't send me," I say. "*I'm* looking for *them*."

"And why are you looking for them?"

"Because," I say, the image of Cardoso House burning in my mind's eye, "they took everything from me." I realise I'm voicing it for the first time, and this sends pinpricks into my chest, but I clear my throat and soldier on. "They attacked and burnt my house. They"—don't say it, David, don't say it—"they... killed my family."

There is silence, as if they hear the grief in my voice and are waiting for it to pass.

"This house," the commander says, softness coming into her voice. "Where is it? Who are you?"

"Cardoso House, off Simpson in Ìsàlẹ̀ Èkó," I say. "My name is David Mogo."

There is another pause, then someone clicks a lighter, lights a lantern and raises it.

We are in a warehouse, alright: a large open space of concrete and cement, storeys high. There are seven of the guerillas in front of me, the commander included. They all hold guns bar the commander. She approaches me, slowly, kneels, then takes off her cloth mask. She is middle-aged, with sharp cheekbones, steely eyes and rough hands, in that way I know she must have once been military. A whisp of greying hair peeks out from under her headwrap.

"The godhunter," she says.

I nod.

"You fought the Wizard at 81 Division."

"That's me," I say, smiling weakly.

"You're Udi Odivwiri's son."

I've never thought of myself as Payu's *son*, but there's a thought.

"Hold on," I say, confused. "How do you know so much about me?"

"Is he really dead? Udi?"

I stare at her wordlessly. She walks away with her back to me, her hands akimbo, shoulders drooped. The others look on, wearing the same fallen faces.

The commander returns to me.

"Why are you here? How did you find us?"

"How did I find...? You guys know you're literally on the road, right?"

"No one like you—no deity of any sort—has come here, ever," she says. "And we've had to be extra careful since the Fiery Ones took over."

My head rings. "Since the *what* took over *what?*"

She lifts her eyebrows. "Oh. You didn't know."

"I've been... occupied. What's happening?"

She looks at me for a long time, something akin to pity in her eyes, then, matter-of-factly, says: "The Fiery Ones took over the State House in Upper Island a few days ago. We no longer run Lagos, godhunter. The gods do now."

THE COMMANDER'S NAME is Shonuga, and after clarifying that I really do come in peace, she unties me from the warded beads. My senses return with a *pop*, and I grab for my esper and flex it with my mind. For the first time since the lightning strike, it seems to be working quite well.

I'm left to catch some badly-needed sleep before the next morning. In order not to alarm the population of the Arena, Shonuga has me sleep in an abandoned bank building her squad has set aside for 'extraordinary guests.' I'm not sure what *extraordinary* means in this context, and I'm too tired and hungry to worry. I end up with some dry garri and water, which I gobble up before bed. I struggle to sleep, of course, but the weariness from walking almost twenty-four hours wins, and I drift into fitful slumber.

Morning sees a late forties-ish man with albinism, thin, dressed in office trousers and a dress shirt, tucked in and everything (the neatest I've seen in a long time) arrive and stand over me while I wake. He's the first person I've seen here who's not armed, and not poised to gun me down. He has new clothes for me, a long-sleeved dress shirt like his and a pair of size 34 jeans, intended to help me blend better into the population of the Arena while Shonuga, who in essence runs this place, figures out what to do with me. I dress behind what had formerly been a cashier's counter. He notices the Lichtenberg figures on my chest, but says nothing about it. Instead, he explains to me that his name is Shonekan, and he is a second-in-command of sorts for the Arena. Then he goes on to explain, in what I consider unnecessary detail, how he first was in the military, then after deciding combat fatigues were not for him, moved on to become a lecturer of history at the now-defunct University of Lagos.

We take a walk around the compound. The Arena is a very modern shopping complex, now converted into a semi-comfortable post-Falling sanctuary. A parallel layout of lock-up shops ("With their own toilets," Shonekan tells me)—over a hundred of them, at a guess—house displaced families, assigned according to need. An equal number of the smaller stalls—traditionally built market kiosks with wooden façades—house singular folk. Behind these are over two hundred square metres of warehouse space, as well as a few odds-and-ends, like the bank where I slept.

Most people are dressed well, as if they've just began their own post-Falling life. They go about their business, which for the most part seems to consist of trying to find people to trade stuff with. We pass by a large general courtyard where small groups of people gather, bending over blankets spread out in the early morning sun sporting signs like, *I HAVE COKE AND WINE. LOOKING FOR SIZE 40 FEMALE SHOES.* Some are selling perishable goods, like in a good old open-air market, while some sell more practical stuff, like lanterns and candles. There is a big, black pot in the corner, with a heap of ash underneath, and sprinkles of jollof rice around.

The Arena is so well kept that for a moment I'm taken back to a time when there were no gods in Lagos, when the mainland too was a haven like Upper Island is now (at least, before the Fiery Ones got there). The Arena might've been one of the government's occasional bids to gentrify the mainland, sure, but for a moment, as we walk around the paved roads and walkways of interlocking tiles between stalls and lock-up shops, I feel like a little slice of heaven is here. Well-pruned shrubbery, glass windows intact, even a good number of vehicles parked around—not moving, sure, but not rundown and infested with scavengers or godlings. A dog barks in the distance; not a howl, but the joyous bark of a dog fetching a ball. As we circle back to the lock-up shops, two children wave to us from a window. Shonekan waves back, and the children giggle to one another.

Shonekan himself is a quiet man with small hands, mostly always squinting behind his glasses. He is a far cry from Shonuga. I guess being someone of fewer words and a demure manner, she always sends him to do the tedious work of building relationships with people.

He takes me back to an empty row of kiosk-style open stalls. He tries a few keys in one lock, and when it clicks open, pulls out the key and hands it to me.

"Shonuga says you should put up here until you two can have extensive discussions about your... mission," he says. "You have a mattress on the floor in there. We don't get a lot of water until it rains, so you might just have to be okay with delaying that bath. We do communal feeding in the evenings, so if you're hungry, be in the courtyard at seven."

"How did you come to be deputy here?"

Shonekan pauses. "Well, I arrived here like everyone else, joined forces with Shonuga, and put my skills to use."

"You're not scared of her?"

He regards me quizzically. "How do you mean, *scared*? No one is scared of Shonuga. Yes, she's a little rough around the edges, but if you've heard what we've heard about what has been happening out there, you will be too. She protects us, and we respect her for it."

"So you all are okay with... what she is?"

"That she's a wizard?"

His directness takes me by surprise. "You know about that?"

"Everyone knows about that," he says, laughing. "We have a governing council, five of us: we're all wizards, including me."

I stop in my tracks. "Wow."

"Wait, you didn't know?" He has a smile on his face.

"How would I know that?"

"We, the pioneers of this settlement, call ourselves Oshodi. Wizards coming together. Our names? Shonekan, Shonuga, Sholuyi? Ọṣó literally means 'wizard.'"

I realise he pronounces the name the exact same way Olokun did, with a stress on the second syllable, and not the first, as I'd done all along. My bad Yoruba is going to catch up with me one day.

"So, Oshodi is a *people?* What about the interchange?"

Shonekan laughs at my epiphany. It's been a while since I've heard hearty laughter. I didn't know I missed it this much.

"Let me tell you a story: Oshodi Tapa, the person who that bus-stop was named after, was a Nupe slave in the 1800s, who escaped Portugese capture and was taken under the wings of the then Oba of Lagos. He became a trading agent, key adviser and military chief for the Oba, and helped defend against the British invasion of 1851, until he got exiled and died in the 1860s. All this land"—he gestures all around—"used to be his.

"Since the LASPAC managed to clear those dirty godlings out, it was first us wizards and just a couple of other people who came here, looking for protection. We did use that name to camouflage what we really are, but at the same time saying what we really are, you know what I mean? So that those who need to find us can. We just hope it won't lead anyone who wishes us ill here."

"Like who?"

He smiles at me the way you smile at a child who's being naive.

"If you intend to win a war, godhunter, you take out the generals first. The Fiery Ones are here in Lagos now. Half the people you see here are refugees from Upper Island; most arrived in the last few days, like you. You and I and people like Shonuga and the council, we're the first to go. Just like…" He trails off.

"Just like Papa Udi," I say for him.

"I'm sorry about what happened to him."

I blink and blink but I'm not even sure I know what to do. Cry? Shout?

"Me too," I say.

Shonekan is quiet for a while, musing.

"They will come here, eventually," he says, a weight in his voice. "I just hope we will somehow be ready for them when that time comes."

What if I stay? Squaring up to Sango is personal; staying here, helping these people repel whatever attack they might face—*that* would be helping people.

But, without Amúnáwá, whatever that might be, I'm very unlikely to make any major impact anyway. I still need to become something more than half-man, half-orisha, if I'm really going to stop this train that I started.

Shonekan, ready to leave, pats me on the back. I get my first impression since the attack: a flash of screaming, crying, burning; the choking smell of smoke and the heavy feeling of loss and despair. The wizard recoils, yanking his arm as if he has touched hot coal. He blinks rapidly, and I know he has seen something too—Does it work that way now? Am I stronger?—and now is desperately trying to unsee it.

He looks up to me, with something more than the respect he's shown me so far. With fear.

"What are you?" he says, putting space between me and him.

Good question, Shonekan.

Good question.

CHAPTER NINETEEN

I DO NOT see Shonekan again until the communal meal that night, and when I do, he frowns at me quizzically and buries his face in his bowl of agege bread and tinned tomato stew. I get a small, round loaf with one sardine fish soaked in oil; a delicacy, because it is my first night here. Cooking and eating is done in the courtyard and everyone just sits on the ground, on mats and ankara wrappers spread out on the concrete. There is a fire, but nothing is cooking on it, and the weather is quite warm, so it's mostly for everyone to get out of the darkness of their stalls, but really to gather and believe together that all hope is not lost.

A young man, about my age, but with artificially-dyed grey hair, shaved low at the sides and top slicked in that way I'm a hundred percent he must've been a pastor before becoming a refugee, starts to sing:

> *The walls of Jericho fell down flat*
> *The walls of Jericho fell down flat*
> *While the children of God were praising the Lord*
> *The walls of Jericho fell down flat.*

Everyone joins in, repeating the song over and over, linking their fingers and holding on to the words as to hope

"Stories that touch the heart, eh?" Shonuga says, settling into the ground beside me. I chose a seat behind the whole crowd; I don't really want the attention. The kind of people here—mostly former upper-middle-classers—might not know too many stories of a Lagos freelance godhunter, but I'm six feet with big arms and a bald head, which tends to draw people's eyes.

"Na real stories that touch," I say. "What do the walls of Jericho have to do with gods raining down from above and making us refugees in our own city?"

"People gats to believe in something, godhunter."

"You can call me David."

"Okay. David."

The singing stops, and the man opens a bible passage and begins to read about Joshua leading the army of the Lord to battle and crumbling the walls of Israel's enemies with their voices alone.

"Your Word is your weapon," he says, spittle flying into the fire. "The Word of the Lord is your sword and shield."

"Why do you let this happen?" I ask Shonuga. "Why do you let him lie to them?"

"But the man dey lie, really?" Shonuga says. "Is their word not their weapon? It's only what they tell themselves they can believe in. The real weapon here is belief, no be so?"

I say nothing. She pinches her loaf and dunks it in stew, chewing soundlessly and thinking.

"Your father, Papa Udi. He taught me that."

"He's not my father, actually," I say, too quickly.

"Abi grandfather, sorry," she says.

"Any one works. You were his student?"

"No oh, not really. I joined LASPAC before, in the very early days, when just those godlings were causing problems. But this government na fuckup, they stopped giving us money. I resigned because I no fit give my life to stupid politics."

I could imagine Papa Udi teaching a bunch of young recruits how to explore their godessence and make recipes and rituals.

"That binding charm you used on me that night, he taught you the godtongue you used to do that?"

She nods. "Nsibidi. I no learn the thing immediately, though. I understood it more only after some crazy practice." She chuckles. "Nsibidi is mad. Fucking difficult. Hieroglyphics no make any sense."

"You're telling me? I grew up with the man and I could never pick it up. I was more interested in getting out into the street and actually helping people than staying at home and practising shapes and how to pronounce them."

"I fit teach you, you know? But you don't have time like that."

I raise an eyebrow. "What do you mean?"

She grimaces, then stands to go get some water from the large plastic tank collecting rain from the roof gutter of a nearby lockup shop. She returns with two cups and hands me one. The water tastes metallic, and I remember the taste of Sango's signature.

"Shonekan saw something," she says. "When he touched you."

"Oh?" I say.

"Shonekan *sees*," she says. "That's his own thing. He does this particular agbo from black oil plants and drinks it everyday—he calls it *nootropic*, say na brain stimulant. He tells us if someone can stay or not."

"Ah," I say. "So, what did he see?"

"Fire."

I scrape off the last of my sardine and gobble it down. The preacher man asks everyone to close their eyes so he can lead them in prayer.

"Fire from me, or fire *to* me?" I ask.

"Around," she says, looking into the distance. "Around you."

"Well. If I'm going to go by all the stories I've heard about myself, *fiery* sounds just about the summary."

"Good fiery or bad fiery?"

"Depends on how you look at it."

"I want to save these people," she says matter-of-factly, sipping her rainwater slowly. "I joined LASPAC because I wanted to save people. This na my second chance; I'm not going to spoil it."

I nod. "I understand. I'll leave first thing tomorrow morning."

"No, you stay." She says this without looking at me. Her jaw is clenched in the light of the night fire. "You stay until we know what you're looking for, make we help you find am. Then we go boot those fucking gods out of our state."

MY NEXT FEW days at the Arena pass in the same way:

New refugees come with new stories. The whole of Upper Island has become godland now, just the way Ìsàlẹ̀ Èkó was. The LASPAC has been overrun, and most have gone into hiding. Everyone else is trekking either *away*, out to Epe and

Ogun State, or *inward*, facing the Lagos-Ibadan Expressway, towards Berger and out of the city. The few who arrive at Oshodi are those who'd heard whispers about the settlement and were brave enough to break away from the exodus and turn off the Gbagada-Oworonshoki expressway to get here.

When a new group arrives, a big bell is rung, the kind used in schools. Three spaced rings, and you know a new group's arrived. Three quick rings, and that's the communal dinner. I ask what happens if there's an attack, and Shonuga says I'll definitely know it's an attack.

The tales from the exodus are not pretty. There are differing versions with pepper and salt added to spice them up, but the throughlines are there. Most Upper Island escapees have not survived the trip to the mainland, falling to hunger, thirst, illness, fatigue, and even suicide. Some tried to drive their vehicles out of town—especially the oyinbo Asians, Lebanese, Europeans—and it did not end well for them. A few of these immigrants managed to join the throng and slip out of Upper Island—I spot an Indian man in day two's group—and they keep asking when they can go back to their country, where they can contact their embassy.

The last piece of news is the one that makes me grit my teeth: the Fiery Ones have deployed a new task force to head off the emigration: they took all the godlings cordoned off in Ìsàlẹ̀ Èkó and turned them into a monstrous plague on Upper Island.

No one can describe what these things look like, because no one has lived to do so.

My afternoons are spent with Shonekan. After grumbling with Shonuga about helping me, then finally coming to terms with the truth that I'm not his enemy, he spends time grilling me for information, helping us dig for clues as to what Olokun wants me to be looking for. So far, we've come up with a good zero of them.

"At least we know what they meant when they said Oshodi will help you," I say on day three. "But, the place where iron lives? Fire smothered by stone? I need someone to make sense, please."

"I think maybe we first need to understand the concept of Amúnáwá," Shonekan says. "You know the legend?"

"There's a legend?" I blink. "Why didn't anyone tell me!?"

"It's not like it's common knowledge," Shonekan says. "Something I found in the archives at the university library."

"There are books about orishas there?"

"There are books about *everything* there, David."

"So why don't we, like, just go there and look around?"

"Have you been inside a university library before? Seen how big it is?"

"Well, no."

He tuts. "Anyway, the legend. Amúnáwá. The Bringer of Fire. Some old Yoruba folksongs tell of a powerful hunter who got lost in an accursed rainforest, and ate a fire lizard when he got hungry. When he emerged, he could breathe fire from his nose and mouth, and fire burned in his eyes."

"He ate a lizard."

"Fire lizard."

"Fire lizard. Like a salamander?"

"Exactly."

"And when he came out, he could breathe fire."

"Yes."

"And you believe this stuff, prof?"

"It's legend, David. Like how the folks who currently occupy the State House are legends."

"Right." I stare at him a moment. "So I find a salamander and eat it. What if I combust from the fire, then? Isn't that what happens? I've heard about them."

He smiles wryly at me. "I know what you are, David Mogo. We all know what you are."

"Okay, okay, let's put that aside. Say I eat a salamander and don't self-combust. What then?"

"I don't know. Maybe the more important question is, when last did you see a salamander lying around?"

"Exactly. I've only ever heard of them, never *seen*. Papa Udi said their dosage of godessence is unrivalled amongst all creatures, more than any human. They must've been hunted to death."

"Not really, though," Shonekan says. "The stories all say to *not* eat them. Other men, in their search for power, tried to emulate Amúnáwá, but they could not contain the fire of the gods."

"Okay," I say, rising to dust the seat of my pants. "Let's say he's right. So, what, I hunt down a salamander, eat it, and become a flamebreather."

"Seems so." Shonekan is drawing in nonexistent lines on the concrete with his finger. He looks like this is a completely pointless venture and he wants to get out of here.

"What do you think?" I ask him. "Really?"

He sighs and rises with me. "I think Olokun is all hogwash, and just wanted you out of their settlement so you could go somewhere and die with everyone else."

There's a moment's awkward silence.

"Did you, like, have family, before coming here?" I find myself asking.

He shrugs.

"What happened?"

"I don't really want to talk about it," he says.

I nod. I don't think I want to talk about Payu and Fati and Ibeji either, whatever has become of them.

"Why do you think these gods are doing, though?" I ask instead. "What do you think they want?"

Shonekan thinks for a second. "I think they just want to go home."

I remember the hunger in Ajala's eyes when he wanted Ibeji, when he had that Yasal bottle around his neck, when he spoke about making a new beginning, a new Lagos. It was greed, yes, but it was mostly longing, a ravenous desire to fill an emptiness inside him.

We stand there and stare at nothing together.

IN THE EVENINGS, by the fire, Shonekan tells me stories. Mostly history stuff, like about the Nigerian Civil War and how people used to hide in pit latrines when the soldiers came. He thinks what we currently face is much, much worse, because the rest of the world looks away, pretends not to notice while Lagos goes under. He says it's the exact same way the civil war started: first as simple unrest, and then the cancer grew and grew until the country could ignore it no longer. By that time, too many had died to douse the fire. He thinks, if we're not careful, we'll end up in the same boat.

Other times, we talk about the meaning of Olokun's words.

Shonuga is there sometimes before she goes off on sentry duty, tying her horse to a stall and petting him to keep still. She says his name is Aburo ('younger one' in Yoruba), and tells us the story of how she found him, wandering on a beach on the island. We gist her about our salamander conclusions, and she thinks the place where iron lives is the Murtala Muhammed International Airport, where all the planes which no longer fly are still parked. Shonekan thinks it's ridiculous to go looking for a salamander in an airport, but I'm not so sure. What *has* made sense since The Falling?

On my fifth night in the Arena, one of the new guys—who used to run a viewing centre for football matches on the island—somehow has a seven-inch portable battery TV still packing hours of charge. After being bribed by numerous parents with a sizeable number of canned goods, he brings it out and fiddles with the telescoping antenna, and after he fails to catch any nearby stations (I seriously dunno what he was thinking, trying to find functioning TV signals with the apocalypse upon us), he plugs in a memory card and selects an old animated film: *Toy Story*.

He plays this for nights five and six, drawing a bigger audience and amassing even more canned goods. By night seven, the adults have done as adults are wont to do and clamoured for their own. The man apologizes, that all he has is the last El Clasico match between Barcelona and Real Madrid that he recorded from the viewing centre's cable TV subscription. *Play it*, they chant. *Play it.*

So the seventh night sees me craning my neck above a sweaty crowd, trying to get a look at the seven-inch screen mounted on an empty refrigerator carton in one of the warehouses. Two-thirds of the Arena is crammed in here. And for the first time since I arrived, jollof rice has been cooked. Some of the new refugees brought in tinned and sachet tomatoes they managed to pack, some lugged big bags of rice. They all donated these things to be stored in the large warehouse Shonuga and her people use as the community pantry, guarded around the clock. It is with these items people buy their way into the Arena. Not like they'd turn away those who have nothing, though— Shonekan used the word *inhumane*—but if someone brings in a 5kg bag of rice, they get into one of the lock-up shops, the cream of the crop of Arena housing.

So there we all are, me and Shonekan and Shonuga and even a couple of her militia and the rest of the Arena, all of us eating jollof rice without oil or sufficient pepper, with only rice and tinned tomatoes and salt, but it's still the best thing we've eaten in decades. We eat out of large leaves with our hands, yellow-red staining the tips of our fingers, our eyes glued to the screen as Lionel Messi zips about and dribbles and people lunge and pull his shirt but he doesn't fall, and his supporters shriek and throw their hands in the air and scream *Merciless Messi, Merciless Messi.* Then Ronaldo does his step-overs and leaps very high and powers a thunder header against the crossbar and the room roars and people dance and say *Cristiano*, reverence dripping from voices. And when the ball gets put in the net, the room erupts and everyone is jumping, screaming, dancing, hugging one another, forgetting who they're supporting, forgetting the match has already been won, forgetting that the land on which they stand no longer belongs to them and they might never see electricity or food or their loved ones or Lagos again; only content to just remember for one night how it feels to be excited about little things and be happy and human and whole again.

Then my skin starts to tingle, and my collarbone throbs and my neck heats up, my esper buzzing. Outside, a crack of lightning flashes out of the sky, and thunder booms right after it.

I fling my jollof rice aside and shoot to my feet.

"David?" Shonekan and Shonuga are looking at me, confusion laced with anxiety written all over their faces.

I feel restless, as if with a fever. I strain my esper, woozy already but pushing it harder, trying to extend it as far as possible in all directions, waiting for a response, but I see nothing, feel nothing.

Then a loud scream, someone calling a warning. Everyone in the room hushes, freezes, waiting for confirmatory sound under the rumble of the impending storm.

Then the bell starts to ring, *klagang, klagang, klagang*. There is one gunshot, two gunshots, and then a clatter like someone took the bell and flung it into a wall.

The warehouse bursts into pandemonium, everyone scrambling to get out, screaming for their friends, partners, siblings, parents, children. Shonuga jumps to her feet and flies outside, Shonekan and her militia following right behind.

I'm frozen. I can smell the lightning, feel its crackle under my skin, my esper buzzing and buzzing like it should find something. I've been here before, and I already know I will be unable to do anything before it's too late, before the Arena and everyone within it is licked to ash and dust by the tongues of Sango's fires.

CHAPTER TWENTY

WHEREVER YOU GO, orisha 'daji, death and destruction follow.

I snap out of it and follow the crowd out of the room. Everyone stands outside, their eyes on the gate, waiting for something to happen, for whatever it is attacking the Arena to come in and claim them.

Then the gates burst open and all the sentries and the militia are running towards us, waving their arms, screaming at the top of their voices, asking people to *Run! Hide!* And there's Shonuga riding Aburo, leaning forward, driving the horse at a hard gallop, Shonekan behind her, his hands tight around her midriff. Shonuga screams over the sky's growling and the lightning flashes for people to get out of the way, to run, to escape, to get the fuck out of this place *now*.

Then the shadows come pouring over the walls.

A flowing, sprawling mass of black forms, like ichor the consistency of tar, the blackness a light in itself, gleaming with all its stolen things: all warmth, all hope, all existence. And out of this darkness, I see that they're not really one thing but two, two-faced but not two-headed, beautiful in the shade, ferocious in the light. For a second, my heart shifts and I think of Ibeji, of

Fati in whom they're housed, and the thought that what I have tried to prevent has come true after all, but the ethereal shine in the eyes of these bearers of madness and energy and chaos is completely unrecognisable.

They move exactly in the same way as godlings, loping with lower limbs like tendrils, rounded torsos bobbing like amoeba as they climb the fence and drop to the ground, galloping into the Arena, smashing everything. With them comes a throaty wail, a mournful anger, like a call to arms braided into a call for home.

But this is not what unsettles me as I watch the horde of shadows spill over the fence. It's that I can't sense them with my esper. They're completely immaterial, even this far away from their centre, yet I can't sense a divine signature at all.

Then the militants are out of nowhere, shots ringing out. The spiked bullets strike one, two, three shadows, and I'm glad to see the shadows go down, squealing as if calling for a parent. But they're too many and there are too few guns, and the fighters are now shouting, calling for everyone to fall back as they're overrun. A shadow plucks a running man and *feeds*. It pulls the man by the neck, lifting him off his feet, and *bites* into his mouth. There is no blood, no fluid; but I see something, *feel* the moment when the man's body loses its firmness, goes limp, and his skin transforms into a waxy grey as all life is sucked out of him. He falls to the ground like a sack of potatoes, completely devoid of all divine energy and existence.

Fuck. The Fiery Ones took the harmless godlings from Ìsàlẹ̀ Èkó and turned them into vampires of godessence. And guess who is the one soul in the Arena with the most essence?

"David!"

Shonuga is before me, circling Aburo around, the horse agitated and refusing to stay in one place, her arm out, inviting me to get on the horse. I'm still numb and unmoving, looking at all of this in slow-motion. Shonekan jumps from the horse; he shoves me and yells for me to "Go now!"

"You too!" Shonuga turns again, reaching for the rifle slung across her back. "Climb."

"Go, go, go," Shonekan is saying, snatching a rifle from a guerilla running past us. "Get out now. We'll take care of everyone."

"No!" Shonuga is saying. "Shonekan, climb this horse—"

"Shut up and move!" Shonekan shoves me again. "You can't carry all of us. Find it. You two find it, and maybe this will not be a waste!"

Then he screams and is off, charging into the horde and firing sporadically, a band of militants in tow.

"Come, David," Shonuga says. Her face is stern, her arm out, not retreating. Getting to Amúnáwá is more important than my feelings about the group.

I take her hand and clamber onto the horse behind her. I get a flash of her thoughts—a stark focus and clarity within the chaos—before her hand leaves mine. The horse's back is bony, like a very uncomfortable chair.

"Hold me," she says, then slaps the horse, which takes off at a quick gallop, sending a shock up my tailbone and through my spine. I cling to her midriff, careful not to allow skin-to-skin contact, almost engulfing her within my embrace. I see the sense in what she says when she balances the rifle in the crook of one elbow and aims it at the horde in front of us.

The rattle of the gun is loud as she fires, bringing down two, four, seven shadows in front of us, as we ride towards the gate. Then Shonekan and his band are suddenly all around, with machetes, guns, anything they can carry; they're swatting, swatting, clearing the shadows.

Thunder rumbles overhead. My collarbone prickles.

"Sango," I whisper to Shonuga. "He's nearby."

Shonuga goes "Hyah!" and Aburo goes at full gallop. We burst out the gate of the Arena, into the expressway, so that the few shadows still chasing are soon left behind in our wake, and with them, the screams of Shonekan and the rest of the Arena militia beating their way to an escape that may never come.

CHAPTER TWENTY-ONE

ABURO IS BONY and rickety, and after over an hour-plus bumping up and down on his back, my pelvis is sore and I'm due for a break. I can't say anything to Shonuga, though, because she hasn't said a word since and I don't want to break the silence.

We are going to the airport, obviously. Shonuga didn't tell me this, but after a few mumbled questions which she didn't answer, I deduced this is where we are headed. I see the sense: an airplane hangar is literally *the place where iron lives*, being like the biggest piece of iron one can find here. The road past Oshodi leads to the airport, if you turn off at the right junction. It is also a place where Sango and his shadows will find it difficult to corner us, so there's that too.

I'm not entirely sure why Shonuga is angry, or at what. There is a point where she stops the horse and asks me to get down in a cold voice, and as I jump down, I half expect her to ride off into the horizon, leaving me standing in the middle of the deserted Lagos-Abeokuta Expressway, but I realise she's only stopping to rest Aburo for a bit and walk a little way ahead to get her bearings. She returns soon enough.

"We're not far." Her voice is distant and impersonal.

"Did I... do something?" It sounds awkward, but I really have to ask.

"No," she snaps.

"So why are you angry with me?"

She doesn't say anything. In the darkness, I can't see her expression. I assume she must be clenching her jaw or restraining herself from punching me or something.

"You think they came because of me," I say. "You think they came for me."

"No," she says again. She goes to pat the horse, who nickers under her touch.

I sit on the ground. Maybe she is right to be angry. Maybe I should just steer clear of everyone.

"I understand if you don't want to come with me," I say to her. "I can go to the airport alone."

There is only quiet between us, before Aburo snorts again, nuzzling her. That's when I hear a low whimper and a sniff, and I realise she's crying.

I'm not the best comforter of people.

"I'm sorry," I say without getting up. "I'm sorry that everything you built has been destroyed and everything you know is gone because of me. I'm sorry for being... me."

Silence, then: "Shut up," she says finally. "Shut up and climb the horse."

I rise reluctantly, dust my bum, and we're off again.

THE MURTALA MUHAMMED International Airport in Ikeja is split into two terminals. Terminal 1, for domestic flights, bears the battered look of a place that's been looted repeatedly, which it has. It only took a few years after The Falling for the airport to stop supporting any sort of air transport, and it slowly dwindled into abandonment, leaving it open to the general populace of Ikeja. The wealthy moved away to Upper Island, leaving a hodgepodge of Lagos touts, street kids and militia groups struggling to protect the few neighbourhoods left from the infestation of godlings. Anything that wasn't bolted in or anchored to the ground—planes, people, equipment— moved swiftly to the new international airport the government hurriedly set up in Upper Island (not like anyone was rushing to fly into Lagos anyway). Most of what was left was looted, swiftly and thoroughly.

I haven't been here in over twenty years, not since Papa Udi brought me when I was seven to see what a plane looks like. I remember he had to squeeze some rolled-up cash into the palm of an airport official who let us in through an alternate back entrance to the runway and let me watch a plane take off, shading my eyes in the late morning sun. From where we stand now, in front of the entrance, abandoned planes peek over the top of the buildings, which themselves look crumbling and unlit, an invitation to death by all kinds of surprises.

Terminal 2, the old international terminal, still retains some of its grandeur and gleam, its edges not yet chipped by age and wear, looking like a younger brother with new Christmas clothes next to Terminal 1. For fear of bringing a whole building crashing down on us, we choose Terminal 2.

Shonuga dismounts and leads Aburo off to one side, whispering softly to the horse quivering under her touch. We leave him and go inside. The lobby of the second terminal is three floors and thousands of square feet of darkness, dust and emptiness. We can barely see beyond our noses, and since I'm not completely sure if this was one of the places cleansed of godlings, going further doesn't seem like a good idea, especially when we're not sure what we're looking for. We also don't have any weapons, having dumped the rifle from earlier for lack of bullets and to reduce load. Before we leave, I extend my esper, my collarbone throbbing, singing, calling, but receiving no response.

We go around to the terminal gate, jumping over a wire fence to the gate and the runway. The tarmac and the runway beyond are no different, dark and deserted. Shonuga and I walk about, my hand extended in front of me, seeking, a walking radar. Nothing gives. We find another entrance (or exit, according to the sign) and go in, only to find ourselves stepping on broken glass and see the shells of rows upon rows of cubicles, metal detectors like forgotten door frames. I move around, checking, bracing, hoping to suddenly pick up something hot, white, icy. Nothing. The airport is cold and dark and dead.

"There's nothing," Shonuga says in the darkness behind me, so suddenly I almost jump. "Just a story. Na lie them lie to you. Or, no be this place. We will never know now."

She turns and walks out, back to the runway. I linger for a bit, disbelieving, refusing to accept that Olokun sent me on a wild goose chase just to get me away from their settlement.

I give up and leave. Shonuga stands outlined in the darkness, hands akimbo, at the edge of the tarmac, staring at the trees and buildings right outside the airport fence beyond the runway, listening to the whistle of the early night breeze.

I want to tell her we need to keep looking until we find something, because the shadows are right behind us and will be with us anytime soon, and if we don't find Amúnáwá, we and the whole of Lagos are doomed, and we'd have failed completely, and the lives of Shonekan and his band and everyone at the Arena will all be for naught...

Then I decide against it, because I'm not sure if it's her I'm really telling these things or myself.

Olokun was right after all, then. Everything I touch turns to dust.

I sit on the hard tarmac and let the breeze whip by me.

We stay that way for several minutes, Shonuga in the distance, listening to the night breeze, the coming of the end of everything as we know it, seeking some peace before we go.

It is the horse that snaps me out of myself.

Aburo comes about onto the tarmac at the far end, galloping and whinnying in that way that a horse only behaves when it is truly spooked. I shoot to my feet. The horse makes straight for Shonuga, who runs towards him and waves, making a loud clicking sound with her tongue and shouting incomprehensibles to calm him down. I get over to her as Aburo arrives, shaking more than he should be. Shonuga calms him in broad, sweeping gestures, but the horse remains restless, pacing, the click of his hooves on the tarmac carrying in the wind. Payu once told me that, next to cats and dogs, horses are one of the few animals who can sense a good load of godessence, and whatever this horse has seen has a truckload of it.

"What're we going to do?" Shonuga asks, looking at me.

As I search her face in the dark, something clicks in me. Since the attack, it is I who have sought help, who have looked up to others. I'm not sure what it is, but in this moment, I realise the attack on Cardoso House did something to me, made me smaller, and I suddenly forgot how I used to be the one with the answers, of how people used to look up to *me*.

The attack made me something I haven't been in a long time: afraid.

No longer. No longer. Bringer of fire or not, let it be known that the godhunter did not go easily. Let it be known that he did indeed bring fire down on these motherfuckers, that he did rain chaos and fire and blood and war, that he did not play fair, that he indeed became Amúnáwá, because by all that is light and living, for all that I have loved and lost, I will stand this down until my very last breath. I will not make the same mistakes I made at Cardoso House and the Arena.

I will not be afraid.

"Thank you," I say to Shonuga, my eyes cloudy.

"For what?" she says.

"Thank you," I say. "Now step behind me."

I stand between them and the direction the horse came in, flexing my esper. My collarbone throbs, my skin heats and sweat starts to pool under my shirt. It all comes to nothing as usual—I am incapable of producing any charms of any sort, and the wave of nausea washing over me is getting stronger the more I hold this up. Now that I think about it, my greatest weapons have all been add-ons—my daggers, Payu's recipes— and without those, I'm left with just myself.

And myself is not strong enough.

I flex and push my esper, willing it as Taiwo taught me. *You must shape your godessence into form,* he said. *Send it across space and time to do your bidding.* Well, dammit, how about we just get past the shaping first? I strain, try to mould the image with my mind, to make it into something tangible, but my mind finds nothing pliable, usable; I feel like I am meeting concrete, like the godessence I need to work with is locked away in a safe that I am unable to crack.

I push harder.

My esper sweeps a wide arc, projecting further than I've ever pushed it. It sweeps the airport, and for a second I'm a human radar, sensing little pieces of divinity in every living thing in the airport.

Then I am picking up two isolated signatures coming towards us, just around the hangars and loading bay, already upon us, moving cautiously, as if they know we're here. One of the signatures is much, much stronger than the other, which is very similar to a human's, like Shonuga's behind me.

Then the two figures come around the hangars, and at first I'm staring at them, confused, then dumbfounded, mouth wide open, and then I am running, screaming, and they too are running towards me, and in the middle of the tarmac in front of the passenger loading bay, I embrace Papa Udi and Fatoumata and Ibeji.

CHAPTER TWENTY-TWO

THIS IS THEIR story:

They fall out the window of the upstairs hallway of Cardoso House, crashing into a stack of plastic jerrycans stacked high on that side of the house, which Papa Udi piled there and procrastinated taking to Upper Island for recycling in exchange for cash. The jerrycan mountain turns out to be their saving grace, breaking their fall. Bruised and disoriented but not dead, they make a quick escape, which involves a lot of Ibeji/Fati pulling Papa Udi with all their might, preventing him from going back into the house, now completely in flames at this point. They manage to find a hideaway within the bushes of Ojo Close. They do not see me struck. They only see Cardoso House burn to ashes and come crashing down like a stack of poorly-arranged cards, submitting sparks and a cloud of black smoke to the sky.

They stay hours in the bush, allowing the dew to fall on them until early morning, before they return to the house. Not finding my body makes them believe I have been captured, and that is what they tell Femi Onipede when she arrives with a LASPAC team. But before they can wrap their heads around a next course of action, they receive word: at the same time that Sango has burst open the barricades at Ìsàlẹ̀ Èkó, unleashing a horde of shadowy godlings, Aganju is at the State House, taking out every single top official, including the State Governor and every single LASPAC official stationed there.

Lagos state officially goes into the godpocalypse.

And because they cannot find me or head off any of the attacks, they all go straight into hiding. Onipede smuggles them into a small safe house in Ikoyi, where they regroup, to strategize, to see if they can get word about my capture. They have nothing, and Papa Udi remains restless, believes I cannot have given up so easily. So they break up: Onipede looks for me near the State House, while Payu and Fati/Ibeji try to track me from Cardoso House.

They do not see Femi Onipede again, because after two days their Cardoso House trail leads them to a lone fisherman on an inland waterway, who says he hears of a godhunter who was in the Makoko Community. There, most people they meet, including the Baálẹ̀, tell them they know nothing of the sort. But then a young boy corners them and points out that I went that-a-way (Hafiz!), and they follow the path in a zig-zag manner, spending days on the road and sleeping in abandoned houses, trying to see exactly where I went. After a while, it becomes clearer: Payu has heard there is a community of wizards in Oshodi and believes I must be heading there for help, and they make haste for the Arena, only to find it up in smoke.

They tell this part of the story in hushed voices. Most of the people at the Arena are dead, or dying. Papa Udi wanted to stay and help, and Fati too, but Ibeji insisted little could be done, so they focused on finding me. One of the militants, gravely injured, told them I escaped with Shonuga in the direction of the airport. They followed the route on foot, and here they were.

PAPA UDI HAS aged a few years since I last saw him. His skin is dry, cracked, ready to peel off at the touch. His head seems completely bald now, and he speaks with a husk in his throat, like he is continually parched. He has lost his usual resist-dye àdìrẹ̀ buba-and-sokoto or khaki up-and-down, resorting to joggers and a women's sweatshirt with *P!nk* written in front.

Fati looks surprisingly rotund, fresh, as if she's been away to a fattening room. I'm not quite sure if it's the gods within her protecting their vessel from deterioration. She is dressed similarly, in trainers rather than Papa Udi's loafers, and in jeans and a tank top. They look like they robbed a high-end sports store (or their Ikoyi safe house *was* a high-end sports store), and Fati particularly looks like an American teenager, which I'm unable to reconcile with the girl I met last year.

Ibeji are still Ibeji: Taiwo is still annoying, and Kehinde is still a pain in the ass.

"Papa Odivwiri," Shonuga says, coming from behind me to bend a knee slightly in front of Payu. It takes me a while to remember she is still here, that she used to be his student, and that Papa Udi still has a surname.

Papa Udi squints in the darkness, struggling to understand who she is and where he knows her from, and then Fati puts forth her hand and opens her mouth and speaks a word in a language akin to the one Sango spoke at Cardoso House, and a ball of light appears in her hand.

"What the fuck?" I say, as Shonuga backs up, quickly. "When did you learn to do that?"

Fati cocks her head and smiles. Kehinde says: "About time she started learning about these little things. Useful if we ran into the Fiery Ones during our endeavours, yes?" She holds the light for a few seconds, and then it goes out.

"I remember you," Papa Udi says now, squinting into Shonuga's face. "You follow come with my LASPAC posting one time."

"Yessir," Shonuga says, reverence in her eyes.

"Thank you," Papa Udi says. "Like say you no help am…" He motions in my direction.

"Yeah," I say. "I realise I never got to say 'thank you.'"

Shonuga looks sheepish, a look that doesn't suit her one bit, while at the same time managing to look broody. Sometimes, I imagine her as a little girl trapped in a middle-aged woman's body.

"The Arena," she says to them. "You passed there?"

Papa Udi and Fatoumata look at each other. Fati looks down and says nothing.

"Are they alive?" Shonuga sounds desperate for any news, any sliver of hope.

"Sorry," Papa Udi says.

"Ugh, you humans," Fati says, Kehinde talking. "Always holding back." She looks Shonuga in the eye. "They're all dead. All of them. Not a single person is alive. The whole place is destroyed. Even the person who pointed us here? Dead."

Shonuga opens her mouth, then turns about and walks away, beating her fists into the wind.

Papa Udi gives Fati a stinky eye.

"What?" Kehinde says. "I just told her the truth."

"You for no talk am like that," Papa Udi says. "Wise god my bumbum."

We watch Shonuga lead the horse away, speaking to him, petting him, her own therapy of sorts. I think of Shonekan, a fine man who gave himself up for a cause that seems to be near useless now. The thought places a heaviness on my heart; I shake it off and turn to Fati.

"Amúnáwá. Tell me what you know about it."

Fati's reaction is visible awe. "Where did you hear that name?" Taiwo asks.

"Olokun," I say. "At Makoko. They told me I would find it here."

Fati cocks her head. "Really." Taiwo's sarcasm.

"Well, not *here,* technically. They told me some stuff we've been trying to interpret and it led us here, but... look, the story is long, but the short form is I didn't find jack here, so tell me what you know."

Of *course* Taiwo already knows about this. Of *course* he tells me the exact same thing Olokun has already said, almost as if they both read it from the same textbook: where iron lives, fire smothered by bone, etc, etc.

"Yes, yes, heard all that, but what does it *mean?*"

Fati looks taken aback. "You mean you don't know?" Taiwo asks.

"Well, we guessed *where iron lives* means here, the airport because, you know, airplanes are metal and are housed here? But of course, we haven't found anything else relating to fire, which we thought was going to be a salamander because of the stories in the history books and whatnot, so."

Fati frowns. "I'm confused," Kehinde says. "*That* is what you came up with?"

"Yes? And not without effort, together and individually. I had a professor and everything."

She looks at me, flabbergasted, then begins to laugh. A duality of cackles; both gods are really having all the fun of it.

"Wow," Kehinde says. "Just when I thought you couldn't be dumber, you prove me wrong. Wow."

I roll my eyes. "Can't you just tell me?"

"Orisha 'daji," Taiwo says, the patronizing teacher tone back in his voice. "Olokun wasn't talking about the airport, or a salamander, or a place, or any other thing."

I remain quiet, waiting for the bombshell.

"Na you," Papa Udi says finally. "Na you be Amúnáwá."

So, HERE'S WHY I'm stupid, Ibeji tell me:

I should've known that *iron* and *fire* were references to war and chaos, the tools of destruction. *Death and destruction follow everywhere you go* was not just a statement of fact or history: it was also prophecy.

I am where iron lives. I am iron and fire because I descend from a god of war, which Taiwo has since told me my mother is. My refusal to come to terms with this has caused my fire to be *smothered by stone*, to be tied up in my physical and become impossible to access or wield. I am my own biggest obstacle.

And to become Anumowa, I must dig deep into myself, into my bones, free that fire from within, and use it. I cannot burn if I do not first become formless and non-rigid, become open, like smoke.

*　　*　　*

I PACE THE tarmac with my hands akimbo, thinking about everything Ibeji have told me. Payu and Fati watch me silently, sometimes whispering between themselves. For a minute, I marvel at how close they have become, at how much of a family *we* have become, and then it hits me that this is what they mean: that I am too human, too rigid, too restricted, too wrapped up inside my own head to understand that I am bigger than what I think I am, and all I have to do is to accept it, accept the divinity within me and make it my one true identity.

To overpower a god, I have to become one.

I return to Ibeji.

"Okay," I say. "I'm ready."

"Ready for what?" Kehinde asks.

"To become Amúnáwá."

Fati facepalms. "David, David, David," Taiwo says. "You cannot become Amúnáwá now. You have spent *years* burying your godessence, placing layer upon layer upon it. To unearth it like that will require a, uhm, a sort of—"

"Kaboom," Papa Udi says.

"Explosion, yes," Taiwo says. "A shattering."

"Like what?"

"Like the attack," Kehinde says. "Did you feel anything after you got struck by all that power?"

The vision. "Yes. I saw my mother in a vision. She was telling me something."

"Well, that is a good place to start," Taiwo says. "Anything since then?"

"Nope," I say. "Dry as a husk. In fact, my esper went away for a while. I couldn't do anything."

"But something is different now, isn't it?" Kehinde says. "We felt you a reaching out from a long way away. It was how we knew where you were."

"If you can get another hit like that," Taiwo is saying, "you might be able to even take this power and turn it. Use it, wield it against the owner."

"Wait, wait," I say. "Am I hearing what you're saying correctly? When Sango finds us here, which he will, like any time now since my esper has dropped a Google Maps pin on our heads, I will have to—what, let him strike me with lightning or something? So that I may or may not be able to take this power of his lightning and use it against him?"

"Precisely," says Taiwo.

"Then make we fight am," Shonuga says suddenly behind us. We turn around at once. Her face is set, angry.

"If we have a weapon, then we must strike first," she says. "Make him come. We fight him here, on our own terms, on our own ground."

The four of us look at one another, hold our eyes in the dark, giving room for the plan.

"This could to be our one chance." Kehinde breaks the silence. "Best not to ruin it."

CHAPTER TWENTY-THREE

CALLING SANGO IS not a problem. Seeing as my esper has become a telecoms network, all I have to do is—under the incessant chants of Taiwo and Kehinde to *push, push, push*—extend my esper as far away as past the whole airport, in a radius almost reaching the Arena. Might've even gone further if I didn't promptly collapse in exhaustion, retching continuously.

Cue a shaken head by Ibeji.

Now we stand, a small army of us five, horse included, at the entrance to the airport, awaiting Sango's arrival. Intermittently, I push out my esper to see if I can catch anything. Luckily for me, Papa Udi has seen fit to bring with him a new War Kit—a small Nike sports bag in which he has managed to assemble an assortment of recipes and a couple of implements done up with some rituals, all sourced from the LASPAC men at Ikoyi. One of these, a worn machete with motor tyre rubber wound about the handle, is what I get to ward off a possible first wave of attacks. Shonuga, lacking her firearms, has to make do with a similar blade, but hers is only a long knife, something quite similar to those that mallams use in selling suya barbecue. Papa Udi himself, diversion specialist, only requires a couple of recipes like water bombs (actually, ebo), as well as one or two powders I'm not quite familiar with. Fati and Ibeji get nothing because they don't need any.

Sango doesn't take long. Soon, I catch the searing signature of an orisha, and I don't have to linger much on it to know it's Sango. I'm not sure if when I got struck, he left some of himself in me, but the Lichtenberg figures on my chest *sing* in the same way my collarbone does, and that's how I know.

Downside, however, is that I can sense nothing else, though I'm a hundred percent certain that shadow horde of his is present too.

"He's here," I say to the group.

"Move," Shonuga says.

I get on the horse. Aburo, of course, does not approve of me riding him without Shonuga there, but she pats him and whispers a few words and the horse snorts and steadies. I have him step away from the group and into the shadows, where I can watch without being easily seen.

Then Papa Udi drops salt in a circle, rounding himself and everyone else off within a ward, speaking quickly, writing quickly in the salt with his fingertip, drawing the Nsibidi symbols. As he speaks, clouds begin to gather, and then the first few rumbles of thunder begin, and beneath the clouds, flashes of light jump and snap.

Then a figure emerges from a cloud of blackness in front of us.

Sango glides forward on a trail of lightning, like a cape of silvery-blue light, his robes wreathed in never-burning white fire. His thick muscles of translucent godskin ripple, the heavy stench of kola-nut hitting us. His superimposed hammerhead statue with the cross-hatched beard frowns down on us in the same way Sango himself does, twirling his thunderstone axe, the àshẹ in his eyes boring holes in our chests.

Papa Udi speaks quicker, quicker, and then Shonuga is down on her knees next to him, helping, drawing more and more symbols, hustling up the ward. Fati and Ibeji ready themselves, beating and singing the beginnings of a charm into form.

Then Sango speaks a command, and out of the murkiness behind him spills a mass darker than nightfall, gunning for us, the shadows hooting in that ululation between victory and pain.

The first ones reach the edge of the salt circle just as Shonuga writes the last Nsibidi symbol, and there's a *pop* as the ward is sealed, and the shadows smack against it. Shonuga slashes at the shadows with her long knife and they howl and collapse to the ground. The next set come, and Ibeji chant a charm into form and slam it against the group, sweeping them away.

A crowd of shadows closes over the ward and soon I can no longer see any of the three, surrounded by the reaching, howling shadows, the odd falling shadow the only assurance that my friends are still alive and kicking.

I turn my attention to Sango. True to word, he is advancing directly for me, riding the lightning like a ghost.

I turn and goad Aburo into a gallop, heading for the runway. Thunder rumbles overhead and lightning crackles, a bolt of light flashes past me and heats up the right of my face. My collarbone buzzes ceaselessly. I glance back and see the orisha following me, then duck my head and drive the horse.

The runway opens up ahead of me as I round the corner. I run Aburo into the middle, dismount and slap the horse on his hind quarters. He neighs aloud, then gives off in chase of nothing.

I turn around.

Sango stands before me, his robes caressed by silver-blue, his axe gleaming. His eyes, as fiery as Ajala's last year. He lifts the axe, points it at me, and in a voice like many cannons, speaks a word.

I open my mouth, my body, my spirit, my self.

The lightning hits me like a thousand hot knives, a thousand wounds doused in boiling water, leaking magma. The strike is one and many, like giant pinpricks, shaking my body like a leaf in the harmattan wind. I feel them travel through my nervous system, hit every nerve ending in my body, and exit my mouth in a throat-rending scream.

I reach around inside myself for my esper, struggling to find it. It's like searching for a pin in gravel on a dark night, buried under all the pain, cowering under the hurt.

The lightning ceases, and my knees give way. I fall.

Sango approaches, slowly, silently, his feet barely touching the ground. Shadow howls fill the background, the eerie death-heralding ululation drowning out every other sound of life in the airport.

"How you live?" he is saying in Yoruba, his voice like a car revving. "How you no die?"

I struggle to my knees, breathing heavily, spittle dangling from my lower lip to the ground. My tongue is swollen, a washcloth in my mouth, tasting like I ate a spoon. My limbs are lead, my abdomen tight like my intestines have worked themselves into knots.

"How you no die?"

I reach in again, sense my esper beneath the pain. I plunge deeper, deeper into the murk and grasp it, but before I can pull it out, Sango lifts his axe again and points it at me.

Thunder rumbles.

Another jolt of pain racks my body, numbing my limbs completely. My neck is stiff, my spine curved into place. I feel the beginnings of a burn on my back, the nape of my neck. My head hurts, my brain going into overdrive.

The pain ceases as I fall on my back, my face to the sky. Wisps of smoke rise above me, smelling of singed fabric. I find myself blinking, of all things thinking, *Why do I listen to gods? Why do I listen to* anyone?

Sango appears above me, a crackling colossus, his face like an angel in a graveyard.

"You're supposed to fear," he says in Yoruba. "Courage without wisdom is foolishness, don't you know?"

"Why—?" I cough, the jerks sending pain ripples along my body. "Why—why are you doing this?"

Sango cocks his head.

"You no know?" he says, matching my English. He goes down on one knee, brings his face closer. "Me and Aganju, we have work to finish here. You're spoiling it. We must finish, whatever the cost."

"But why?"

Sango seems to be confused, as if he's never thought of it before. Then angry, as if I'm forcing him to think of something he doesn't want to.

"Because you people think you're something," he says, waving his axe over me. "We can't go back, you know? Orun is gone. We must make new home here. But you people make it difficult, running around like cockroaches, refusing to accept your limitations. You want to control us, control things bigger than yourselves. You must understand, you people *deserve* to be corralled, and those who refuse, put down. You, most of all."

He rises now, points his axe at my nose, a glint of finality in his eye.

"I don't know why my brother say you're special," he says. "War god, my foot."

I see the lightning leave the axe. I smell the metal in the air, feel the heat of the silver fire. I close my eyes, breathe, clench my esper in my grip, his last word washing over me:

War god.

Where iron lives.

War god.

Amúnáwá.

War god.

Firebringer.

The lightning strikes me on the bridge of my nose, snaps the cartilage in two, flows down to my cheekbones, into my skull, down my neck, down my spine, the whole of my skeleton, every piece of flesh, every tissue, is on fire.

But I *am* the fire. And what burns does not burn again.

I let go.

My esper sinks, into the murkiness, burrowing deeper and deeper into the darkness built from every fear, every attempt to bury the divinity within myself, every struggle to plaster it over with a search for more humanness. I give in to the murkiness, death by every mound heaped over my true self, every brick laid over my divinity.

I sink, sink, burn, burn.

Like a phoenix, David. You know what those are?
Yes, mother, yes. I know what those are now.

SINK. COLD. FLOAT. Pain. Fear.
Pain. Fear.
Fear.
Fear.
Fire.

MY ESPER CRACKLES, ignites, a fount of divinity, a gathering of flames, a raging beast too big to be contained. The heat of life and warmth and godessence sweeps through me, and suddenly I am no longer dead to myself. I am no longer David Mogo, no longer half of anything.

I am the one who brings the fire. I am Amúnáwá.

I rise, slowly. There is no pain in my body, no sensation, because everything burns within. My clothes hang off of me like tattered flags.

Sango is walking away, his back to me. He stops and turns. I can't help but catch the slight twitch in his expression. He raises his axe. Thunder rumbles overhead. Lightning tears through the clouds and makes right for me.

I draw on my godessence, will it into my hand, reach up and catch the lightning bolt mid-air.

Sango's jaw goes slack.

"Surprise," I say.

Then I push the power in my bones, my teeth, my flesh, into my fist, and hurl it, all together with the lightning, at Sango.

He doesn't move. I'm not sure if it's surprise or disbelief or pride. But he stands his ground as lightning and fire burn through the air between us and smack him in the middle of his belly.

Sango moves four, five feet, levitates for an instant, before dropping back to the ground in a crouch. He raises his head and looks at me, furious.

He throws his axe.

The thunderstone cuts through air, whining like wind through a whispering pine.

I have just enough time to swerve, so that the axe nudges me on the shoulder as it flies past and knocks me to the ground. I rise quickly, just in time to see the thing spin around in a tight arc and come back for me like a boomerang.

"Oh, for fuck's sake."

I reach out and grab it just when it's a hair's breadth from my face, but it doesn't stop, swinging around and pulling me along the tarmac, my soles scraping the runway. Silver fire sears my hands, burning with an intensity greater than I could imagine. I grit my teeth and hold on, the axe pulling me forward, into the waiting arms of Sango...

...who leans back and plants his foot in my chest.

I fall flat on my back, coughing, struggling to pass air into my lungs. Sango catches the axe and brings it down. I turn, and the thing sinks deep into the tarmac. He pulls it out and strikes again. I swivel. The axe buries in the road.

I push myself off the ground with my hands, reach out, grab his neck, and ram my head against his. The orisha staggers, giving me time to plant myself between him and his fallen axe.

I should've thought of this sooner. Same way I'm little to nothing without my daggers, this guy is likely not much to contend with unpaired from that axe. If I can keep it that way…

He comes for it immediately, and I duck under his punch and ram a fiery one, all my godessence in it, into his side. He doubles back and comes again. Same pattern. Shuffle feet, block, duck, punch, punch, punch. He grasps his sides, snorting mist, his face a contortion.

He charges, and I grab his shoulders and push him back away from the axe. He strains against me, and I'm pushed along the tarmac again, my soles struggling to gain purchase as he leans his weight against mine. I'm moving, sliding back, and the axe is right there behind me. I'm doomed if he gets to it.

His face is screwed up in complete focus and purpose. He will not stop until I or him or everyone else is dead.

Well, so be it.

I let go and sink.

My godessence dips, like a match into fuel, then bursts out, ferocious. My pores ignite, flames pouring out of every hole in my skin, every pore a snorting dragon, my body a gas cooker.

I grab Sango in an embrace and take him down with me, my fingers interlocked at his back.

We burn together, the high god screaming atop me, slamming my face repeatedly with his fist until I can taste my teeth and the metal of blood from my nose and cut tongue, but I do not lose my grip. I clamp my legs behind him, locked at the ankles, and give in to the fire, burning, burning. My skin starts to give way in patches, first like a fever, then like the faintly sweet smell of roasting meat.

I do not let go.

Slowly, unlike the flash I get when I touch human skin, an impression washes over me. It's similar to that which I saw with Ajala, but after a moment, I realise it's from a different perspective. I'm back in the formless place of divinity, bubbling with spiritual energy but still formless. I am arguing with another god whose voice is like a loudspeaker and whose face is too bright so I cannot see it, and I am defending someone by my side. Before the vision fades away, I look beside me and realise I have seen the face before: Aganju's.

Then we are back at war, fighting, burning, falling, and then I'm in a darkness, alone, unable to find my centre, my way back. Then someone, Aganju, is pulling me out of the void, welcoming me back, telling me that we do not need to find our centres because we do not need to go back at all. We must make new home here, where we will make the rules for what we want, and indeed I agree. But first we must rid it of these infestations that if given the chance will treat us the exact same way we were treated, bullied and cast out of Orun. Better to strike first, yes?

A shift, and I am leading scores and scores of the shadow horde, claiming one piece of this place after another. And with every place claimed, Aganju pulls another god from the void and places them there, and if we continue this way, we will make this place home in a way Orun never was, yes?

And then the vision vanishes, and I'm left with the raw, unfiltered emotion of the impression: an agonizing pain, but underneath it sadness, the sadness of never getting to see the end, of never knowing what one has built. This regret washes over me, so that I am suddenly too late, too late, and my heart is too heavy, so heavy.

The impression fades. I open my eyes, and atop me is nothing but ash and embers and the metallic smell of burning stone.

CHAPTER TWENTY-FOUR

I LIE FOR a while, watching the stars twinkle silver-blue, as if they are made of lightning too. If this is where all things divine come from, are the stars divine too? I think about all the things I've never allowed myself to think before: where do gods come from? Where are they when they're not down here causing havoc?

Then the pain in my body brings me back down to earth. Every inch of skin and bone feels like it's been rammed and torched and I'm not sure if I do not want to move or if I am simply unable to. The burns on my back press into the tarmac beneath me. I lie there, unmoving, until a flurry of footsteps reaches me, before I remember I left the group back at the airport entrance.

I push myself into a sitting position, slowly, carefully. The figures running toward me are more than the three I expect, so for a moment I worry they're being pursued by the shadows, or that my eyes are no longer working properly and my brain must've doubled them for some reason; but then they arrive and I realise I'm looking at Papa Udi and Shonuga and Fati in front, calling my name as they arrive, and behind them are a group dressed in the blue LASPAC uniform. Leading this group is Femi Onipede, dressed in the same uniform.

"David," Papa Udi says when they arrive, then kneels to check my arms, my legs, my clothes, my body. "You don burn!"

Fati is smiling, nodding. "You did it," Ibeji say, a chorus of voices.

I can't open my mouth to make any words. I just look at them and struggle to breathe.

"They finished many shadows until the rest went back," Shonuga says, answering my unasked question. She points to Femi Onipede and her band. "They saved us."

Femi Onipede steps forward. She has lost some weight, so her deepset tribal marks rest below sharper cheekbones. She no longer wears her spectacles, and I'm not quite sure if she can see me properly. She nods in my direction.

"Good to see you're still pushing," she says. "We were worried about you."

I look from face to face in the group above me. In their eyes I see reverence, respect, a look of awe. They seem to all be waiting for something. For me to lead them.

To lead them where?

Papa Udi rips what is left of my clothes, to get a better look at my burns, which are beginning to stink of rotting meat. The LASPAC group reconvenes, Shonuga joining them, standing next to Femi Onipede like a second general. The two women look at each other, and I'm unsure if it's smiles I see exchanged there.

Then, the hot-ice, searing signature of a high god flashes about. Ibeji and I feel it at the same time, because Fati/Ibeji whips about, alert, head jerking like a dog smelling the air. I put up a hand and grab Papa Udi's arm.

"Someone is coming."

All heads turn to me, then to the direction I'm looking.

Down the runway a lone figure arrives, dressed in long, red robes, with a lengthy cloak wrapped about its head and flowing down its neck to below the waist. I put out my esper, which is weakened but functional enough, and it prods, searches. I get an image of a palm tree swaying, its fronds in the evening breeze. Then a dog barks, and suddenly there is blood, gore, the smells of intestines and death. The sounds of swords and spears clanging one against another.

I rise, slowly, and the group repositions with me, behind me, an army. They stand poised, ready, intent brimming in their eyes.

The high god stops a few yards from us all, then raises its head and lets the cloak fall.

She wears the form of a woman in her forties or fifties, eyes grey like iron. Her head is bald and without speck of hair. Now that I think of it, the red dress and cloak *are* like an Indian sari. She is a warrior, she is a bosom, she is home.

I don't need to ask who she is.

"David," she says, and her voice is like the wind.

"Mother," I reply, and the word is honey on my tongue.

WARMONGER

CHAPTER TWENTY-FIVE

I'M IN LOVE with the darkness.

Not the dark, not the simple absence of illumination. I'm talking the *darkness*, the older brother to the after-hours. Something sentient, something that moves, something that lives under your bed. A gaping hole where other things should be, an emptiness in your chest where a heart should be beating. It changes, it grows, it builds; something that takes away and stuffs nothingness into the spaces left behind. It's black, but also shining in its own way. It feeds the night. It *is* the night.

I love it so much that I have locked myself in a coffin. As a child growing up in the only occupied house in an abandoned neighbourhood in Lagos Island—with a foster-grandfather-wizard who was always away and disinterested in parental care outside the traditional African quad of feed-clothe-shelter-educate—I've had a lot of practice cramming myself into small dark spaces for long periods and sliding into the rabbit hole of tangled thoughts. It's left me neither claustrophobic nor afraid of the dark, making me enjoy what most people consider agony.

It's technically not a coffin. It's the overhead baggage compartment of an airplane. A big one, a massive international carrier. It's my first time in a plane, which is sad, considering it's abandoned, left to rust in the Murtala Muhammed International Airport in Ikeja, Lagos. I found it parked in one of the abandoned hangars in the abandoned airport in a technically abandoned Lagos.

I hear footsteps. Tentative at first, as if testing the ground, but then I realise they're finding footing in the dark. Then the sound of bare feet on the metal floor, first loud, then again tentative, as if realising they are making too much noise. The footsteps grow louder along the aisle of the plane and stop outside my compartment. That my esper cannot pick up anything says I'm dealing with a full-blown human here and not a god of any sort, so I'm not surprised when there's a soft knock on the overhead luggage cover before it is opened.

The inside of the plane is just as dark and I can't see jack, but I already know who it is, because there's only one person who knows the exact luggage compartment I usually crawl into.

"Yes?"

There's some hesitation, then Fatoumata says: "Your mummy say I should call you."

I WILL NEED to back this up a bit.

Fatoumata can talk, yes. She speaks only Yoruba and very broken English, yes. The twin gods, Ibeji, are no longer in residence within her, no. She has not died from the force of their exit, no.

Two words: my mother.

I wait for Fatoumata to climb down the rope we tied to the exit door and then climb down myself, fearing the same thing I do every time—that the thing will snap and I'll crash to the ground. None of that happens, though. I get down and follow the soft footfalls of bare feet on concrete flooring in the darkness, and once at the smaller exit from the hangar, walk into the blistering June afternoon sun glistening off the tarmac of Murtala Muhammad International Airport's Terminal 2.

Things have changed in the ten days since we first arrived at the airport to battle Orun's fiercest lightning god. More people have heard the tale about a community of gods and wizards who were able to defeat the deadly Sango and his horde; some have braved the move from whatever hole they'd previously been hiding in and taken up residence in various parts of the airport. Terminal 2 was filled with refugees on that first day, but most have drifted into various crannies of the airport now, quickly claiming territories and marking them their own.

The airport no longer has that creepy, abandoned feel; now it's full of bodies and the things they bring with them—a lost slipper, a piece of clothing spread on a line in the middle of nowhere, a fresh mound of human faeces. A woman and a little child, both dirty with dust and mud and black smudges from some kind of journey, pass by and greet us in Yoruba. The woman genuflects, and I wince.

Around the corner of the hangars is a small walkway taking us through the back door and into the main building via a small exit. The air in here is cooler but just as humid. The singlet I'm wearing is plastered to my back, chest and under my armpits. From here, I can hear voices in the main halls, where the largest body of refugees have settled near the booking desks, immigrations, customs and departures. We do not go that way, though, but turn off into a succession of narrow corridors up to the first floor, take the back stairs and a few more turns, landing us in front of an old open office that once housed the Federal Airports Authority of Nigeria.

Since our arrival at the airport, the workstations have been taken out of the FAAN open office, leaving us with a large room with a few desks and partitions, and open spaces now given over to bedding. We kept the chairs too, creating a collection of small living spaces arranged according to taste. Papa Udi, who has never had much use for privacy, is one of the few who don't bother to cordon off their mini-quarters. He has a bed made of bundles of fabric from ratty curtains and clothing all around the airport, all wrapped around a wooden door without hinges. All his other belongings, which are few, are stacked around the door-bed in a horseshoe-shaped cocoon. The man himself is seated on the bed, working on a ritual, twisting pieces of thatch around his fingers over and over, a deep frown on his forehead. Ever since Sango's death, he's been obsessed with keeping us, the airport, hidden from Sango's brother, Aganju. He's made countless wards and rituals to keep us in and keep god-like powers out. He will never stop until we're hidden from the whole world.

Onipede and Shonuga own two spaces beside each other, kept very minimalist, very barracks-like: a hard surface for a bed, with everything they own wrapped up and used as a pillow. They aren't here now, since, along with Ibeji, they help coordinate the refugees' affairs and keep all fracases from blowing up. Fati's own space is a sprawling mass of odds and ends, as if she just learned the freedom to own property and is scavenging for everything and anything she can own. Save for Papa Udi's corner, they're all congregated around my mother's space.

Papa Udi and my mother look up as we enter.

I have had countless visions about my mother, and none of them have prepared me for the form she's chosen to wear since she's arrived. This form is much less powerful, so much that it is too jarring, too much to take. The hair I'm used to seeing as wild and free, spread out in the wind, is not even there—just a bald, shaven head. Her face is unnaturally smooth, without pimple or wrinkle, but lacks sheen, so that it looks like plywood left to the mercies of the sun and rain and wind. The fat of her arms droops, languid. She has very small hands and feet.

I cannot believe this is the almighty Ogun, the almighty god of iron and fire and blood and war that everyone speaks of with so much trembling; the almighty Ogun, who many fake wizards at the Sura Divineries pretended to invoke and got people scrambling; the almighty Ogun, worshipped from here to the ends of the earth. There she sits, silent and contemplative, like an old woman counting down to the days of her death.

That thing about never meeting your heroes? I get it.

Her piercing eyes of iron, grey and unrelenting, watch me as I approach. They are the only things that have remained from the visions.

Fatoumata goes and sits at her feet. My mother draws her in and strokes her head like a pet, and Fatoumata snuggles in. I find the whole thing so weird. And it's not just Fati; save for Papa Udi, who never really knows how to act in the presence of new friends anyway, they all always *sit* at my mother's feet, like she is Buddha to be worshipped. Everyone somehow feels that urge to snuggle into her safety; everyone except me, her one and only son, the one person who *should* feel the urge to sit at his mother's feet.

"You sent for me," I say, after we stare at one another for a while.

"I was wondering where you were," she says. Her voice, too, is different. In the visions, it was something divine, something otherworldly, something that rang in my bones and sang in my teeth. This is a flat monotone without depth or nuance, too human.

"You know where I was."

She calls me a name and sighs. That name, it's something I can never pronounce or remember after she's said it. No matter how I try to listen, to grab hold of it in my memory, it darts from me like a mosquito.

"You should be staying with us," she says. "You can't be hiding in the dark out there in that plane."

I look at her for a second, watching her pat Fatoumata's head. The day she came, she immediately recognised Ibeji within the girl. Ibeji, too, knew her for who she was, and dropped Fati to her knees, bowing her head, whispering in a godtongue that scratched at my ears. My mother walked over to her, slowly, and patted her head in this same way. And before anyone knew what was happening, my mother grabbed Fati by her neck and stuck her hand down the girl's throat.

I swear we all thought she was killing her, and went in all fires blazing, but before we could act, there were these flashes of light and bursts of sound, and our skins crawled and we smelled earth and burning and rum, and then Fatoumata was lying there on the ground, and standing beside her were Taiwo and Kehinde, wearing their respective forms. When Fati got up and opened her mouth, even she was surprised when words came out.

Maybe that was the thing that bonded them all, caused everyone to gravitate towards my mother like fireflies to a light. Maybe she *is* a light to them; maybe they see her as the one who will take us out of this bondage we're living in. It's just that if she is, she's a light I cannot see.

"What do you want?" I ask. I'm not sure if I'm asking her why she wanted to see me, or why she's been here for so long and hasn't told me why she's returned, what she's looking for. Maybe I'm asking her all this at once.

"Come stay with us," she says. "I want to see your face often."

"Is that all?"

She calls me the name again, and the memory of it is gone before it even begins.

"My name," I say between teeth, "is *David*."

She studies me for a second. "What are you angry about?"

Papa Udi slowly clears his throat in the background. This suddenly feels like a very traditional family; the peripheral father keeping the child in check, the front-and-centre mother doing the talking. I'd never thought about it before, but I feel like I have *parents*, and the whole idea sends a wave down my spine.

"Is there something you want to tell me?" I say, addressing them both.

"David, calm down," Papa Udi says in a low voice. "Make she talk."

"There's a war out there, with actual things happening, people like you"—I point to my mother—"taking everything from everybody, and you're down here, wanting to *talk*." I shake my head. "I don't even know what I'm doing with you people."

"What do you want, then?" my mother says. "What do you want from me?"

The truth, maybe? I really don't know *what* I want. I want my doubts erased, my world back. I want *home*. I guess I hoped that when I found my mother, I'd find all these things. And I'm angry that I didn't.

"I'll be in the hall," I say to no one in particular, turning away. "When you're ready to do actual things, you know where to find me."

CHAPTER TWENTY-SIX

THE END OF the world as we know it does things to people. Everyone forgets who they were, abandons their past life and tries to align themselves with the new state of things, tries to form new connections with people, tries to unearth some new version of themselves. Some change a little, most change a lot.

Not Nigerians, though, especially Lagosians. The end of the world hasn't changed them much. They are still unruly, uncouth, unabashedly rude, and disinterested in any sense of community or structure. Or maybe this is just the same way every end-of-civilization is.

As I round the corner back into the main hall, I can already hear shouting, complaining, mostly in thick Yoruba that's beyond my limited understanding. In the main hall, there is a major gathering of all kinds of people, which is expected. For the last few days since the increased arrival, Femi Onipede and Shonuga (whose first name I've learned is Ifelola, but I've been unable to get over how unfitting that is, so stuck with using her tougher sounding surname) have both been working to bring order to the growing populace. I'm not sure if it's scratching an itch from their military backgrounds, but I quickly saw the sense in it. If order isn't established quickly, the airport will devolve into a toxic space before long.

They stand before the complaining crowd, trying to get them to calm down. The twin gods, Ibeji, are trying not to interfere. Taiwo, back to his lanky seven-foot form, looking like a stick of ice lolly in those warm-red-almost-pink robes, has his head down. I can hear his constant tut-tutting from all the way over here. Kehinde, on the other hand, has her arms crossed, her forehead in that perpetual frown that's just a part of her face. She too has returned to her blue robe over jeans, but has ditched the heavy suede monk-buckle wedges which were always terribly out-of-place. She and her brother have gone for almost-matching laced boots, a more practical option. I'm unsure if they found those or if they came with their new forms.

Most of the crowd have gone more practical too: jeans or cargo pants, hats and beanies, fanny packs, utility and military belts, ponchos and pashminas, denim or suit jackets, heavy laced shoes. The newcomers look like experienced travellers who took the time to pack before leaving. (The earlier groups weren't so lucky, some arriving in nothing more than singlets and boxer shorts. One woman arrived in a nightgown and no shoes; one in a wedding dress.)

I walk over to the crowd, and the noise dies down to almost total silence as they spot me. It no longer surprises me; instead of hiding, I should be using this influence to help in any way that I can.

"What's up?" I say to Onipede, ignoring the whispers among the crowd and the many eyes following me as one, like a school of fish.

"We're still trying to explain why we need these groups," she says. "They're refusing to listen and I'm tired of explaining."

I look towards Shonuga, who nods firmly.

The two women have, in the last few days, developed a relationship that's almost symbiotic; unsurprising, understanding their backgrounds, but still jarring, having spent some time with them both beforehand. They've almost completely ditched their I-can-save-the-world bravado, and simply settled into doing their parts in something bigger. They're almost *becoming* one another, dressing identically: they clipped each other's hair close to the scalp, snipped their combats into shorts, military-style belts still on their waists, and topped the lot with matching dainty flower-print blouses I believe they must've traded with some newcomers.

They're still strong, still command respect, but something has shifted within them. They've become more interested in simpler things, often seen taking walks down the runway during sunsets, fingers interlocked, smiles playing about their lips. A few people have mentioned seeing them kissing at the far end of the runway, but no one is sure and no one wants to ask. It's the end of everything anyway, who cares?

"What d'you want to do?" I ask them.

"We need everyone to join a group."

I look to the people. "Everybody, outside."

No one even blinks. They move as one, hurrying into the sun, now beginning its descent. I motion to Ibeji and everyone else to follow me. Outside, I arrange them into rows, then explain why we need groups, and why everyone here must be treated with respect. Then I lay down a couple of threats, specifically that anyone who refuses to pay attention to what Onipede and Shonuga and Ibeji have to say will answer to me.

Femi calls out the required groups, starting with security and running through scavenging, food, water, pantry duty, hunting and scouting, clothing, shelter preparation, the likes. Truth is, we're most interested in security, but we don't want to tell them that outright; it'd put put everyone off. Everyday brings newcomers, and it's only a matter of time before someone shows up, human or divine, that isn't interested in integrating but in conquering.

Then, of course, there's the lingering issue of Aganju and his horde.

There have been rumours of a preparation for an attack on the airport, that he's coming for me—for taking out his first vessel, then his brother. He has even more of that shadow horde Sango did. He's managed to take over the State House in Upper Island, bent humans to his will; and those who couldn't escape and wouldn't join his cause have gone 'missing.' With the current exodus from Upper Island, a lot of it currently leading here, we expect an attack at any time and need to be prepared.

Once everyone has chosen a place and dispersed, we're left with five volunteers for security. The three tough-looking men in front explain that they used to be part of the Federal Special Armed Robbery Squad. It takes everything in me not to pounce on them. Before The Falling and Aganju's attacks, the FSARS was the deadliest and most unchecked police force group, kidnapping and torturing young men all around the state just to extort money from them, in the name of tracking down suspected armed robbers and internet fraudsters. Amnesty International published several reports about their atrocities, and the public hated them. Before they even start to say anything, I ask the men to turn around and leave the airport immediately, but not without adding a threat that if I see them return, I'll kill them myself. They walk away slowly, shuffling, muttering between themselves and casting glances back at me.

The two left are a woman who used to be a Federal Road Safety Corps official and a man who used to be a gated estate security guard and local vigilante. He knows how to shoot a gun, so we take him. The woman doesn't, but Femi offers to teach her.

"So," I say, "all in a day's work, eh?"

The two women and gods look at me as if I'm delusional.

"What?"

"You shouldn't have sent those men away," Kehinde says. "That was foolish."

"Those men are killers," I say. "We can't have such people in our camp. Small thing, they would start bullying everyone here."

"You should've given them a chance," she insists. "They were assets."

I look at the other three. "You people think I'm harsh? Am I being irrational?"

The two women look away. Only Taiwo says, "Yes, you are."

"That's not true," I say. "I'm not angry."

They just look at me.

"Let's look at any new group tomorrow, abeg," I say, turning away. "You people know where to find me."

I'm on my way back to the hangar, back to my plane and my darkness, complaining to myself under my breath about how everyone's acting crazy, when I hear someone following me. Kehinde.

"What d'you want now?"

"You need to stop this. You need to go and speak with your mother."

I stop and turn. "What did I do again?"

"Everything," she says. Her eyes are bright even in the late afternoon sun, shining with àshẹ, the divinity of the gods. "You are doing *everything* wrong."

I sigh, arms akimbo. "What do you people want from me?"

"Talk to your mother," she says, frowning. "You two need to settle. Then you'll see not what we *want*, but what we *need* from you."

I watch her walk away, her blue robe swaying in the breeze of the tarmac.

I wonder if anyone cares what *I* need.

CHAPTER TWENTY-SEVEN

EVENING COMES WITH its usual lights and sounds. Somehow, Shonuga, with the help of Femi Onipede, Ibeji and Fatoumata, have managed to recreate the Arena in miniature here on the tarmac of Terminal 2. The whole airport community comes out in the evenings to settle around a big bonfire. For the last few evenings, I haven't joined them, but Kehinde's words have pricked me someplace uncomfortable, so I seek a little light this evening after all.

I go to the hangar door and look out to the sunset, which is always beautiful from this part of the world. The sky is like flames mixed with harmattan's dry red sand, giving off a reddish-orange glow as the clouds put a blanket over the sun. Most people just sit on the ground, but some bring blankets, clustering in family or friendship. There are very few children—my guess is many could not make the long walk—so we mostly have couples, some trios, and a few odd bands. Femi and Shonuga, resting on one another shoulder-to-shoulder, form a pair, their pastel blouses standing out in the crowd. At some point, they get up and leave, murmuring some excuse about going to check on Aburo, who's tied up at the very far end of the runway.

The most interesting cluster, however, is my mother, Ibeji and Fatoumata. That one takes centre stage at the fire. My mother barely speaks, but Taiwo is always front-and-centre, regaling the airport community with tales of things that happened long before the great-grand-parents of most people here were even conceived, and of things had have happened in the last few weeks. Fatoumata embellishes the more recent tales, chipping in here and offering a demonstration there. Doesn't matter what they're saying. The people are enthralled enough by three gods just sitting there. They should be. These are the only divine beings they've ever met that haven't tried to kill them.

I leave my safe spot at the hangar and head out to the fire, but I do not go to that cluster. I seek out Papa Udi, who sits off to one side. He has resumed his chewing, becoming more and more of his old self before this whole thing began. He has also resumed his delight in solitude. Something tells me I might've learned a thing or two from him.

He's in the back of the crowd, listening to Taiwo tell about the time Sango came to Cardoso House, when I sit by his side. He doesn't acknowledge my presence. We sit that way for a while, with his chewing and Taiwo's voice and the crackling of the fire and the giggles and gasps of the audience, before he says:

"How body?"

And that's all he needs to say, really, and I feel warm inside. Maybe I was looking for warmth in the wrong place all along.

"I'll be fine," I say, sighing. "Just having a rough couple of days."

"I understand." He chews a bit. "That thing wey you do with Sango, your body suppose don scatter."

"I feel like say pessin carry my body knack am for ground, arrange am back," I say, glad to be back to the old us. "The thing dey pain, I no lie."

"This Amúnáwá thing," he says, "don change your body. I for surprise if the thing no pain you."

I think about that for a while. "But what if I no wan change, you know? I'm not sure I like where all of this is taking me. I'm not sure I want to be that person."

"Na why you dey run from your mama be that?"

I eye him sideways. "No."

"You know say she go tell you the truth. She go tell you the same thing whey those two"—he points to Ibeji—"don dey tell you since."

"Which is?"

"You no fit run from this thing, David. You gats to end this thing last last."

"Ugh." I'm tired of hearing this.

"Point one person for this place whey go fit face Aganju."

I stare into the fire, listening to Taiwo talk about falling out the window and onto a pile of jerrycans. Now Kehinde and Fatoumata are laughing and adding the motions. It's like a badly scripted three-man stage play, but these are the same people who love Nollywood, so they're easy to please.

"Go talk to your mama," he says. "We no get time to waste. Una two need to plan how we go do this thing."

"Why us two?" I ask. "Why us?"

He gives me a sceptical eye.

"Fine," I say. "You nko, why haven't you spoken to her?"

"We don talk."

"Oh? When? And what did you talk about?"

Apparently, I've been missing out on all the good stuff. It seems everyone has gained closure with my mother, especially Papa Udi. He tells me she explained why she chose Aziza, because he was from a pantheon outside hers and was a god no one wanted to interact with. The whirlwind god is apparently something of a mischief maker, someone no one wants to be known to be associated with. As a god of thresholds, it was easier to get him to slip me from her pantheon down here. She didn't know, of course, that Papa Udi was going to be the one getting me, but after I was grown a bit, she was able to come back and spy on me from time to time without compromising our safety, until I was grown enough to take care of myself. She *was* there, even when neither of us knew it.

I look at my mother through the fire now. She looks weary but peaceful, a small smile playing at her lips as she listens to the story. She doesn't flinch when they speak of violence and destruction, and maybe that's because she already knows.

She looks across the crowd and meets my eyes, and I look away, into the darkness of the bush at the far end of the runway. She can see me, see through me; she can find me anytime. If she hasn't come seeking me yet, she must be waiting for me to come to her. In my experience, Ogun always has a reason for doing things.

I retire into my airplane early. On my way, I pass Shonuga and Femi, returning to the fire huddle, the smell of ethanol on their breaths. They're laughing, and I realise this is the first time I've ever heard either of them laugh, and the happy sound in the wake of a near-death experience and the promise of more doom to come is a breath of fresh air. I realise everyone seems to have settled into this hope, this belief that everything will be okay, and all of it hinges on my mother and me being here.

I don't go into the overhead luggage yet; I just sit in first class and let my thoughts settle. I'm there for two, three hours before I let out a deep sigh and think: *Fine*.

I descend the airplane. It's pitch black, but I know where to go already. I don't even need to feel for the hangar door as I go around it.

Outside, there's a fire-hot icy signature burning a few yards from my door.

"I have questions," I say, moving closer.

"Good," my mother says. "Let's take a walk."

GROWING UP NIGERIAN, nights without lights are not new to me. Even before The Falling, the Power Holding Corporation of Nigeria never provided power beyond a few hours a day. But the nights since The Falling have been extra dark, extra-stocked on bad promises. Losing the occasional warmth of Cardoso House has further adjusted my eyes to the darkness; I have become part of it, as it has become a part of me.

My mother and I walk down the runway in this stifling darkness, wrapped around us like a blanket. Above, there are stars, a rare occurrence these days. I keep my eyes on them as my feet scrape on the tarmac.

"I want to know why you left," I say. "I want to know why you abandoned me and didn't come back, why you kept teasing me with those visions."

Even in this dark of night, I sense Ogun's eyes of steel on me.

"I'm sorry, David," she says, finally using my earthly name.

"I know that's not enough, and nothing I say or do will ever be, but I'm sorry. But I want you to know that if I had to do it again, I would do the exact same thing."

"Eh-ehn?"

"You do not understand what I had to protect you from," she says, "and still must. I'm sure the twins already told you what some pantheons do to people like you, and gods like me, when they find out. And they always do. I had to keep you safe, keep us safe."

"And what pantheon is this?"

"All of them," she says resignedly. "I, too, have suffered a shared world like you. From my first taste of existence, I was brought forth to be shared between pantheons. One of them is Orun, of course, that's why the twins know and recognise me. But I have also been claimed by several others, from the Loa to the Vodun to the Candomblé. The Bini people of Edo consider me fully theirs, and their Erimwin Nohuaren don't hesitate to remind me of that every time. That is how I even met Aziza, from when the pantheon was still one with the people of the Delta."

Her feet slow for a second. "It might seem glorious to anyone that so many pantheons claim me as theirs, but what you might not understand is how that means I belong to no one and I am welcome nowhere. I have existed in the interstices for a long time, and I have only longed for something of my own. And this is why I sought to make that happen."

I stop and stare at her, my mouth open.

"Selfish, yes, I know now, in retrospect. I unwittingly bestowed upon you the very thing I hated, the burden of struggling to find a place, torn between allegiances, doomed to live a life filled with confusion. This is why I say I am sorry."

We walk for a bit. The night is full of the sounds of crickets and frogs, and there are one or two rustles in the grass, but aside that it's all stillness.

"So, let me guess. My father isn't anything special to talk about, then?"

"No," Ogun says. "He was a pitiful man, a drunkard. I'm not sorry to say I picked him because brute strength appealed to me then. I simply thought it'll be nice for you to have, that it could come in handy in the future. Besides"—she looks at me—"I wanted to know I had someone to take over who I am if I'm no longer... here."

"To become god of war?"

"If you put it like that."

"I don't want to be your god of war."

She cocks her head. "But if you think about it closely, David, you already are."

When we walk a little again, I say: "David is just some name Papa Udi gave me, right? I've heard you call my True Name."

"And never been able to remember it, right?" She chuckles. "Even I cannot remember it until the exact moment when I want to say it; I forget it right afterwards. There are unique beings in Edo called the Oboihoi—beings of memory and divination, who answer only to their supreme keeper. I was able to convince them to do this for me. It was they who shaved my head, and as long as I have no hair, I can never remember your name, and neither can you. If you or I keep it in memory, then that memory can be attacked; if your True Name were known, you and I would've been discovered a long time ago. Imagine all those pantheons looking for you, believing that their own god of war created an abomination. It would've been madness. We would not have survived as we did."

"Is that why you've kept this... glamour?"

"Unflattering, isn't it?" She snickers. "Sadly, no. I have fought many wars, my son. These wars have taken their toll on me, they have made me old and battered. I am weary now, and since I found the joy in creating something, for a long time I have no longer cared about destroying things. This form you see me in? This is who I truly am, a god who wants only to savour everything. I long since abandoned the taste for war, for blood, for iron, for fire. I am no longer that god, David."

"Wow," I say, almost laughing at myself. "So, you appeared all the way here like a badass, like everything is okay now because the god of war is here to protect us, and now you're now telling me you don't even want to fight?"

"No," she says. "I didn't come here to fight Aganju at all. I came here to help *you* fight him."

Now I do laugh, a derisive, dry thing that punctures the night's stillness. I'm not even sure why I'm laughing, but when I'm done, I realise it's because she is right, and I'm going to have to do this shit after all because, point anybody for here whey go fit face Aganju, right?

"All this time, I have watched you. I have lived in echo realms, in the spaces between, keeping you from recognition of who you were. During the wars, Obatala put cloaks around the realms, and I've been trapped in those in-between spaces since. That's why you could see me only in trances, in dreams and visions. Those were the only places I could reach you.

"Then, after you killed Sango, Aganju split the cloaks open, and suddenly I was free again to return. This is why I'm here."

"You don't sound so excited about that."

"No," she says. "Do you know why Obatala put those cloaks?"

"To prevent the outcast gods from returning to Orun?"

"Exactly. Now that there is no more Orun, where do you think most of the castaway gods have come to?"

I sigh. "So, what do we do now?"

"Aganju knows we're here," my mother says. "You killed his brother, and you have become a firebringer. He knows you're a threat to his plans to establish his own version of Orun here in Lagos. He is going to come for you."

"Then let him come," I say, gritting my teeth. "I'm ready for him."

"Don't be foolish," she says. "Aganju is not Sango. He is a cunning, intelligent god. He will not underestimate you. And he is no longer alone. He has freed many gods who have joined with him. Like Sango's sisters: Oba, Oya and Osun. They are just as notorious as their brother. They will finish you off at his command." She draws a breath, as though steeling herself. "David, we must prepare to go to war."

She stops and waves her hand. Suddenly, she's holding two things: a thick chain of heavy iron and a bolo machete with gold and silver worked into the grip. The iron gleams even in the dark, reflects the stars, the weapons alight with the fire of the gods, the àshẹ of the divine.

"I *was* the god of war, my son," she says. "But your time is now. This mantle belongs to you now, and so do these."

"No, mother," I'm saying, shaking my head, stepping back. "No. I'm not ready. I can't do this."

"No, you cannot do it alone," she says, moving closer to me.

"This is why I have returned. I am here for you now. We will do it together. You have the twin orishas of all abundance. You have two wizards with you, and you have the humans of Lagos behind you. You, David, have gone in the ashes and arisen a firebringer. You are iron and war and blood and chaos. You will lead us to war. You will lead us to victory. You will save us and this part of the world."

She places the weapons in my hands. They are cool, then hot, the same feeling I get when I sense an orisha. They are heavy, but do not feel so. They feel natural in my hands, like something I've been missing all along and did not know. They feel like a part of me has returned.

I squeeze the iron in my hands, and the godessence within me roils, gurgles, blazes in response.

Shit.

I'm the fucking god of war now, dammit.

CHAPTER TWENTY-EIGHT

THE FIRST THING they make me do as the god of war is draw blood. *They* are Ogun and Ibeji, and the blood is mine. Taiwo calls it *activation*, says I need to build a connection with my weapons. So Kehinde cuts me with an ebo-tinged knife and smears my blood all over the chain and machete. She tells me I will need to do this every time, that there must be blood on my weapons, either mine or others'. She says I am at the height of my power when I have drawn blood. I look to my mother, who nods in confirmation.

The first time I do it, my insides boil. I'm like a worm wriggling in salt, with the pain of almost bursting, of power that feels like it will consume me any second. The weapons themselves are difficult to hold once charged with blood, becoming hotter and hotter until I have to drop them. I push my godessence into my hands to try to cancel out the heat, but before I know it, my fire has ignited the weapons, and I feel like I have taken cocaine and all my nerve endings and pleasure centres are activated, and it is the most pleasant thing I have felt in ages, but also the strongest need to *murder* that I've ever felt, so that I feel like I'm having an out-of-body experience.

I vomit once it is over. I also realise I have ejaculated into my trousers. My mother regards me without expression, but Taiwo and Kehinde let me have it, laughing their heads off, pointing at my crotch and threatening to share stories about it at the bonfire.

My days are split three ways here on out. Taiwo takes me first in the mornings, sitting on abandoned boxes in my hangar, which I've now opened up to everyone. Fati likes to hang around in the plane, and she usually comes with Taiwo in the mornings.

Taiwo provides me with all the details of history, information about pantheons and gods, and carefully breaks down my complicated self to me.

"See, first you were astride a threshold, right?" he says. "Neither god nor man, but both. Then opening up the well of fire in your fight with Sango shifted your godessence closer to the divine. With these"—he taps my weapons—"each battle you fight will take something of what you currently are and replace it with the god within."

"Hmm."

"War is blood, fire and iron, and you are all three," he says, animated, excited to be teaching. "You bleed, and that makes your connection stronger. You have unlocked the fire within, and as you connect to iron through blood, you become unstoppable."

Afternoons are for Kehinde, Femi and Shonuga. Kehinde (and sometimes Ogun, when she's in the mood) teaches me how to reach into myself and use my fire. She teaches me to channel it into different parts of my body, to use it as a weapon. She takes me through her own bodybeats, showing me how she channels them into her arms and voice and weaves them into charms. After failing spectacularly for the best part of three days (burning off half my eyebrows and my choicest clothes), we settle on channelling out of my hands only. She shows me how to shoot it out of my palms, how to pull it out in the middle of a fistfight, how to use it as a decoy or to dissuade an attacker, how to propel myself above the ground like a jet engine. We practise all this out on the runway, and everyone stays away.

Some afternoons, Femi and Shonuga bring over the airport force they're grooming and we train together. More people have come to our little settlement since, some with weapons. Along with the few LASPAC guys who arrived with Femi, the airport force is growing. There are lots of skilled people now: ex-servicemen, former vigilantes, former policemen (they begged me for these; I almost sent them back again). There are a few teenagers hardened by the streets and a few thugs who joined more reluctantly, having never been bossed before.

We practise shooting and combat and formations, Femi and Shonuga putting all their years of experience into us. Femi draws the awe of the group every time she picks up a rifle, hitting tin can targets further than anyone, even against the wind. Once, the wind knocked over her target, and she hit it as it fell.

Shonuga is more into close combat, teaching us how to use our ebo-tinged weapons toe-to-toe. In the heat of the sweltering sun, our backs glistening with sweat, we duck and swipe and swivel and thrust and jump and kick and duck.

Fati joins us in these sessions, always next to Taiwo, who comes just to humour her. The two have developed a weird relationship, where Taiwo just talks and Fati just listens. I see how being unable to make words for so long could make it feel like work to make them now. Fati is full of one-liners, but I only really see her animated out on the runways. Here, her face is set, fierce, focused. She yells when she kicks, when she punches, when she shoots. She yells only then.

In the evenings, I sit with Papa Udi, while he makes ebo and other recipes, amulets and rituals. Papa Udi is always out all day, scavenging for materials, then returns in the evening to select the best to dice, grind, mix. On the days the force isn't training, Shonuga goes with him, with her gun. Papa Udi doesn't like it, but she lies to him that she's also interested in re-awakening her wizardry training, and that lightens the man up.

Much later, we realise doing all these by the fire unsettles a lot of the community who aren't familiar with his wizardry and otherworldliness, so we make our own special fires elsewhere.

The community grows into something bigger than us. The whole of the airport seems to be occupied now, including the old domestic terminal; new arrivals cleaned out that portion a few days ago and settled there. Femi and Shonuga have to work overtime to keep the peace, but the airport force does its job well. My mother goes sometimes, a god presence that does its job just by appearing. The biggest culprits are the former street gangs who have already forgotten their fight for survival and want to try their hands at some bullying.

But the biggest vices here cannot be solved by gods. There are petty quarrels and personal feuds that involve things like people rubbing shit into other people's belongings. People are always stealing stuff, with food, water, clothing and soap at the top of the list. People are always fighting and need to be broken up. People are always hungry and irritated and ready to start something. I ask Shonuga how she dealt with all this at the Arena, and she replied, "We had food and separate quarters, oga. We didn't need to."

But for the most part, a certain sense of belonging has settled into the airport community, the way one lives in a big house with family members whom they dislike, but know they must live with anyway. Despite the drama, most people care for one another in a way that says, *I hate you, but I hate the gods who took my life more*, and that is just fine enough for me.

But peace and contentment don't last long in Lagos.

One day, my mother calls me into the plane and tells me we need to leave the airport.

"Why?"

For the first time since my mother has arrived, her face shows some other emotion than her usual faint smile. Today, her brows are furrowed in concentration. This is the first mark I've seen of the real Ogun.

"I've been keeping my ears to the ground on Aganju and his band," she says, "following the gods he's been able to convince to join his cause."

I don't need to ask what his 'cause' is. As Taiwo says, they just want to go home, right? I also have not seen my mother leave the airport in days, but I don't ask how she's getting this information because she's *the* Ogun after all.

"And?"

"He has made himself some very powerful allies," she says. "Allies that are capable of wiping everyone here off in one go."

"And our response is to run?" It sounds so weird coming from her since, last time I checked, she used to be the god of war.

"No," she says. "But whatever we're doing here will not be enough. I hear he has started expanding into the neighbouring states in the west. Their governments sent forces against him, and he decimated them, every single one. He's expanding his base, making more space for his conquest. It's no longer a question of your precious Lagos now, it's *everyone*. And it's only a matter of time before he turns his sights back this way."

"We will be ready," I say. "*I* will be ready for him."

She tut-tuts. "Few weeks as a god of war and your blood already boils."

"As it should. We thrive on chaos, remember?" This is the first time I've used the collective to describe my mother and me. The word tastes strange.

"Yes, but Sango's sisters are leading the army."

Taiwo has described Orun's pantheon tree to me and often mentioned Sango's three sisters, but nothing about why they deserve attention.

"What's so special about them?"

"A lot." I've never seen my mother look this serious. "Many of your people down here will know them as Sango's 'wives' from the folklore they've passed down. But the stories have been downplayed, made them softer. Don't be deceived by that; their ferocity knows no bounds. Sango was slow, methodical, brutish and arrogant. His sisters are fierce and intelligent and they do not waste time asking questions. They will kill you before you can draw breath."

"Ehn, let them come," I insist. "I can take them."

"Shut up and listen to me," my mother snaps, the growl of a battle commander present in her voice. "I have known these gods for as long as I have lived, and I have lived for very long, David. Long enough to know what living without someone or something to care about is, and I do not want that anymore. I do not want you to die."

I blink, shocked at the display of affection. It's a strange thing to accept, like an old wool sweater that prickles. All my life, I've had one person in Papa Udi show anything akin to love for me, and mostly in a backhanded way. Since she appeared, she's just picked up where Papa Udi left off. This is new, and I'm not sure how to react to it.

"Okay," I find myself saying.

An awkward silence engulfs us for a moment, and we shift uncomfortably, trying not to look one another in the eye.

"What are they like?" I ask, finally. "The triple gods."

"They are the best warriors Orun ever had, better than Sango even. They left Orun a long, long time ago and never returned, because they disagreed with Obatala's systems. I have no idea where or how Aganju found them. I'm sure it mustn't have been hard for him to convince them."

I nod. "And Obatala? Do you know where he's been all this while? Why he has allowed all this to happen to us?"

Ogun sighs. "All I can tell you about Obatala is this: there is nothing he is more interested in than keeping his kingdom. Since the war, he has sealed off all of Orun from everything and everyone, so not even those who once called it home can find their way back. He will keep it that way if it ensures that those who sought to destroy it never return, even if the rest of the world perishes as a consequence."

"So we're on our own."

"Yes." She holds up a finger. "But. We're not done yet."

"What do you advise?"

"Well." She rises like an old woman, slowly, her robe rippling. "He found allies, yes? Maybe we can find some of our own."

"Are there any gods left who haven't joined him? Who might be interested in joining us?"

Ogun cocks her head. "I might just know a few."

CHAPTER TWENTY-NINE

FOR THE FIRST time in years, I almost shed tears once I step out of the airport and see the bare, charred wasteland of Lagos. Everything is rust and smog and dust and death. We pass a few corpses by, some lying prone, their faces at peace as if they died in their sleep; some bent low in submission to the elements, unable to go on any longer. There are no animals, and only the odd tree struggling to survive. The only thing I recognise about Lagos is the smells of open gutters.

Once in a while, we hear the shuffle of things in hiding, and we're not sure if they're human or divine. We figure that, whatever refugees are still out here might've become dangerous, robbing and murdering if they can, stealing if they can't. But we believe that even if we come upon such a band, they too must realise, after one look at us, that it will be in their best interest not to interfere.

Our troupe consists of Ibeji, Papa Udi, Shonuga, Femi and me, led by my mother. We are going to meet Aziza, who my mother has found a way to summon. He refuses to meet us in the airport, my mother says, because he isn't sure if he is being lured into a trap. So he has opened a small threshold a few kilometres outside the airport for us to step through and meet him where he is. None of us have ever walked through a threshold or travelled between worlds before, so we're all nervous and unsure.

But no one is as nervous as Papa Udi, who has unfinished history with Aziza. This was something he never talked about at Cardoso House, but all of a sudden he's fidgety now that he gets to meet the god whose work he used to perform, in his early years as a hot-blooded, powerful wizard. Whatever rift opened between them, Papa Udi doesn't say, but it's such a big deal that he almost refused to go. He got into a hot argument with Ogun before we left the airport, but finally succumbed to her steely eyes and grudgingly came with, chewing furiously and mumbling endless things to himself.

We snake though the streets, clinging to the shadows of the evening. The sky is grey and expressionless, blotting out the sun and all its warmth and light. We're all wrapped in identical hand-knitted ponchos, a gift from the newly-minted clothing group of the airport community—partly for taking them in, but mostly courtesy of Femi and Shonuga guilting them into it. We amble along in a line like nomads in a desert. Ogun insisted we all come along, that if we were going to convince anyone to join our war, it's better if they see who they're fighting with. We left the airport in the hands of the most loyal airport security personnel, but I especially asked Fati to get into the airplane, shut the door, lock it and not come out until we return.

We get to the appointed place just before dusk, a four-way crossroad in a clustered neighbourhood, parallel to the expressway but closer to what used to be the Agege neighbourhood. Now it's just a jumble of abandoned buildings, brick and zinc shanties skewed at various angles and lacking any sort of planning. The perfect place for an ambush.

At the edge of the crossroads is a small pile of food: mangoes, guavas, a small watermelon, five fingers of plantain, and a clay pot with roasted yam in it, spread with palm oil. Scattered amongst them are large chunks of chalk in different colours.

Ogun goes over, picks up a piece of the chalk, chews it, draws a line in the road, steps over it, and vanishes before our eyes.

"Shit," Femi and Shonuga say together.

Papa Udi sighs, then repeats the action, chewing the chalk, drawing a line, stepping over it, and is gone as well. Ibeji follow next, Taiwo and Kehinde performing the rite together, like two halves of the same person.

I let Femi and Shonuga go before me because I'm the one with the machete. They hold hands and steel themselves before doing it. I go last. The chalk tastes like what I imagine brick dust would taste like.

When I step over the line, there's a *whoosh*, like I'm standing atop a high-speed train, but without the wind. Then I'm standing in the exact same spot, at that crossroad in Agege, but this isn't really the Agege I just left. This is something else, as if someone took an eraser to everything human and possible and existent and perceptible, and left it with a drab, soulless background, like I'm standing on a beach without the sand in my toes or the wind in my face, the rush of the waves, the salt in the air. It is like I'm standing in space, and Agege is a grey, static painting wrapped around me.

Before us is a one-handed, one-legged dwarf. Every inch of his body, from his dreadlocked hair to his nailless toes, is smeared in white powder, presumably more chalk. His face carries the weight of ages, but is unlined. He stands smack in the middle of the crossroads, resting his weight on a stick, which looks like it's made of wood but also like it can slice iron.

"Ukrobogbowovo," my mother hails him.

"Ọsìn ìmọ̀lẹ̀," Aziza says. His voice is like a ripple, like blowing air through a cloth. Now that I think of it, so does my mother's. We likely all sound this way here.

"Thank you for having us."

"Hmm." His eyes run across us, then stop at Papa Udi.

"Odivwiri." He says it like he's working on a piece of chaff that needs to be spat out.

"Ukrobogbowovo," Papa Udi says, then goes on a knee.

"Keep that praise out of your dirty mouth," Aziza says, his eyes flaring. For the first time, I see the àshẹ behind his pupils.

"I only honour you, Aziza," Papa Udi says, his head still bowed, refusing to look at him.

"I don't need honour from the likes of you."

"Okay," Ogun says, her tone snipping the conversation like a pair of scissors. "Aziza, you can do that later. Just say if you'll join us or not."

"I wanted to get a good look at them," he says, roving his eyes across us. "I'm not impressed."

"We are all that is left," my mother says.

"Then you are not enough," Aziza says. "You want me to go up against Aganju, of ash and dust and magma, and against Sango's sisters of wind and water and making, with *these?*"

Everyone is silent.

"Do you still believe in me, Aziza?" Ogun asks.

"You are the mighty conqueror. I can't stop believing in you, my old friend."

"You have supported the decisions I have made in the past. Without hesitation."

"Without hesitation."

"And none of those choices have failed before. If anything, they've birthed bigger, stronger, better things." She looks at me as she says this, and I step forward. Aziza studies me, nodding approvingly.

"He makes a fine complement to you."

"Not complement," she says, looking at me with—is that pride? "He is of me. He *is* me, but even better than I have been. He *knows* these people. They are as much his people as we are. He is best to lead them, much more than I am."

Aziza keeps his eyes on me. "So it is you we follow."

My first inclination is to be modest, to say, *Ah, well, you know.* But something in me straightens my spine, keeps my feet on the ground.

"Yes," I say. "I will take Lagos back for us."

He chuckles. "You don't have to pretend with me. I can see how fear washes over you. You are afraid, because you care about these people, this place, and you are afraid that you will lose." He nods. "That is good. Use it."

His eyes remain on me for a beat, then move, surprisingly, to Papa Udi.

"You have done well, Odivwiri," Aziza says. "You have done your part in a task that you did not ask for, a burden you did not need to carry for me, and for this, I have forgiven you. You have shown me what it means to be loyal." He turns to my mother. "I have been loyal to you, conqueror, for a long time. I will continue to. I will stand with you in every battle, this one and those to come." He taps his stick on the ground twice, as if to seal it.

There is a sense of tension easing, a collective unvoiced sigh of relief, and Papa Udi, who never rose from his knee, rises now, his back straighter than ever, the glistening of tears in his eyes and on his cheeks.

AZIZA OPENS UP another threshold, and we step through and are back in the airport runway. I half-expect him to have abandoned us, but he is right there in the airport. He has ditched the one-legged, one-handed form, and has all limbs complete, but has retained the stick-sword, the chalk, the dreadlocked hair, the dwarfism.

Femi and Shonuga go on to check with security, discussing a prank to scare them to test their reflexes, then deciding against it after realising they could get shot. I head right for my plane in the hangar to check on Fati. Ogun suggests Aziza goes with me and stays in the plane as well, until we can announce to the community that we've been hiring. I agree, because just the look of Aziza alone will scare the living daylights out of the residents.

Fati is indeed in the plane, but she didn't shut the door as discussed, and I see why: the whole plane is smoky with the fire from a makeshift lamp she's managed to make from a hollowed-out sandstone rock, burning twisted tree bark in a pool of fat. She regards me with a bored look when I get into the plane, and I see she's been reading a book.

When Aziza comes in right behind me, I expect her to yelp, but she only starts, then watches him carefully, like one would a tamed wild animal. I see her other hand reach behind her for one of Papa Udi's long skinning knives, hidden under the seat.

"It's okay," I say. "He's the one we went to meet."

Aziza pays her no attention, but instead navigates to the very back of the plane and stretches awkwardly in a seat like someone who has never been in a plane. He probably hasn't.

"What're you reading?" I ask Fati.

She flips the book, cover to me. *We Should All Be Feminists* by Chimamanda Ngozi Adichie.

"Where did you get that?"

She shrugs.

"You know how to read?"

She shakes her head. "Only small small."

"Here, lemme read to you."

She hands me the book reluctantly.

I read a section where Chimamanda says men and women are different biologically, and how men being dominant historically was based on physical power, but physicality is not required to be stronger in these days, that intelligence, knowledge and creativity are not defined by hormones, and that anyone can be on top. Fati listens intently.

"You believe?"

"What the book says?" I shrug. "I guess, yes."

"So I can good too, be on top?"

I want to tell her that our world has changed a lot from the one Chimamanda was talking about, but I don't bother to complicate things for her, so I just say, "Yes."

"So why you no take me? Because I'm woman?"

I want to say I left her behind because she's a teenager, but then remember there are teenage boys in other groups in the airport, from security to hunting and gathering, and Fati is not assigned to any of these. I'm forgetting this is a girl who literally walked into a heavily guarded house where I was held captive and rescued me.

"You know what? I'm sorry," I say. "From now on, we do things together, okay?"

"Okay."

"I'm going to see Papa Udi, then we're going to see if we can find another god. Want to come?"

She nods.

"Good." I rise, and after a pause, say, "Come with your knife."

PAPA UDI IS nowhere to be found until the evening bonfire, when he reappears, looking very tired. I realise it's not just him: apparently, travelling across thresholds has left all the humans fatigued. Even Shonuga and Femi suddenly have bags under their eyes, accentuated by the flicker of the fire.

While my mother gathers the community to explain Aziza's presence and unveil him alongside our plans, I find Papa Udi and settle beside him without comment, both of us silent. Fati finds us and settles between us, a welcome change from her being glued to Ibeji or my mother. For a moment, it feels almost as if we're back at Cardoso House.

My mother rises and stands before the airport community, standing behind the fire so it lights her properly and downplays the àshẹ in her eyes. She has altered her form slightly, now in an iridescent sleeveless robe the colour and texture of palm fronds. Her head is still bald, her forehead and scalp shining by the fire, but her arms are covered shoulder to wrist in tattoos, all of them faces of people frozen mid-scream. The combination of the firelight and my mother's steely eyes and stoic demeanor sends a hush through the crowd.

She opens with the story of the tattoos. They are reminders of the wars she has fought, she says, of the conquests she has made as the god of war. They are her reminders of why she no longer makes war. They are the repercussions of all the pain she has already caused, and she will continue to bear them as a symbol of who she's supposed to be.

"But this war we have is one I will fight," she says, "and becoming the person I once vowed to leave behind is a sacrifice I will make, if it will prevent further destruction. And every one of us"—she points a finger at the crowd, pricking every chest as if it's pointed at them alone—"will have to make a sacrifice like this."

With that, Aziza appears out of thin air to stand by my mother. This provokes a gasp from the crowd, and more murmuring and whispers. My mother watches silently until they die down.

"Aziza, Ukrobogbowovo of the Urhobo pantheon, will join us. Many more will in the coming days. And I do not compel you, but if you have something to offer, we will need it. We will need everything we can get, if we are to go against Aganju and his army."

No one says anything, until one woman rises, carrying a child in her arms. She starts talking quickly in Yoruba. Most people nod in understanding.

"She say she can make…" Fati translates, struggling for the word. "Long stick-and-knife."

"Spear?"

She frowns at me. "What is spear?"

After the woman, more people come forward and explain

what they can offer. I use this time to turn to Papa Udi and say:

"So you go tell me now?"

He looks at me. "Tell you wetin?"

I motion with my chin towards Aziza.

"But you already know."

Well, I did see some of what happened between them when he mirrored a Reveal charm at the 81 Division. I know he was chased out of Isiokolo for doing something bad, and Aziza abandoned him at about the same time. He came to Lagos and built a life and never returned.

"I don't know what you did, though."

He hesitates a second, then taps Fatoumata. "Go meet Ibeji."

Fati eyes him, but Pap Udi puts on his mean stare before she reluctantly rises and shuffles over to where Ibeji sit a few feet from my mother. They ensconce her between them.

"So?"

Papa Udi sighs, chews a bit, then sighs again. "My wife and my two sons. I kill them."

My chest lurches. *How* and *why* leap to my mouth, but I ask nothing, and just wait for him to chew some more.

"At that time, I reason say I fit do anything. For the whole of Isiokolo, only me get power. I use my power help sick people, heal them. I protect them from thieves, from attackers, from even police. Na me be their Odibo, their Seer. Na only me fit connect to Aziza."

He spits whatever he's chewing. "And I dey like try new things, most especially charmcasting. I start, small small first. People warn me say the thing dangerous, especially Karo, my wife. She say make I stop Odibo completely. Aziza too tell me once, say make I no take this thing too far. Even the local chief then, call me come the palace, tell me say if I no stop him go send me commot. But the thing just make me vex, so I even try bigger, bigger things.

"Then one day, one of my stupid experiments scatter. I join one new ritual with one old recipe whey I no too understand. I no even remember wetin I dey make, but I remember say the thing just dey boil, dey boil. Then the whole thing just explode for my face. My whole house, fiam. Almost half of the village, fiam. Just like that. Like say I no cast ward around myself, na so me too, fiam."

He puts a stem in his mouth and begins to chew. He offers me one, for the first time ever. I'm about to decline, then decide last minute that I'd like him to keep opening up, so I take the stem and roll it around in my mouth without biting. It's tasteless, exactly like a fresh stem should be.

"When them hear say I survive, them come for me. Them for roast me alive like say I no run."

I watch him tell the story without emotion, as if he's spent so many years burying what he should feel that he no longer knows what that is. I realised why he was so incensed with Ajala—the man's ebullience, his self-destruction must've reminded him too much of his own younger self—and I wonder the kind of trauma the burning of Cardoso House must've brought back to him. I wonder if this is why he decided to live apart from everyone else—did he fear himself too much?

"And Aziza left you after this," I complete for him.

"Yes. He say him no fit give him power to person whey go use am destroy. I no know whether Isiokolo find new Odibo later, but I no hear from Aziza again. Until you."

I wonder how much of my life was about him making

reparation to Aziza, to his lost family and town, to himself. I wonder if he's now found what he's been looking for.

Papa Udi rises. Almost everyone is up now, having something to offer Ogun. I rise too, looking at my mother, who stands behind the fire, her face back to her permanent faint smile. She looks across the crowd at me, and winks.

CHAPTER THIRTY

OUR NEXT TARGET meets us at the airport runway in the wee hours of morning, away from the prying eyes of the terminal. Aziza pulls out his chalk, draws a line on the tarmac, speaks some words in another arcane godtongue, then steps across it and is gone. We wait one, two, three minutes, then he reappears on our side of the line. And someone is with him.

Eshu is the picture of the biblical angel. His skin is so fair it's almost white, and his hair is albinism-white, in large kinky curls. Even his eyebrows are white. And everything combines to make the àshẹ in his eyes so bright you almost have to squint when you look at his face. *Radiant* is the word. He is dressed in an all-white robe without a speck of dust, cinched around the waist with a golden belt. His feet are bare and unsoiled. He is perfect in every way, except for one tiny thing: he looks exactly like a mirage, like a mirror reflection without a subject. He is either an old man or a young boy, or both at the same time; it feels almost as his identity is a choose-your-own-adventure game, where you decide what you're seeing.

As one, we slightly bow our heads and greet him with the praise song Ogun has taught us:

Ìbarabọ̀-o mojúbà
Ìbà kò ṣe ọmọ dẹkò
Ẹlégbàále
Èṣù tiriri
Ọmọ́júbà
Bara abẹ̀bẹ̀
Tiriri lọ́nà

The god throws his head back and laughs long, hard. It's a striking laugh—literally, like the clatter of metal sheets in heavy wind. If he were completely human, spittle would've flown out of his mouth and he would've held his chest and gasped. But he laughs and laughs without taking a breath; and the longer the laughter lasts, the longer the winds beat against zinc in our ears, the more goosebumps rise from our skins.

When he finally winds down, he looks at Ogun.

"You know," he says, and when he speaks, there's a whiff of black pepper in the air. All the humans amongst us blink rapidly and sneeze. He laughs again. "Learning the words is good, you know, but without the right enunciation, what a loss, eh?"

Ogun was right. I don't like this guy at all. He stinks of bad news and laughs like a fucking psychopath. But what was I expecting? This is one of 256 iterations of Eshu, the god of pathways and manifestations, Orun's version of Aziza. This guy is not a person—he is an *it*, a thing, a hologram. He cannot be trusted.

The tricksters are very tight across pantheons (even though Aziza warned us never to use the word *trickster* to openly describe any single one of them), and Aziza was the first to offer the news that Eshu hadn't yet joined any side. He seemed like a clear fit for Aganju's army, so we wondered if he'd already joined but was only faking to get into our ranks. We wanted to meet him fully armed, but Aziza pushed against it vehemently. And now we're standing right in front of him, open to his pocketful of deceit.

"We welcome you," Ogun says without expression. "We come in nothing but peace."

"Sure," he says. "Very sensible thing to believe, coming from a god of war and"—he turns to me, studies me for a second— "and another god of war! How many of you *are* there?"

Nobody responds.

"Well at least if you're going to welcome me, you should come without weapons." He raises his hand, and there's Papa Udi's—now Fatoumata's—long knife in his hand. Fati, who's standing next to Ibeji, gasps, then reaches behind her and pulls... Papa Udi's knife from the band of her trousers.

"Ha!" Eshu says, and giggles. The knife in his hand disintegrates before our eyes.

"Caught you," he says.

Fati's face grows dark. Taiwo slowly pulls the knife out of her hand, and she lets go reluctantly.

"You know why we called you," Ogun says, impervious to Eshu's antics.

"Yes," he says. "And I'm here to tell you, without any hesitation whatsoever, that I'm ready to join your cause."

We look at one another. Now, that's unexpected. And not worrisome. Not worrisome at all.

"Why?" I ask. "What do you get out of this?"

Eshu regards me properly for the first time, and I realise I can't stare at him for too long. His dual face creeps me out, and the whiteness of his face hurts my eyes.

"What if I told you I have nothing to gain or lose?"

"Then we're done here," I say. "Thank you, Aziza."

"David..." my mother says softly.

"No," I say. "I don't like this guy. Coming in here, trying to shit on all of us." I point at him. "I'm not fucking scared of you, you hear me? Go and join Aganju if you like. I will see you there, and I will rip you to pieces."

"David," Papa Udi says. "Easy."

Eshu has a smile on his face, and then he laughs again, clapping his hands.

"Now *this* is who I want to be on the side of! You know what Aganju and his lot lack? Creativity."

"Is this a joke, though?" Kehinde says, her frown deepening. "Everything is just a game to you, Eshu, isn't it?"

He shrugs and shows his palms. "Nature, Kehinde. You can't fight it."

Ogun gives all of us the eye, and we calm down. She returns her attention to Eshu.

"Fine. We will need one more thing from you, then. Show how you can help us and that you mean good."

Eshu cocks his head. "Which is?"

"Take us to Olokun."

OGUN HAS EXPLAINED our plan of attack a long time ago. The one thing she's learnt from all those battles, from the Nigeria-Biafra War to the Orisha war and everything between, is that there are three ways to win a war. The first is to outnumber the enemy and crush them by the strength of numbers. The second is to outsmart the enemy, to defy expectations and surprise them into defeat. Sadly, we're bound to fail on both counts with Aganju, so our plan is the third way: try to match the enemy in every way possible—resources, strength, turf, et cetera—and hope for the best.

So far, we've established that when it comes down to it, I'm to face Aganju the way I faced Sango, one-on-one, while Ogun, Kehinde, Femi and Shonuga will lead the force's charge against the rest of the horde, supported by the offerings of Papa Udi. But there remains the little issue of Sango's sisters, and hence our recruitment drive to find people to match them in their respective abilities. Aziza, being the god of whirlwinds and thresholds, will meet Oya in the air. We picked Eshu, who is god of manifestations and mirages, to match Osun's powers of fertility and rebirthing. And to negate Oba's whirlpools of destruction, we need a water god, and what better one than Olokun, who's already aided us in the past?

So, with all of us armed and ready, Aziza and Eshu combine to convey us: Aziza does his chalk magic, while Eshu manifests a large door on the runway right in front of us. He opens it, we all step through with the now familiar sense of disorientation, and fuck it, we're suddenly standing on a deck back in Makoko.

The place has not changed a bit. The smell of faeces in stagnant water is still there, overpowering. Papa Udi, Fatoumata, Femi and Shonuga cough and choke, wrapping their palms around their noses. Mosquitoes buzz around us. The familiar swish of lagoon water is a welcoming sound; I've missed it, holed up in that airport for months. I get a flash of Hafiz's orange ankara cloth and Justice's *Pasuma Wonder* t-shirt, and realise

I've missed them too—I should stop by and greet them once we're done here.

The flimsy scrapwood deck we're standing on sways under our weight. Everything is literally unchanged. Everything is peaceful and calm, and that is exactly the problem.

There's not a single sound that says humans live here. Not a human being in sight.

"Something is wrong," I say.

"Trap..." Ogun says softly as if thinking aloud, then turns back to us all and yells: "Trap!"

CHAPTER THIRTY-ONE

SHE DOESN'T NEED to say it twice. From the first word, the water in the channel next to us bubbles, becomes choppy, twisting into a tempest, a raging monster; then it opens its mouth and yawns, forming the largest whirlpool I've ever seen, and tosses three wildly grinning, massive crocodiles at us.

The first one crashes onto the platform, the creaky pier finally giving in to the weight and breaking in two. Kehinde grabs Fatoumata and hops onto another platform, Taiwo following with that smooth sailing motion the gods use, like bees flitting between flowers. The impact hurls Femi onto the opposite platform. Shonuga and Papa Udi are standing right in front of the croc's massive jaws as it turns to face them.

The second croc lands with a massive splash of smelly water in front of my mother and me. The third lands in front of Aziza and—

Eshu. Not there. Gone.

My mother yells something that sounds very much like a battle cry, and then her arms are lit and burning, the fire within her hot and consuming. She fires one, two, three darts at the croc in front of us. They strike the animal right in one eye with pinpoint accuracy, leaving a large, burning hole. The animal reels like a hurt dog. Then I hear a gunshot, and another. Femi's gun is smoking, and the croc in front of her retreats. Both crocs sink back into the whirling water.

Papa Udi is screaming; I turn to see the first croc pulling at his leg, his calf disappeared into the thing's massive jaws. His hands hold its massive jaws, veins straining with the effort. Then Aziza is there, rotating his stick, and there is the fiercest of sharp winds, a tight dust devil that knocks the croc off Payu. Aziza sails on the whirlwind and plants himself between man and animal. Holding his staff like the rod of Moses, he dips it in the water, and a barrier of air—a sort of shimmer sheet, knocking the returning croc back—shuts off the whirlpool and separates us from the danger.

Shonuga pulls Papa Udi away from the water. He's not fatally hurt or whimpering, but he's an old man with a wounded leg. His tightly clenched teeth and blood dripping onto the wet wood of the broken platform are bad enough.

"Weapons!" I call through my teeth.

Everyone draws their respective poison. I pull out my cutlass and chain and charge my godessence for the ready.

Then something I've only seen on TV emerges from the whirlpool and walks on water.

Eyo masquerades, part of the Eyo festival—held in honour of an Oba or ruling family member's death, or to add colour to an event at a ruler's request—are barely ever seen up-front, but every Lagosian knows what an Eyo looks like. The thing that emerges from the water is an exact representation, covered from head to toe in white cloth: a flowing, white agbada, from neck to calf, with an arópalé beneath covering calf to feet and trailing behind. It wears the fìlà, a wide-brimmed hat, white with black stripes and frills dangling from the brim like wind-chimes. Hanging from inside the hat, draped to cover its face, is the ibori, a lace veil with holes for eyes, though I see no eyes there. Usually, there is an ọ̀pámbátá, a long staff, the one thing that strikes fear into every Eyo watcher, but this one carries none.

The Eyo stands atop the water and stares at us for a moment. Then a second Eyo arises from the same place, identical in every respect, so that we cannot tell them apart. Then a third. All three stand on the water and watch us.

I try to reach my esper across Aziza's air barrier and read them, but apparently the thing is some sort of ward, preventing godessence from passing through either way.

"It's Sango's sisters," my mother says aloud, as if sensing what I'm doing. "We've been delivered into their hands."

"And that's not the worst part," Taiwo says, and the colour's completely drained from his face, something I've only seen once before, when it was I who hunted him. "That's Oya, Oba and Osun; yet we have no idea who is who, and who can do what."

I turn to Aziza. "Can you get us out of here?"

"Yes," he says. "But, I have to drop this barrier before I can open a threshold."

Ogun shakes her head. "They're waiting for us to do that. They will come for us once this thing goes down."

We stand there for a beat, our minds racing. The three Eyos don't move.

"Aziza," I say, "listen carefully. You are going to drop this thing and open a threshold. You're going to get everybody out of here."

"And you?" Kehinde asks.

"My mother and I will hold them."

"They will kill you in seconds," Taiwo says matter-of-factly.

"I'll be right behind you guys."

"I'm not going anywhere," Kehinde says. She steps forward and stands between my mother and me.

"Nor I," Femi says, and cocks her rifle. Shonuga does the same without a word.

Fati steps forward to stand in the front line with us.

"No, eh-ehn, no," I say, shoving her back. "Go with them. You take Papa Udi to the medicine group." I turn to Taiwo. "You too."

"Oh, I wasn't staying before," Taiwo says, pulling Fati to him, who resists, her long knife tight in her grip.

"Go," I say, sterner. "Go. Protect them."

She glares at me, then gives into Taiwo's pull. They huddle next to Papa Udi, behind Aziza.

There's five of us on the line now. The Eyos still haven't moved.

"Aziza, on my word."

The whirlwind god nods.

And then before I can open my mouth to say the word, the first Eyo steps forward.

I'm not sure exactly what it does, I swear it does no more than touch the barrier with a finger, and the whole thing shimmers and fizzles, and we're suddenly staring into the void where its eyes should be.

"Go!" I yell at Aziza.

I push flames onto my weapons and charge into the water. Ogun and Kehinde splash closely behind.

The first gunshot goes off, from Femi or Shonuga. The Eyo waves a hand, the abgada sleeve collecting the wind in front of it, and the bullet strikes an invisible barrier, emitting sparks.

Oya, god of whirlwinds.

Kehinde darts off to face her in Aziza's absence. I reach within myself, charge my godessence, shove fire onto my chain, and hurl it at the remaining Eyos.

The second Eyo steps forward, draws water from below and opens up a whirlpool in the air. The end of my chain goes right through it, returns like a boomerang and slams straight into my chest. I'm in the air, then suddenly in the water, my chest hurting like fuck.

Oba, god of waves and whirlpools.

I come back up to see one of the crocs before me, charging on stubby limbs with an open mouth. I raise my cutlass and aim for its head. The thing dodges, then leaps for me, jaws parted. I shoot fire into its mouth. It drops and is pulled back into the whirlpool. Another gunshot, Femi and Shonuga firing at the second croc, which takes their bullets in its hide. It lashes out at Shonuga, who lands in the water, the whirlpool pulling at her. Femi fires one, two shots, then leaps into the water and grabs her.

I fling my chain at the second croc and catch it on the head; the thing turns to me. I fling again, and the croc snatches my chain it in its jaws, pulling me. I'm *this* close to ts jaws when I lift my machete and bring it down on its head. It screams and slinks back into the whirlpool.

I rise and turn, expecting to see the last croc, but instead am just in time see Aziza's threshold snap shut. A severed tail splashes in the water.

Shit, shit, shit. The croc followed them.

Kehinde is cornered by Oya, her blue robe rippling in the goddess's whirlwinds, large and small, from every angle. The twin goddess is working hard, beating charms out with hand-claps and body-beats to counter the wind. Femi takes aim and fires a shot at Oya, who waves her arm in another wind block, then conjures a whirlwind to lift Femi and dump her somewhere in the channel, away from the fracas. Shonuga screams and follows the wind, wading and splashing in the water.

I turn back. My mother has engaged Oba, fashioning a whip out of fire and lashing out at the god, who sidesteps and lashes a whip of her own, sometimes water and sometimes ice, trying to catch my mother and pull her into the whirlpool. There is a lot of steam between them, obscuring their fight, and they soon disappear into the mist.

The third Eyo, which hasn't moved since, stands up and faces me now.

Osun doesn't come at me. Instead, the god spreads her legs wide and howls, something inhuman, ear-rending. She howls again, and suddenly I'm not sure if it's just me or if there are black wisps of cloud gathering about her, preparing to rain death.

The bottom of her agbada ruffles and I see the imprint of a palm, and I realise the howls were the pain of bearing offspring. A hand reaches down to touch the water. There is a plop, like a huge wad of faeces dropping; then something is swimming towards me, swift and sure.

I raise my weapons again, charging fire to them as the creature leaps out of the water and flies at me. There's just time to see claws and hair and teeth and ugly and know what it is.

Shigidi. A fucking shigidi.

I check its flight with the chain, catching the demon-goblin's midriff. But the little creature latches on to it instead and is suddenly hanging a few inches from my face. It claws my cheek, and I feel my skin peel from ear to lip, burning. I swing my head back and crash my forehead into the thing. It lets go and tumbles into the water, but rights itself quickly to stand and grin at me.

Fucking nightmare creature with that fucking open-toothed smile; fucking death messenger of the gods. This one has a thick, blunted cone of clay for its head, black hair covering every inch of its twisted body except for its clay head, and teeth and claws for tearing. Black shadows float about the creature, and I suddenly realise Osun must've offered Aganju her own essence, the essence of these shigidis, to turn those godlings into shadows. Hence their ability to sap godessence, like shigidis do.

Osun screams again. Another shigidi plops into the water. The two shigidis come at me together.

Shonuga, behind me, takes aim at the first one and fires. The bullet rips its head open and the thing melts into a thick mass of black smoke. The second is close behind it, but I catch this one in the belly with my machete. It dissolves into smoke, and my godessence charges, like a battery plugged, like a fire fed petrol. Osun yells, drops two, three more shigidis in the water, and then suddenly there are too many shigidis to shoot, to keep count, to escape from.

We retreat, stepping back into my mother, who's emerging from the mist the other way. Oba backs away as a wall of water, a towering whirlpool sucking all of the channel into itself, rises to separate them. Kehinde, to my left, is flung back by a gust of wind; she rolls over and scrambles towards my mother and Shonuga and me.

Then a figure rises out of the water, back to us, and stands between us and the three gods. The figure's dreadlocked hair is held up with seaweed and water stones. The back of my tongue tastes of fish and grapes, and I smell raw, wet incense.

Olokun catches the first shigidi by the neck, opens their mouth wider than I'd ever think possible, and bites into the shigidi's neck. The demon-goblin squeals, squirms, and then Olokun bites down and tears its head off with their teeth, spitting hair and black smoke. The rest of the shigidis launch at them, and Olokun swats at the shigidis at they come, grabbing any they can by their stubby limbs and tearing them apart, scattering black smoke.

Suddenly, someone appears before Shonuga and Kehinde, then there is a flash, and both are gone before my eyes. Before I can think anything, there's that flash again, and my mother is gone too.

Then Oba and Oya shoot wind and water and ice at Olokun, and Osun drops one, two, three shigidis in the water, and suddenly they're all over the water god, who has just enough time to turn to me with that jerky motion and blink those fish eyes at me.

Then someone places a hand on my shoulder, and suddenly I fall on the hard tarmac of the airport runway.

CHAPTER THIRTY-TWO

ALL I HEAR for a second is coughing and water dripping onto the solid tarmac. I blink and count with my eyes. There's Ogun, standing next to me; Papa Udi and Fati and Taiwo and Kehinde. The errant crocodile lies next to them, bleeding, Fati's blade lying bloodied further away; there's Shonuga kneeling next to Femi, trying to get her to breathe as she expels water from her lungs; and there's Aziza in front of me, standing next to Eshu.

I rise, my essence charging with anger and fire and blood. I bring the machete to my palm and slice. The wound tingles, the blade lights up in flames. I turn and face Eshu.

"You bastard." I move in on him.

"David," Aziza is saying, getting between us. "Now, you calm down…"

I take a hand to the whirlwind god's shoulder and shove him harder than I expect. He scrapes along the tarmac, stilling himself with a swipe of his windstick. Eshu steps back, looking around.

"People, people…" he's saying, frantic.

"David," Ogun says softly.

"You sold us to those things," I say.

"What?" Eshu's angel face twists. "What, no, what?"

Good actor. Bastard. "What did they offer you?"

"What?" He steps back again, looks to my mother.

"David," my mother says again. "Calm down."

I whip the chain, light it up, dragging fire along the tarmac. "You're dead, you hear me? Dead."

"David, calm down," Kehinde says.

I whip the chain in the white god's direction. He turns, swivels, dodges the end as it reaches him, the chain snapping at air like a hound's iron teeth.

"Ogun, help!"

"David, stop it now!"

I whip the chain at him again. He dodges. His face twists, his immaculate form giving way to something darker, more primal.

"Last warning, orisha 'daji," he says.

"Fuck you," I say, and go for him with my machete. He's right before me when I swipe, but when the machete comes down, it swipes air.

"Told you," a voice says behind me, then a heavy blow slams into the back of my head. I grit my teeth, sweep around to find nothing.

"Stop this," I hear Kehinde and my mother chorusing, and then another blow to the back of my head. I turn and wait, wrapping the chain around my fist, then reach out behind me just as Eshu reappears. I catch him by the arm and jam my chained fist into his chest.

The immaculate god skids across the tarmac. I follow him, readying my machete, when a large gust of wind sweeps him further away and raises dust to block my vision. I power through Aziza's dust devil to find nothing on the other side.

Then my mother is in front of me, a massive frown on her face.

"Stop it, right now," she says, taking hold of my arm. "Stop."

I spot Eshu reappear in the corner of my vision. I shrug my mother off—her grip is strong; her arm doesn't leave—and I want to head for Eshu, to finish him off, when I realise it's not one of him I'm looking at but two, three, four, a multitude.

We're surrounded by the 256 iterations of Eshu, their foreheads creased and jaws set as one.

"Stop now," Ogun says. "I won't repeat it."

"He wanted to kill us," I say to her, anger burning in my chest. "Can't you see?"

"No, oga," Shonuga says. "He helped us."

I look from face to face. Everyone's eyes are on me, laced with fear, their bodies tense as if poised to defend themselves from me, as if I'm a rabid animal set free.

"He delivered us to the sisters!"

"I delivered you *from* them!" the multitude of Eshus hiss back, a company of snakes. "They ambushed us. *All* of us!"

"It's true," Femi says, her voice weak. "He rescued me. He also rescued Olokun. They had Olokun bound."

"He got all of us out of there," Aziza adds.

I look back at the Eshus, who shake their heads in return, glaring at me. "You're not worthy to hold those things," they chorus, all pointing at the weapons in my hand. "You're not worthy."

They look up at the group, their eyes shining with the àshẹ of the gods: "And you are not worth fighting for if I will have to watch my own back the entire time."

The iterations pop out as quickly as they appeared, and we're looking at one immaculate god. Eshu turns about on a heel and walks away, reality pulling at the seams and gathering about him, fabric warping, as if opening its arms to embrace him, and then he has walked right into the air in front of us and is gone.

We stand in silence for a beat.

"It's good riddance, anyway," I say. "His loyalty had a question mark on it."

"Oh, stop it!" Kehinde snaps. "Just stop. You messed up and you know it."

"How, how?" I turn to face her.

"You want to come for me too?" She steps from the group to lean down from her seven-foot frame and put her nose in front of mine. "You want to attack me too? Because you're strong now? Come, then, do it."

"Stop that," Ogun says, sterner than before.

"Look at your son," Kehinde says to her. "He's drunk on power. Is this how he's going to lead us? By killing us every time he gets angry?"

"I'm not killing anybody," I say.

"Oh, aren't you? Look around." She sweeps her arm at the group. "Look at how they look at you."

I do not look. I already know what I'll see.

"It is you we cannot trust, David Mogo," Kehinde says. "It is you."

We stand and stare at one another. Aziza turns, whips up a small dust devil and disappears into it. When it fades, he's no longer there.

"Come," Kehinde says to Femi, Shonuga and Fati. "Let's take Payu to the healing group."

Femi and Shonuga help Papa Udi rise and hang an arm between them, Fati supporting him at the waist. I watch them leave, Kehinde darting hot glances in my direction. I turn my back to her so I won't see, and point to the crocodile, looking at Taiwo.

"Fati," he says, gesturing towards the discarded long knife. "Eshu helped her finish it off."

Ogun comes to stand by me. "You will need to fix this thing that you have broken."

"Whatever."

"Not *whatever*," Ogun says. "You will need to fix this, and fix it quick."

"Because?"

"*Because*," my mother says, turning me by my arm so that I face her, "you see that?" She points to the crocodile's black blood congealing on the runway. "That thing is one of Osun's children. And she knows where every single one of her offspring in this world are, dead or alive. As long as they live or breathe or bleed, she knows where they are."

"Oh, no," Taiwo says, his hand to his mouth.

"And what do you think Aganju will do with that information?"

"No, no, no," Taiwo says.

"Get your people together, David Mogo," Ogun says. "The time has come."

THERE IS NO communal bonfire in the evening. The airport is cold and dark and miserable, and there is a grey sheet of rain for the remainder of the day. Most people stay indoors and pack up, say goodbyes to those with whom they've formed bonds of friendship, family and romance.

I stay in the plane and do not get a lot of visitors, neither do I visit the rest of my group in the FAAN quarters. Taiwo and Fati come by once, tentatively, to check if I'm okay. Then later, when the rest of the airport has wound down, Ogun comes to visit.

"Odivwiri will not be going with us," is the first thing she tells me when she settles into the plane. She is now dressed in a red tunic, decorated in symbols from various godtongues I cannot read, over a green pair of long shorts, bound at the calf with strings of cowrie shells, similar to those tied about her biceps. She does not carry any weapons, but I'm sure she will be wielding something eventually.

Fati's animal fat lamp still burns in the plane interior, ensconcing us in an otherworldly cocoon of smoke.

"Guessed as much," I reply. "He was badly hurt."

We sit in silence for a while.

"You will have to be careful," my mother says. "You only have a few more chances before you lose their trust."

I can't blame them; I am no longer even sure of myself.

"What is happening to me?" I ask her.

"Nothing. Everything," she says.

"Is that good or bad?"

"Neither. You will need to be that person again when the time comes. It will be in the best interest of those you protect that you do not hesitate then."

I observe her for a moment. "Has this happened to you? Do you make terrible decisions on impulse?"

She nods. "It is the only way I've lived. The curse of being part of chaos, I believe."

"Is that why you stopped?"

"Maybe." She stares off, towards the darkened rear of the plane. "But it doesn't guarantee anything, really. We are fire and blood and war. We do not have the luxury of family or friends. Sooner or later, the heat drives them away. Sooner or later, we ruin everything."

Unless, of course, I reject this new aspect of myself that offers me so much power, and let the whole of Lagos and everything I know and love be overrun.

Either way, I'm screwed.

"Story of my life," I say, and rise. "Good night, mother."

CHAPTER THIRTY-THREE

THE LONGEST BRIDGE in West Africa is officially named the Ibrahim Babangida bridge, but no one calls it that. Snaking out of Oworonshoki, the Third Mainland Bridge curves away from the many fishing slum-villages and into the lagoon, giving way to the concrete and glass graveyard that is the Lagos city-island, a once densely-populated, resplendent metropolis now empty and deathly silent against dawn's misty breath.

We cross Aziza's threshold at the Murtala Muhammed Airport in Ikeja, and step into the middle of the Third Mainland Bridge, heaving and retching from vertigo.

The morning is cold and the sea breeze is unforgivable. Not much has changed since I was last here. The once-vibrant LED billboards have finally lost their power. No one has bothered to remove the years-old political feather banners, still flapping in the wind, advertising aspiring governors that have since abandoned Lagos to its own devices. The skyscrapers in the distance are old and broken and monolithic and silent. Nothing has changed, yet everything has.

Shonuga, riding Aburo with Femi Onipede holding tight to her waist behind her, half-appears on the bridge. The horse refuses to cross over completely, whickering, spooked. He stands there, snorting and petulant, his forelegs over the threshold, his hind quarters still at the airport. Shonuga tries to goad him into crossing, then threatens, but neither do the trick. So she dismounts, places his head in her hands and her head to his, and speaks to the horse in low, comforting tones, until he takes one step, two, and is finally over the line. Aziza steps over the threshold last, then closes it up.

That's the agreement. Whatever happens today, the airport community remains safe. We told Papa Udi and Fati to move them to a secure location that not a single one of us knows. Fati was terribly upset with me and refused to speak to me until we left, no matter how I explained that I needed *her* to stay and help the force we left behind protect the community.

The rest of us stand in the middle of the Third Mainland. Femi leads one group, spearheaded by her remnant LASPAC men who blended so well into the airport community that I forgot they were there. They're to focus on long-range attacks: guns, slingshots, spears and arrows. Shonuga leads the other group, prepared for close combat, armed with short knives, machetes, clubs and axes. I lead with my machete and chain, smeared with my own blood. My mother looks as she did yesterday, now sporting a machete similar to mine and a thick iron shield. Kehinde appears with nothing, as usual, but Taiwo carries Fati's long knife.

We wait.

Aziza and Ogun have our intel. They did some reconnaissance together in the dead of night, reporting that a shadow horde was indeed on its way from Upper Island, but not visibly led by anyone—not Aganju, not his generals. They seemed very focused, very much on a mission. No points for knowing where they were headed. Given the number—a couple of hundreds—the two have advised us on how to approach.

Shonuga dismounts and leaves Femi on the horse to offer her a good vantage point for her shooting. The two spend a few minutes whispering things to each other that everyone pretends not to notice. They embrace for a long time, as much as the height difference allows them. When Shonuga leads her faction away to rally behind me, I think her eyes might be shiny with tears. The exchange seems to set people off: Kehinde hugs Taiwo tight and kisses his forehead, and others in the group follow suit, embracing one another, holding hands, kissing lightly. My mother and I look at one another.

"Be careful," she tells me.

"Sure," I say.

We wait.

The first sign of the horde comes almost a half-hour later. The slowly brightening dawn sky sours quickly, the morning blue succumbing to a thunderstorm grey, with black clouds scudding in on the fringes. The lagoon on both sides of the bridge breaks into small, choppy waves, as if someone turned on a turbine underneath.

Around the bend come the shadows, vampires of godessence, galloping like a band of tar primates. Teeth, claws, formless middles rippling, catching the morning light and turning it into something... wrong. They see us and charge, crying from the depths of their larynxes, wails for survival, calls to warfare.

"Ready!" I say, surprised at the sound of my own voice, the anger it contains. Scenes from the Arena flash before me. I draw blood, drawing fire.

The lagoon's waves grow choppy, and I already know what lies beneath it. I breathe and move. The force comes with me, charging, yelling. We crash into the horde.

My machete blade meets the first shadow. The tar-like creature of night cries and dissolves into a substance like black sand, and power courses through my body like an electric charge. I inhale it and fuel more fire in my weapons. Slash, slash, slash. I whip my chain in a circle and take out five, six. The sounds all around me: sand on concrete, flashes of gunshots, my mother's fire, the screaming, the iron.

Then two Eyos are suddenly right there in front of us. Ogun and Aziza peel away from the shadows to stand with me. I move on them, my machete and chain dripping fire, beating shadows out of my path. A few feet out, I swing my chain at the Eyos. They break their stance. One rises into the air— Oya—and Aziza follows with his windstick, brandishing it like a sword. Oba pulls a wave out of the lagoon, rearing above us. The airport force shows its first signs of fear when the shadow of the huge wave falls over us; and that hesitation gives the shadows their first opening. The first humans fall within seconds, the life sucked out of their very beings.

"Fight, fight!" I'm roaring, right before the wave crashes over the bridge.

Osun's massive crocodiles drop out of the wave like falling mangoes in fruit season. The force of the water sweeps some of our men off the bridge and into the lagoon. The crocs, happy to be near so many breathing, bleeding human bodies, catch two, three in their massive jaws. Femi's band peppers them with bullets.

Shonuga and her band go past me, screaming head-first into

the oncoming horde. I whip my chain out and clear a path for them, and they run into burning dust and embers, slashing as they go.

Ogun emerges from the midst of the crawling mass and swings at Oba. My mother's machete catches the Eyo on one shoulder, ignites her agbada. Oba reels, screeches, and it's a thousand nails scratching into concrete. Ogun runs, shoulder behind her shield, and checks the Eyo. Oba grabs the shield, and both of them tumble over the parapet into the lagoon.

Kehinde, next to me, claps her hands on the head of a nearby shadow, and the thing dissolves into black sand.

"Osun!" she screams.

I look out to the end of the bridge. The shadows are like an endless loop, always coming. Something is *producing* them in real time, and no prizes for guessing who that is.

Kill it at the source. If we can take Osun out, there won't be any new soldiers for Aganju.

"Come with me," I say.

She shakes her head, slams another shadow into dust. "Taiwo," she says.

Right. She has to stay by her brother. It seems I am on my own.

I look back at the airport force. Just as we planned, Aziza has engaged Oya and my mother has engaged Oba. Shonuga and Kehinde lead the combat line, while Femi and her shooting gang clean up from behind. The force is working through the shadows like a spear through flesh. Now is the best for me to get to it, before they tire out.

I sheath my machete and track back to Femi, who is taking pot shots and hitting shadows with ebo-tinged bullets.

"I need the horse," I say.

She dismounts without hesitation, and I heave myself on and charge Aburo forward, past the fighters. I whip my chain left and right as I ride, iron and fire catching the shadows that dare to come close. My insides boil hot, my hands scalding. Sweat stings my eyes like mosquitoes. My tongue is parched and the wind blows concrete dust in my mouth, but I'm no longer in touch with my senses. There is only wind in my ears, and chaos in my head. Embers of fallen shadows settle about me like soot from the sky, and I am a fiery hound burning them to dust, moving too fast to keep pace even with myself. With every shadow fallen, I feel myself slip, overwhelmed with the desire to kill, to destroy.

Ahead, I can see the white of the Eyo agbada through the mass of shadows, the fìlà perched delicately still, despite the fact that out of the bottom of the agbada pours forth an endless stream of shadows, a conveyor belt of evil child-soldiers birthed by the now reversed-fertility orisha, Osun.

One swipe of my machete is all it'll take.

A few yards from the Eyo, I swing one leg off the horse, slip away and let him run off. I land on the tarred road, tumble and find myself squatting in front of the bowed head of the Eyo, sitting cross-legged, the fìlà lowered over its face, frills dangling like a bamboo curtain. I pull my machete from my sheath.

The Eyo throws its head back and lets the fìlà fall off.

"Boo," says Eshu.

Every single thing around me pops out of oblivion. The Eyo, the shadows on my side of the bridge, everything. I'm suddenly standing in front of thin air.

My collarbone sings for the first time in a long time. My

senses are overwhelmed by a *whoosh*, a dry, hot breeze as if I'm standing in the desert on a sunny day. I grind my teeth and taste fine dust. Suddenly I'm sweating from invisible heat and I smell burning, but not of the kind that comes from dry fire; I smell ash, choking gas, melting—the kind that comes from a liquid, flowing fire, as of melted iron in a furnace.

I turn around.

The figure before me, his back to the ongoing battle between the real shadow horde and the airport force, is robed in red, in the same manner as my mother was when I first met her; except his is only a half-robe, with the front open and displaying black armour, built for a warrior that is not him, so that it seems ill-fitting. He holds two swords—not machetes like me or my mother, but short, narrow swords with blades that look like they're constantly in a hearth, as if magma flows within them. When he breathes, smoke comes from his nostrils, like a dragon's on a misty morning. Energy crackles about him in the same manner as Sango, and I taste metal in my mouth. Unlike Sango, he is not bald; his hair is woven up to the back of his head in traditional shuku cornrows, decorated with cowrie shells in the same way Olokun's was, so that it makes him almost normal, almost human, almost not a monster.

Aganju's signature is too familiar for me not to remember it. From the touch on Fati's fingers at the palace last year, to my battle with Ajala at the barracks; I remember it all.

But I have no time for nostalgia.

Aganju turns away from me, lifts up both swords, and plunges them into the tarmac of the Third Mainland Bridge.

There a string of little explosions, like bombs under the bridge breaking apart the concrete. At first it creaks, then slowly cracks appear, snaking from where his swords have entered the ground. The fissures hiss and liquid fire flows from the blades into them, and they crumble, a yawning gap opening up in the tarmac.

The third mainland bridge severs into two.

Half the shadow horde falls through the hole, but so do half of the airport force. Before my eyes, another huge wave crashes over the top. More of the airport force topples into the water.

The horde descends on those left. I can't see my mother or Kehinde. Shonuga creams for her men to retreat, retreat, and then Femi is trying to reload and shoot at the same time, and she's screaming for Aziza to open the portal and get everyone out of here, but Aziza is nowhere to be found, in the flurry of arms and blades and black sand and blood and grey skin.

Aganju faces me again, grinning, and I realise this was his plan all along.

"I told you we will meet again," he says, then moves. I ready myself, chain wound tight around my fist, gripping my machete.

Aganju rolls both his swords, takes one step, two steps, then disappears into thin air.

What the—?

There is the heat of fire on my face, like a blacksmith's hearth, and before I can think, Aganju materialises before me and brings down a sword. I have enough time to parry it with my machete, but the second sword comes too fast, and sinks into my ribs.

My whole body sets on fire.

I should know fire. I *exist* as fire. But the fire that consumes me now is not mine, is an *impurity*, like a fever tearing through my body. I feel the sting of Aganju's magma flowing within me, threading through me like it did the tarmac. I grit my teeth and fall to my knees.

My vision dims. I see the shadow horde overrunning our airport force in the distance. Grey and black, sucking the life out of everything they touch and consuming every last ounce of life Lagos has left.

Aganju kneels before me, his face right in front of mine.

"You should've minded your business," he says, clicking the back of his tongue.

That stupid smirk on his face and the unnatural pointiness of his canines are the last things I remember before it all goes dark.

CHAPTER THIRTY-FOUR

I'M IN LOVE with the darkness, but the darkness does not love me back.

This is the first thought that pops into my head as I wake up, my forehead split across the middle by a migraine. It takes a lot of blinking to realise I'm somewhere completely dark, very much like my overhead luggage compartment back at the airport. There is a running sting in my left side, as if I have a burst appendix. I feel terribly hot and cold at the same time, sweating as if with a fever. My stomach burns in the pit, like the embers of a night fire left into the morning, unquenched.

I try to move. I cannot.

I'm not bound. For a moment, I'm taken back to my time of in captivity at Ajala's palace. I know Aganju would not stoop so low as to use a wizard's rituals when he can charmcast liquid fire forth from himself. Yet there is so much familiar about this: I'm unable to move any part of my body, save to blink and lick my lips. There is a stiffness in my neck that I cannot creak to solve. My esper is not only unreachable, it is completely absent, inaccessible. The déjà vu is too strong to ignore.

The first thing I try to do is not get delirious. But the passage of time in the dark is a tricky thing, and a few seconds, minutes, hours or days after, I feel like I am a bodyless entity spinning in an endless vortex of darkness, and I soon lose grasp of which way is up or down and I think I puke on myself a bit, and I smell urine before I realise I've pissed on myself too.

I might've cried a bit too, who knows? Me, David Mogo, godhunter of Lagos, son of Ogun, heir to the mantle of god of war: I've lost my powers twice within a year, been captured as many times and pissed myself in the process. Some god of war, that.

I sleep and wake several times, seeing nothing but my mother falling over the bridge with Oba, me calling out her name. Seeing the airport force overwhelmed, the airport community destroyed by shadows, seeing Fati looking for her knife right before the life is sucked out of her by the horde. I wonder if I've had the essence sucked out of me by a shadow, and my useless human husk left behind as punishment, to almost taste true power and then have it yanked from beneath my nose.

I sleep, and the next time I wake up, it is because I am yanked out of the darkness and dipped into liquid fire.

IT STARTS AS a sensation in my side. Pain bites hard into my consciousness and I snap awake, straight into a throat-rending scream.

"Welcome," Aganju says.

The State House is no longer the State House. The place that once used to house the governor and his administration has been remodelled into a semi-palace. I kneel in front of

Aganju in what used to be a massive boardroom. The large meeting desk is still right there with its accompanying swivel chairs, coffee corner, floor-to-ceiling remote-controlled blinds and lights embedded in the ceiling. There is air conditioning, working perfectly, something I have not felt on my skin in a very long time—I get goosebumps instantly. Save for the throne at the far end of the room—a real throne, cut from a glittering, unrecognizable stone, igneous in nature, shaped like a mountain with a seat within it—this could literally be any Upper Island office after The Falling.

There are faces cut into the throne's stone, many faces I cannot recognise, and they seem to move, blink; their eyes flicker every now and then. The room has a very high ceiling, and I can see the pale squares on the walls where the photos of the president, governor and everyone else has been taken down. In a few places, splashes of black soot surround white human outlines on the wall.

Aside from rolling my neck, I'm still unable to move of my own accord. I struggle to get up, gritting my teeth. Aganju, who sits in the throne, says nothing, watching me. Standing next to him are the three Eyos, still and watchful.

After a while, he raises his hand and flicks it at the wrist, and immediately, my side starts to burn again. I grit my teeth, my joints stiff as stone. I feel warm fluid trickle down my side and patter on the floor.

"David, David, David," Aganju says, shaking his head. He's not a terrible-looking fellow at all; his form is much better off than his brother Sango's. He is dressed almost in the exact same way Ajala was—in a long, flowing jalabiya, except his is not white, but a flowing red with black stripes, which makes him look like a priest. Maybe that's what he considers himself: some sort of priest, saviour, messiah.

"Stop struggling," he says. "Painful to watch you do that, like a fly in a closed fist."

"Then free me," I say, gritting my teeth. "See if you can take me when we're the same size."

He laughs, a schoolboy chuckle. He sounds quite refined, almost like Taiwo, but with a lot more edge, something that tells me this is the kind of person who will stop at nothing to get what he wants.

"You think I care about fighting you?" he says. "I'm not my brother, you get? I'm not you or your kind. I'm not concerned about battle, just about winning. The less stress winning costs me, the better." He waves his hand at the Eyos. "Besides, I have people to do the fighting for me. And I have this."

He balls his hand into a tight fist and my side burns. My body doubles over, struggling to contain the pain. Aganju chuckles again.

"Where are they?" I manage to ask, licking my lips, spittle dripping down to the marble tiles in front of me. "What have you done with them?"

"You'll find out soon enough," he says.

"I'm going to kill you. You know that, right? One mistake, and you will not last another minute."

He chuckles again. "Don't overestimate yourself, David. There's a lot of me, and so little of you, you know?"

"What do you want?"

"Now this is the kind of question I don't like," Aganju says, and he sounds genuinely angry. "How can you be asking me this, David? After all this time we've spent dancing about one another, you're asking me what I *want?* You know what I want, David. You've always known."

"To go home?"

He claps. "See? Smart little people, all of you. Yes, it's that simple. We"—he waves his arm at the whole room—"just want to go home, David. Just like you. We all want the same thing."

"No, we don't. You are a mass murderer and I'm trying to save Lagos from being obliterated by your stupid quest for power."

"Power?" He sounds as if I've accused him of stealing meat from a pot of stew. He looks to the Eyos. "Look at this man, talking about power. What power? I said, we all want the same thing, David. I'm trying to save my people, and you're trying to save yours."

He rises from the throne. "Tell me, Mr Saviour, what is it that I have done that you haven't? I've been locked out of my own home, and the first thing I tried to do was get into a corporeal realm; this one, to be exact. I was trying to use a proxy to do just that, but you killed him. You killed him to save your people. *You*, David, started the killing here. *You* are the murderer."

"Is that what you tell yourself?" I say, my anger roiling. "That you're just trying to save your people?"

"All I've ever wanted is just to find home here. But then came you, chasing after me with everything you had. And your band of police too, who made it their duty to not only round up my project—creatures I spent half my life working on—but also to thwart every effort I made to get back into this realm, and to bring all my people here, in one place. Your Lagos just happened to be the place, that's all. Most of us were already here, anyway."

"What are you saying?" I scowl. "This is *our* home, and you came and destroyed it. Why don't you go to *your* home?"

"*I* didn't destroy your home. It was Obatala—you should meet him by the way, you two would love each other; big on saving the world, you two. *He* cast all of us here, including all my creative projects you guys made meat of. We did not choose to come down here of our own accord, my friend. Orun was sealed off from us the minute we popped out of it and were thrown into our different realms. If I know Obatala, he really wants to keep us out of it forever."

He paces for a beat. "Tell me, David, if it was you, wouldn't you try to get your people settled into a new life too? Wouldn't you want to make things better for them, try to stop them from getting killed by hostile forces in the land in which they have found themselves? And tell me, if you had the advantages I had, wouldn't you have used those advantages, to prevent the oppression of your people, even at the cost of others?"

I'm speechless, stunned at how he has rationalised it all for himself. In his story, *we* are the enemy. I am the villain.

"So, what do you want with me, now?" I say. "What do you want with us?"

He shrugs, returns to his chair. "You'll see. Maybe you'll figure it out for yourself, if I show you how your people can suffer when you're not there to help them; maybe then you can understand what I want. And after that... maybe you will even help me."

He balls his hand into a fist, and my side *sings,* and I find myself on the floor. One of the Eyos comes up to me then, places a hand on my head, and I'm suddenly plunged back into the prison of darkness in my head, with only the pain of fire in my side to remind me I'm still human.

CHAPTER THIRTY-FIVE

Aganju takes me on a rollercoaster ride of pain.

First stop is Aziza. I wake up in the prison in my own head, a place that I have by now made my own, somehow familiar. I hear the scream of the whirlwind deity, a grating, throat-rending sound. First, a whimper that pulls me out of sleep (or not sleep, which is something you do on purpose, but unconsciousness, slipping into the void) and I find myself listening to something like a dog in suffering. Then there's a scream.

It sounds like someone losing a finger. First, the yelp of surprise, then the scream of disbelief, then the wail of resignation and horror. I want to rise, but I cannot. I'm unable to move, to help, to do *anything*.

"No, no, no," the whirlwind god is saying. "No, no." Then, another long piercing scream.

I don't know what they're doing to him, and I'm not sure I want to know.

Before long, I find myself weeping for Aziza, whimpering with him. And before I can find respite from this, it suddenly stops, and I'm back alone with myself. But rather than be grateful for the silence, I find myself craving his voice, wishing to hear something, anything that tells me he is no longer suffering because of me.

But when voices do indeed return, it is not Aziza. Two women's voices. It takes me a while to recognise Femi Onipede's voice, cracked and hoarse from a lot of screaming.

"Ifelola," she is saying, Shonuga's first name. "Ife, please answer me."

There is a weak groan in response, and I realise Shonuga's trying to speak. I listen closer. The voice, reduced by pain to a small, wheezing thing, is repeating, "I love you. I love you. I love you."

The cycle goes on and on, interspersed with moments of silent weeping, first by one party and then by the other, and then Femi is screaming, and though I cannot hear her thrashing about and banging on something, I imagine her doing so. Once, Femi says: "Stop hurting her, please. Stop. I'll do anything you want, just stop, please!"

I listen to this over and over until it becomes background noise, and I don't even know when it stops. I only become aware when the voice changes, then I'm hearing the same thing play out between Kehinde and Taiwo, with Taiwo being tortured in some way, and Kehinde pining and screaming. Kehinde is calm at first, as if trying to contain the effects of the torture, then snaps suddenly and becomes completely feral, screaming her lungs off as her brother whimpers and yells and weeps.

I find myself wondering why I am not going through the same thing, why I have not been earmarked for torture. I am the lead instigator, leader of the resistance. If anyone should suffer, it should be me.

I can take it. Give me the pain, I can take it.

* * *

"Do you understand now?" Aganju says the next time he pulls me out of the prison of darkness in my head. "Do you understand what it's like to stand by and listen to everyone suffer? To watch everything unfold before your ears, but you can neither see nor touch nor help?"

"Please stop it," I find myself saying, kneeling in front of him in that throne boardroom. I've spent so long—Days? Weeks? Months?—in that darkness that I no longer know the difference between imaginings and reality. I believe this must be real.

"Stop making them suffer. Make me suffer instead. I'm the cause of it all. I hunted your godlings. I killed your wizard. I killed your brother. Take it out on me. Please."

"Oh, but I am," he says, smiling, showing his pointed canines. "I *am* making you suffer."

He comes close, puts his face to mine. Being so close stirs up something in me, a faraway response from my esper long gone. I cannot even feel his breath on my face.

"Don't you know that the best way to make someone lose all hope in life and existence is to remove everything worth fighting for? That is what you almost did to me, David Mogo. You took away my first chance to return to this world when you killed Ajala. I was stuck in a void, a realm of nothingness just like the one you're stuck in now. Ajala was how I interacted with *this* realm, with the corporeal world, and you took that away from me. Then you and your friends locked up my lifetime project and took away the key. Same project that I lost my home and my loved ones over, that I was ridiculed for and branded a usurper. I lost everything, David Mogo. If I hadn't found a way to get out of that place, I would've given in to despair."

He walks around the room, hands akimbo. "Then, as if that was not enough, you went and killed my brother."

"He tried to kill my father and sister," I find myself saying.

"Yes, he did," Aganju replies. "Because you would not leave me alone. You had to be removed."

We stare at one another for a moment.

"I know *exactly* how you feel, David Mogo." Aganju's voice is now soft, placating, very reminiscent of Taiwo when he's lecturing me. "I'm not doing anything to you that I haven't already experienced. But I want you to see it for yourself, see that it's not always about you. I want you to know what it feels like to be a fallen god."

He leaves me in the room. I find myself staring at the empty throne of faces, wishing that I could see a face, just one, that I can recognise—my mother, Papa Udi, Fati, Femi and Shonuga, Ibeji, Aziza; hell, anyone at all from the airport.

I realise that, without knowing it, I have already built a family, already built something worth saving. I was just too busy trying to save a whole world to notice it. If I could take it back, I would focus on protecting what I have, trying to live my life in peace, in my own slice of the world, instead of clinging on to power and the thirst for chaos.

I failed on all counts. I'm done and over. And so is my family and Lagos.

Or, perhaps, I did succeed.

I succeeded in destroying everything.

*　　*　　*

THE CAROUSEL OF tortured voices continues.

When Aganju brings me out for the last time, I'm already spent. I have no words left, no more spittle to make them. My throat is too parched. My head is too heavy, my heart too light, my soul too empty.

"This is good," Aganju says. "I don't like blood, you know? I can hurt you, yes, but I don't like to see your humanity spilling onto the floor. I'm a thinker, not a brute."

I bow my head, and thick spittle dribbles over my lower lip.

"That shard in your side, it's the same as my brother's thunderstone. Remember the axe that dissolved with him into nothingness? Well, this one isn't going anywhere. This one will remain buried in your body, will offer me control of you for as long as I want, as I have had over so many people. So get comfortable, David Mogo. Consider yourself fallen forever."

He stops short then, listens for something. The three Eyos are suddenly standing there in front of him, silent, but their postures tense. Aganju stares at them for a beat, as if communicating telepathically, then the three of them leave the room, though I'm not sure how.

I might as well have been in the darkness because I do not know how much time has passed of if anyone else enters or leaves. Which is why, when I hear my mother's voice whisper in my head, I'm not sure what to make of it.

"Wake up, David," she is saying. "Wake up."

No. Not you too.

"Shut up," she says. "Wake up!"

Then I hear a familiar voice, whose owner I knew so long ago that I no longer remember.

"Get up, David," it says. "You can do it."

I strain my body, my mind, trying to fix on the voice, reach for it with my esper which is so far, so far away.

"Come on, David," it repeats. "Try. Try."

"Get up!" Ogun screams.

I strain, so far that I feel like I am separating my soul from self, and then there it is, my esper, just within reach.

The faint smell of black pepper stings my eyes and hits my nose. I sneeze.

Eshu. The voice is Eshu.

What the fuck is happening?

"We're coming, is what," Eshu says, and then the walls and the air-conditioning and the boardroom table and the throne collapse in front of my eyes and suddenly the whole room is filled with thick, black smoke, pouring right into my lungs and choking me to the ends of the earth. I fall to the ground coughing. In the distance, I can hear pandemonium, shouts and running and gunshots and impact sounds. Fire crackles around me, eating up fabric, iron, wood, cement, concrete; eating up the State House and everything in it.

CHAPTER THIRTY-SIX

GETTING UP IS difficult. My limbs feel like they have not been used in ages, and there are pinpricks in my muscles each time I move. But I keep remembering my mother's voice, *Get up, David! Get up!* and Shonuga saying, *I love you, I love you, I love you,* and I know I have to get up, I have to.

I'm trying, but my limbs are like lead and my joints are too stiff.

There's a noise, and hands are soon on me, lifting me. I'm too weak to resist. Smoke obscures everything. The hands drag me along what used to be a hallway, now falling apart with flaming rubble raining down from above. They stop once or twice to ward off attackers, then pick me up again. Finally we're outdoors, in the open, where we're greeted by a colossal racket, clanging and smacking and thudding. I'm dropped on the ground and abandoned. Projectiles fly, there are shouts and cries, and I hear the familiar sound of the shadow-things wailing and dying.

It all dies down soon. There is the shuffling of feet as dust and smoke settle. I'm still lying on the ground. Someone lifts my arm and places something in it—a cold piece of metal.

My blood stirs.

Another piece of iron in my other hand. I recognise this one—a chain.

My esper responds to the iron like a long-distance phone call, slowly returning to me.

There's a sharp slice on my palm, and the other palm, and the warm flow of blood follows. Then the hand clasps mine over the weapons.

My chest ignites. Warmth and life spreads over my veins, my skin, my bones. All the darkness, all the gloom, burn away.

I rise. I blaze.

Ogun steps up to me, venturing into my sphere of flame. She is still holding a machete and her shield. She seems to have shed all glamour, all form. She is still bald-headed, and has the tattoos on her arms from the night at the airport, which move and wriggle like the faces on Aganju's throne. There is black dust in her hair, mixed with the sweat on her smudged face, where a wry smile is plastered.

"The phoenix, David," she says. "They rise in fire."

I breathe and simmer down, and the haze from the fire clears. Around me is death and dust. There is an amount of humans dead that I last saw on TV back when Boko Haram and groups like them were rampant in Nigeria. Blood everywhere, in splatters and pools in the concrete. There have been rumours for years, that these men and women served the gods willingly, but I never thought they were this many or would go this far; fighting *against* the very people who sought to liberate them. The sight makes me sick. It's an odd feeling: repulsed by death and joyful for life, at the same time.

Someone runs over and embraces me, then leans back. Fati.

"They say you die," she says. Her long knife is stained with black dust and drips blood and ebo; the garlic stings my eyes even in the smoke. I blink my teary eyes and see Papa Udi too, behind her. He is smiling, his crow's feet prominent, his War Chest strapped to his back like a backpack. Behind them both, over a hundred iterations of Eshu grin back at me. There's a large number of people around that I don't recognise; they're dressed in very old clothes, too raggedy to be from my airport bunch.

I see a splash of colour, and two people step away from the group.

"Godhunter," Justice says. He carries a hefty, misshapen club, splattered with black dust and dripping with blood as well. Beside him, Hafiz, still in his orange ankara, is similarly armed and plastered with gore. Justice and Hafiz bow together, and the rest of what I now realise is the survivors of the Makoko community bows with them.

"How...?" is all I can muster, looking back at my mother.

"No time," all the Eshus say together, in that creepy groupspeak. They're coming."

"The others..." Ogun says to me.

"I don't know where they are," I say.

"We split as before," Ogun says, taking the lead. "Eshu, find them. Meet us in front. The rest of us, we press our way out."

The Eshus snap back into the one, and the white god nods, then slips out of what I now realise is a semi-courtyard. We're still inside the State House.

"Come," my mother says. "Let's survive."

*   *   *

ONE THING ABOUT the new State House in Upper Island: it's a complete replica of the one once used by the Federal Government back when Lagos was the national capital (school excursions will do that—my history class visited the house back in King's College). The original was a British colonial-style three-storey affair with no basement; a central Victorian façade sporting the Nigerian coat of arms flanked by two long wings, housing offices and meeting rooms. This one has all the exact trappings: if I'm right, that puts our courtyard right in the middle of the building. Navigating our way out of the building should be easy, through the neat grid of the corridors. The large grounds outside might pose more of a challenge.

The smoke is everywhere, and we get turned around once or twice, blocked by fire and falling debris. We run into a group of godling-shadows—weird beings caught mid-transformation so that they have the darting, pleading eyes of godlings, but their skin is already turning black and they have the ability to absorb godessence with their touch—and have to go through them.

The battle is short and intense, lacking space and packed with heat. There's grappling, stabbing, swiping. One of the shadows breaks loose from the fracas and heads for me, screaming and stretching out a spindly arm. I backtrack, rolling my chain but not swinging it. The thing advances, caring too little about its own wellbeing, running to death.

"David!" My mother's voice. I know she's calling on me to swing, but I'm suddenly no longer thirsty to feed my iron. I'm no longer chaos defined.

"David!"

I swing. The chain catches the creature in the neck. My bones respond and my teeth and blood chime, urging me on. Fire awakens in my belly, antsy, happy to be summoned.

The thing howls, clutching at the chain, still reaching out, grasping my arm, and suddenly my body is screaming, calling out for help. I hear myself howling like the shadows, and I hurt exactly like I did with Sango's lightning strike.

I pull back my machete and plunge it into the godling-shadow's body. Its hand leaves my neck, and the fire in me responds, igniting the machete and consuming the creature as it falls to the ground.

Ogun hurries over to me.

"I'm okay," I say. "I'm okay."

"Don't hesitate, David," my mother says quietly, placing a hand on mine. "It's kill or be killed."

"I know," I say, sighing. "I know."

We move, slower now, all of us feeling the exertions of battle, spent godessence and torture. Surprisingly, we meet no more resistance: Aganju's human allies are no doubt fleeing for their lives, and the rest of his shadows are nowhere to be seen.

We come out into open air soon enough, happy to breathe fresh air that isn't tainted by smoke. We're to the east of the front façade, where a water fountain gushes water in the centre of a roundabout, the broken pieces of a statue half-fallen into the water. If memory serves me right, that should be the statue of Herbert Macaulay, one of Nigeria's pioneer fathers. Something tells me Aganju ordered it taken down.

There's movement to our far right, and we form a cluster, poised for another skirmish. Then, out of a cluster of tall palm trees, we first see Eshu—just one of him—then Kehinde and

Taiwo, holding on to one another, coughing. Femi and Shonuga follow behind them, doing the same. Eshu has a long face.

Fati runs over to Ibeji and embraces them tight. I nod at Femi and she nods back.

"I thought you were dead," Kehinde says, looking at the group. "All of you."

"Me, too," Ogun says. "Where is Aziza?"

Eshu, for the first time, looks serious. It's an odd look on the white god. He shakes his head slowly and looks away.

"No," Papa Udi and my mother say together. Papa Udi buries his face in his palms. Ogun curses loudly—I don't understand the language, but swearing sounds the same in all languages.

"He's gone—for good," Eshu says. "I can no longer feel him."

We stand about awkwardly, avoiding each other's eyes, unsure how to feel about the news. The only sounds are the crackling flames within the State House, and the occasional crash of falling debris. I watch my mother's face, devoid of any expression, and wonder if I'd be the same if any one of us died today.

There's a large splash behind me and I turn again, and there stands Olokun, their body gleaming in the late afternoon sun, glowing water stones in their dreadlocked hair. They cock their head and fish-blink at us, their àshẹ like a panther's eyes if they shone at noon. The Makoko people gasp together, lay down their weapons and hunker down, averting their gaze and mumbling praise.

"Seriously, though!" I say. "Will someone tell me what the hell is going on?" I point to Olokun. "How are you even alive? I *saw* you attacked."

"It was in the plan," my mother says. "We needed an infiltrator in their ranks, and we needed them to think we were dead. That was the only way they would lay down their guard."

Everyone looks at Eshu, who gives us a sad smile. I return to Ogun. "So we were *pawns?*"

"No," she says, looking away from me. "I didn't think they were going to capture you. I just wanted us to look defeated."

"That was why you went missing during the battle," I say, getting infuriated. "That was why we got overrun."

"I didn't go *missing,*" she says. "I had Olokun hide Aziza and me. Only us three and Eshu knew of the plan. That was the only way to make it look authentic."

"You sacrificed us? People *died* because of this!"

"It was the only way!" Ogun snaps back. "If they didn't believe they'd defeated us, they were never going to leave the airport community alone. *More* people would've died."

"We could've won. We could've fought and won."

"And what do you know about war that tells you so?" she says, stepping up to me. "What did we have over them that tells you we could've beaten them, once and for all, on that bridge?"

I stare at her. The whole group watches us, anxious.

"Aziza is dead. Because of you."

"Aziza understood the sacrifice. He chose to give himself up."

"How can you be this calm?" I step closer to her. "How can you be *okay* with this?"

"Because we're all the same, all of us," someone says.

We turn towards the voice. Aganju, flanked by the three Eyos, is standing by another cluster of palms and mangoes, overhanging the road to the exit. There are no other gods with him, and no humans at all.

"You and me, what's the difference?" Aganju says, waving his hand at us, ambling forward. "You kill people and burn them, for a *greater good*. You sacrifice people, for a *greater good*. But when I do it, it's evil." He chuckles, wags a finger. "All of us, we do whatever it takes to make home, to keep it safe."

As he speaks, shadows drift out of every nook and crevice— from the trees, from the smoke, from the rubble, as if they've been within the walls, waiting. Fuck, why do these things have no goddamn signatures?

"So the question here today, really, is who gets to be more evil than the other?" The Eyos walk with him, and the shadows flow around our flanks, encircling us. "And the one who is most ready to sacrifice everything to keep their house is the one who gets to stay."

"This is not your home," I say.

"And neither is it yours, orisha 'daji." There's extra bite in that last word. "But here you are, destroying everything in the name of saving it."

"Everything was fine until you came along," I say.

"Everything was fine for *me* until *you* came along," Aganju retorts.

The shadows have circled us proper. Their faces are full of hunger, the thrumming life in us all like a vicious thirst on a scorching day, their lips dripping with the anticipation of sucking the life out of us.

"If you leave now," I say, the chain in my hand turning red, "more blood will not have to be shed."

"Ha. And who has done the more shedding? Who has

destroyed more lives?" He points to the building, the fire—burning highest near the back of the building—now encroaching on the front, now visible through the windows and in the smoke billowing up to the sky.

"He is trying to get into your head," my mother whispers. "Don't let him."

"And you aren't?" Aganju says to her. "Aren't you all fakes?" His eyes sweep across us, then stop at Eshu. "And you; I thought I had an ally in you."

"Ah, well," Eshu says, smiling like a bashful child. "You know I only serve my own interests, Aganju."

Aganju shakes his head and clicks his tongue. "Well, it seems you have all chosen death." He shrugs. "So be it."

The shadows take that as their cue. They screech, shriek, howl like monkeys. I put myself between the Makoko group and the shadows, the burning State House behind us.

"Eshu," I say, "take every human in this place to the airport." I look Ogun in the eye when I say: "Us gods started this. Let's finish it."

Ogun nods.

Eshu splits into a number of iterations and six line up behind me, fencing the Makoko group off proper. Ogun steps up beside me with her shield and machete ready. Kehinde follows, holding her side, but with her jaw set, ready.

Fati, Taiwo, Papa Udi, Shonuga and Femi stand right there with us, saying nothing, but making no moves to leave. I'm this close to asking them to go back to the airport with the others, whom Eshu's iterations are busy swiping off, but I stop myself. Osun knows where they're going already. If we fall here, they will not be safe anyway.

I look at them and nod. Femi pulls out a revolver—she must've swiped it from a guard here at the house—opens the chamber, shakes out all the bullets and hands them to Papa Udi to douse in ebo.

I step forward.

The shadows respond to Aganju's wave and charge, the Eyos breaking apart, all heading for us. Femi opens fire, Shonuga, Fati and Papa Udi charging with her, Eshu's iterations right behind them. Taiwo and Kehinde head for the first Eyo together—Oya, who springs into the air and rains potshots down at them. Olokun raises a wave and brings down Oba, who responds in kind, the pair of them turning the water fountain into a hurricane. Ogun slings one fire bolt against the last Eyo—Osun—who flings half-formed shadow creatures in response. Ogun checks one after the other with her shield, swipes with her machete and sends the creatures back to black dust.

For a third time, I find myself face-to-face with Aganju.

I breathe, reach for my godessence. The heat stirs in my belly, a gathering of flames hungry to lick the life out of anything my iron touches. There is excitement in my teeth, in my bones, in my flesh.

Aganju takes one step, two, and then disappears into thin air.

I shut my eyes, pushing my esper, trying to sense him, smell him. I smell his ash, feel the heat of his magma, the sting of his smoke, the rock-solid feel of his muscle, of his fist and swords.

When I feel the heat right on my face, I step aside and swing my chain, fire whining through air. Aganju appears just at the last minute and bats it off with his sword.

"Ah, figured it out." Cowries bounce on his plaited hair as he nods.

I swing the fiery chain at him, and he parries. I swing again. Parry. We do this dance a couple of times. I catch a glimpse of the human-and-Eshu gang striking down a line of shadows out the corner of my eye. At the same time, Olokun wraps Oba's head in water, trapping her.

That lapse in concentration is enough for Aganju to parry again and come at me with the other sword. He's so fast, both swords flashing, that I have to block, block, block, until one blade smacks my hand and my machete flies away. I'm suddenly on the ground, my butt bone slamming the pavement with a painful thud. Aganju is over me in an instant, glowing swords raised. He squeezes his hand, and my side—I'd almost forgotten about it—burns again, so that I curl up on the ground, liquid pain shooting from my side into my brain.

"I don't even know why I show you any respect," he says. "I should've ended you a long time ago."

He raises his sword.

Then something weird happens. He stops and turns around.

All around us, the shadows are crumbling into black dust, wailing long and hollow, pleading for help, for home. Aganju's gaze shifts, as does mine, and there at the east end of the tarmac is the reason.

Ogun has arms wrapped around Osun, her fingers locked together behind the Eyo's agbada. They're both burning, a halo of fire about them. Osun is a foot off the ground, her scream rending the air as she burns.

Shadows everywhere crumble with her, and the humans and Eshus plough through them.

Aganju turns from me and flies towards my mother.

I collect myself and swing my chain at his back, catching him in the shoulder blade. He staggers, but does not fall. I follow him, the pain in my side stabbing with every step, but I press on. He is a step or two from my mother, who is completely oblivious and is gritting her teeth, trying to survive the heat, as I did with Sango back at the airport.

I fling the chain and catch him about the neck just as he raises his swords, and I wrap my end around my elbow and hold him there. He strains, but I wind the chain under my armpit and over my shoulder and pull back, like a plough. He scrapes across the tarmac, gritting his teeth, grasping at the iron tight around his neck.

He he doesn't need to breathe, technically. But if I can hold him there...

The last of the shadows drops into dust as the àshẹ in Osun gives way, fading into nothing. The god droops limp, and like Sango fades slowly into ash and embers, leaving behind the stench of a midwife's bathwater.

Aganju's rage builds—I can sense power in him growing, growing, and then he drops a sword, reaches behind him with one hand, grabs my chain and yanks.

The chain breaks.

I hit the ground. Aganju hacks ferociously at my mother. She has enough time to raise her shield, but she has no machete, nothing. She fires one blast, two at him. They smack his chest, but do nothing. I rise and reach for my own machete, but Aganju turns then and thrusts his hand out at me. The shard in my side ignites and *moves*. I double over to my knees, the machete clattering to the ground. Blood pours into my palm as I grip my belly tight.

Then Ogun checks into Aganju with her shield, and he

staggers. My insides are melting, but as he thrashes at her, clattering against the shield, she pushes forward. He steps backward, and again, closer to me, closer.

I lunge for my machete. Aganju turns, lifts his sword. I ignore it and swing my blade up under his guard. He sees it coming, drops the sword into his left hand, and buries it in my chest just as my machete severs his right arm.

Pain like liquid iron engulfs my chest like so that I can't breathe, the glowing sword searing my organs as it drives through my chest, coming out under my shoulder blade. I scream, as does Aganju, a black void where his right arm should've been, spraying a clear, viscous fluid. We're right in each other's faces, eyes to eyes. I reach for my godessence, but it is depleted, too strained to pull out fire without harming me, because I am too weak, too contaminated by Aganju's power in me.

Then the chain around his neck tightens, and Ogun is behind him, twisting, twisting. She lights up the chain, so that embers rise from his neck, forming a blackened ring on his skin. Aganju grits his teeth, yanks his sword from under my shoulder, reverses it and makes to stab behind him.

With great effort, I lift my machete again and knock the short sword off. He clenches his fist in response, and the shard in me moves again, cutting, cutting. My eyes tear up, blurring my vision, and I feel the wet warmth flowing down my belly.

Only one thing to do.

I look at my mother. Her eyes are focused.

Let go, I tell her.

Her narrow with understanding. She lets go.

I close my eyes, and sink.

A Phoenix, David. They rise in fire.

I sense Aganju turn as I stagger back. He swings with his remaining arm, ready to catch her, but Ogun ducks just in time.

I open my eyes, and push with my mind.

Fire comes from within, the dregs of my godessence, the deepest reserves of everything that is me. My machete ignites, blazing as ever, thirsting for blood.

I swing.

I do not miss.

The blade catches Aganju clean in the side of his neck, passes right through it, and comes out at the other end.

The head tumbles down, smacks on the tarmac and rolls away. His body stands for a moment longer, then slowly gives way, abandoning its human form and cloak and displaying the god beneath: a flowing, burning mass of magma and rock. Then it crumbles, melts, disintegrating into a pile of ash from neck to arm to body to feet, and finally Aganju is gone without a scream.

I feel the shard disintegrate within me too, as does the head a few feet away from me.

Suddenly I can see too little, breathe too little. I look around desperately, trying to grasp anything, hold on to something as life slips away from me.

As I fall to my knees, I see Taiwo and Kehinde, backed by the now liberated Eshu, holding down Oya, who is struggling in their arms. At the fountain, Olokun has Oba bound, seaweed wrapped about her agbada like a bundle of bedsheets. The rest of the humans stare at me, their mouths agape, slowly confronting the reality of their warrior, their hero, dying before their eyes.

And in front of me, as I fall, Ogun, my mother, running over, calling my name. Not David. My True Name.

Sadly, I cannot remember it, and I never will.

CHAPTER THIRTY-SEVEN

I WAKE UP in a bed.

At first, I think I'm dreaming, but it is indeed a bed. On closer inquisition, a mattress, which is on the ground. But I'm outside, because I'm looking up into an evening sky, and the sun is low. A dry, hot wind blows.

I've never been happier to take in the smell of a coming harmattan. I breathe in a lungful of hot, deserty air. Nothing like a question mark on your mortality to remind you of how the little things matter, even if they involve a nosebleed risk.

I try to sit up. The stinging in my belly flares, and my fingers reach for it in instinct; then another sting, from my shoulder. They're both patched, and I feel a sticky salve applied around each wound—either that, or it's my blood. There is a dull ache underneath them both, a feeling of healing already begun.

"Easy, easy," a voice says, then Papa Udi appears above me, a hand on my chest. There is a bag open on the ground beside me. He settles on a stool by me, tracing his fingers across my now exposed torso, along my Lichtenberg figures.

I look around and see a large pile of rubble. I figure we're still at the State House, but then I look the other way and there it is:

the guava tree that started it all, outside Cardoso House. It is no longer whittled down to a skeleton, but sports a thick crown of leaves now turned yellow by Harmattan's unforgivable onset. There is the barren tree now fruitful, a flag of victory flying, a symbol of hope renewed.

"We won," I say to Papa Udi.

Papa Udi's eyes dart towards the tree, then to the debris of Cardoso House behind him. He shrugs.

I sigh, rest on my back and look around. I am under a makeshift shelter fashioned of sacking nailed across a stick frame, under a zinc roof. There is an identical bivouac next to it, and Papa Udi's neatly-piled belongings, as well as a small firepit. I see two beds.

"Fati?" I ask.

"I am here," a voice says, and then she is standing right there, next to Papa Udi, her frail figure unflinching. She has shaved her head, like my mother.

She smiles.

"Good to see you too, kid," I say.

The sun is low in the evening sky. I didn't expect it to be this blank, this bleak, the day we eventually won this war. I expected to feel joy and celebration. Instead, I feel like a heap of rubble myself, one more casualty in the ash, like it wasn't worth it after all.

"Look at us," I say. "The survivors of Cardoso House."

"Hmm," Papa Udi says. He's back to grunts and gestures and little else, a slice of normality that I welcome with an open heart.

I try to rise again, but he puts his hand on my chest and shakes his head. "Wait first," he says. "Give am time."

"Am I... getting better?"

"Hmm," he says. "Maybe."

"How long have I been unconscious?"

"Days." He pushes me back down.

I drift off, and it is night when I open my eyes again. There are voices all around me, and a fire crackles.

"He's awake," someone says, and then someone lifts a light. I smell the animal fat of one of Fati's lamps.

Faces block out the light: I can see Ogun, Kehinde, Taiwo, Femi, Shonuga. Papa Udi and Fati are by the fire.

My mother smiles, the light in her eyes dancing.

"They rise from the fire," I say.

She nods and looks away, like she's trying not to cry.

"Welcome back, bro," Taiwo says, patting my shoulder. Femi and Shonuga give me nods. Kehinde looks like she wants to smile at me but doesn't know how to work the muscles for it.

"Where are the others?" I ask.

They look at one another. "Which others?" Femi asks.

I realise I'm thinking of everyone we've lost; Shonekan, Aziza, the airport force; everyone who gave themselves so that even if we lived like refugees, in the rubble of our own home, we would at least be free.

"Eshu, the airport community, the Makoko people," I lie.

"They're good," Taiwo says. "Everything is fine."

"Olokun is back with the Makoko people," Shonuga says.

"And the sisters?"

"Eshu took care of them," she says, without turning to face me.

"Took care how?"

She turns. The àshẹ in her eyes is brighter than ever. I'm not sure if that's how gods cry.

"Well." She clears her throat. "Remember how there are realms between this one and others, slips in time and space? Eshu knows how to get in and out of a few of them. Let's just say he's mistakenly left them there."

"And where is he now?"

They all look at one another, and end up looking at my mother. She shrugs.

Of course. What should I expect?

The stars are out, and we turn our attention to them, saying nothing. It's been a long time since anyone saw stars in this city.

"What happens to the airport people now?" I ask.

"Well, the government—" Femi starts.

"Government ke?" Shonuga interjects. "Which government? Abegi."

"The *new* government," Femi presses on, "is a committee of experts offering the federal government headways for a new triple-R approach: reconstruction, rehabilitation and reconciliation."

"Wetin that one even mean?" Papa Udi asks.

"I guess they'll rebuild what needs to be rebuilt and offer people, like the airport community, some refuge and maybe some money to start over."

Shonuga scoffs. "Is it not this Nigerian government?" Papa Udi scoffs with her.

"Well, at least they're doing *something*," Femi says.

"And what about you people?" I say, realising too late what I've asked, forgetting I, too, am a part of *these people*.

The gods look at one another and say nothing.

"We are home," Ogun says, standing next to the blackened skeleton that used to be Cardoso House, looking up at the stars.

Another beat passes, and Kehinde says: "Besides, Obatala doesn't want any of us back anyway, so."

"Is the *government* happy with this choice?" I ask Femi. "Considering there are a lot of... *us*."

She tilts her head. "I believe the last R was reconciliation? We'll see how they handle that part, right?"

We continue to look at the stars above the Cardoso House rubble, at everything that was, is, and will come. I sit up painfully and join their gaze.

"Home," Ogun says again, and we all know exactly what that means.

THE END

ABOUT
THE AUTHOR

Suyi Davis Okungbowa is a storyteller who writes from Lagos, Nigeria. His stories have been published in *Fireside*, *PodCastle*, *The Dark*, *StarShipSofa*, *Mothership Zeta*, *Omenana*, and other places. Suyi has worked in engineering and financial audit, and now works in brand marketing, where he gets paid to tell stories. He is also associate editor at Podcastle and a charter member of the African Speculative Fiction Society.

FIND US ONLINE!

www.rebellionpublishing.com

/rebellionpub   /rebellionpublishing   /rebellionpub

SIGN UP TO OUR NEWSLETTER!

rebellionpublishing.com/sign-up

YOUR REVIEWS MATTER!

Enjoy this book? Got something to say?

Leave a review on Amazon, GoodReads or with your
favourite bookseller and let the world know!